DEPARTURE

Departure

A Novel

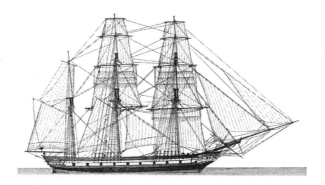

Janet Stevenson

Blue Heron Publishing, Inc.

Book and cover design by Dennis Stovall

Illustrations of ships and knots from: *The Art of Rigging* by George Biddlecombe (Marine Research Society, Salem, Massachusetts, 1925), *The Book of Old Ships* by Henry B. Culver and Gordon Grant (Garden City Publishing Company, Inc., New York, 1935), and *The Arts of the Sailor* by Hervey Garrett Smith (Van Nostrand, New York, 1953).

Published by
 Blue Heron Publishing, Inc.
 24450 NW Hansen Road
 Hillsboro, Oregon 97124

Library of Congress Cataloging in Publication Data

Stevenson, Janet.
 Departure.

 I. Title.
PS3569. T4558D4 1985 813'.5484-25231
ISBN 0-936085-37-1

ALSO BY JANET STEVENSON:

Weep No More
The Ardent Years
Sisters and Brothers
Woman Aboard
The Undiminished Man

AUTHOR'S NOTE

I wrote *Departure* because I stumbled upon a small historical nugget in a book called *Women on the Frontier*, published in Hartford, Connecticut, in 1878. It described the achievements of an unnamed woman during her voyage from the Sandwich Islands to the West Coast at midpoint of the last century. I felt instant empathy with the woman who has become Amanda Bright, in part because I live within sight of the climax of her ordeal, in part because my own experiences at sea and at the bar of the Columbia gave me some understanding of what hers must have been.

But more than a century had passed between her voyage and mine, and although the ocean and the winds haven't changed, most everything else has. I spent months trying to find more factual detail about the real woman and her vessel—and came up empty-handed. But in the process I proved to myself that the story I had read was true. Other women of that time had accomplished feats enough like Amanda's to justify my inventing her story within the bounds of the givens.

Exploring those bounds became a full-time research project. In it I had help from institutions and individuals I've wanted for a long time to thank.

I began in Washington at the Smithsonian Institution, where I was able to examine the specifications and models of many ships of the period and eventually to select one—the *Cohota*—to use as a model for the *Maria M.* (The name is an invention of mine, a tribute to Maria Mitchell, another New England woman who pioneered in a "man's province.") I spent a lot of time in the library of the National Institutes of Health, in Bethesda, reading medical guides of the sort nineteenth-century ships' captains carried with them and talking with people who could diagnose the illness that incapacitated the ship's officers on the basis of the clues in the historical account.

Then I went to the maritime museum at Mystic Seaport. In the

G. W. Blunt White Library there I read the journals and letters of whaling captains' wives and other contemporary eyewitness material. I spent time exploring the vessels kept on exhibit. And best of all, I had the help of the Assistant Curator of the Museum, John Leavitt.

As a young man, Mr. Leavitt had shipped aboard one of the last full-rigged ships, and he was a living encyclopedia of knowledge on the subject. He was also a fine draftsman and enthusiastically sympathetic with my project. He spent hours working out with me every aspect of the incident at the Columbia bar, and he gave me, when I left, a pencil sketch of the *Maria M.* That sketch hung on the wall above my typewriter all the time I worked on the book. Mr. Leavitt died within a few months of my visit to Mystic, and it sobers me to think of how I might have managed if I had gone to Connecticut too late.

There are others I want to thank for lesser but important help—Henrietta Moore, who gave me a safe harbor in which to write the first draft of the book; and Freeman Dyson, of the Institute for Advanced Study at Princeton, who gave me the sort of tutoring in navigation that Amanda needed but had to do without.

Finally, here in Clatsop County, I have had the help of many librarians, local historians, and some of the pilots who bring the great ships across the still-dangerous Columbia bar. Over the years it took to finish the book I imposed most often, and depended most heavily, on Captain Raymond H. Collins. He answered, by letter and viva voce, questions that must often have seemed stupid, with patience and clarity.

Hammond, Oregon
August 1984

de-par´ture, *n.* [OF *departeure*]

7. *(Navig)* **a.** The distance due east or west made by a ship in its course. In plane sailing the departure is reckoned as the product of the distance sailed and the sine of the angle made by the course with the meridian. See SAILING, Cf. DEAD RECKONING. **b.** A ship's position in latitude and longitude at the beginning of a voyage as a point from which to begin the dead reckoning. It is ascertained usually by taking cross bearings of landmarks.

I

Jonathan Bright,
Master

THE FIRST DAY

Bark, Maria M., Jonathan Bright, Master
Home port, Boston, Mass.
Bound for Nootka Sound from Ouwahoo, S.I.
September 1, 1851
  Weighed anchor, Honolulu Harbor, 10:45 A.M.
  Weather clear and mild.
  Wind NE $^{1}/_{2}$ pt N at 10 k.
  Barometer 29.62" and steady.
12 noon
  Diamond Head bearing N.
  Course SE by E, full & by.

The first of the big swells caught the *Maria M.* broadside. She lurched a little, then slowly heeled, like a lady of quality acknowledging an impudent greeting, with dignity and in her own good time.

The timbers of the hull were tuning up, and Amanda could feel her own muscles tensing to regain their sea posture, almost lost during the long harbor stay. It was one of the rare moments when she felt a kinship with the vessel; both of them would make the adjustment, because they must, but not without strain.

She had wanted to stay on deck this morning to watch the great headlands of the coast approach, each in turn brightening, disclosing patterns of dark and light: paths, patches of timber, the desolation of old lava flows in contrasting shades of brown and yellow-gray, green-black, and red—each in turn dropping away, blurring, and fading into blue. But there was no place where a spectator in the bustle of departure could station herself and not be in the way. So she had braced herself in the entrance to the companionway where—by craning her neck a little—she could catch glimpses of the shore beyond the bulwarks of the ship.

Diamond Head had already disappeared, and Koko was slipping out of range of her vision, but forward loomed the indigo bulk of Makapuu, the last point of land. Little by little it too would sink until the bowl of the sky would fit down tight, and the ship would be pressed against the sea, hammered with sun or rain or sleet, fixed with needles of starlight, while time piled higher and higher and all movement ceased. For time did not pass under the bowl. It piled up into a terrible mass under which the heart could hardly beat or the breath come and go.

At the start of this voyage Amanda had wondered at herself for feeling so. Later she wondered at those who did not, who sang paeans to the freedom of

The sea, the sea, the open sea,
The blue, the fresh, the ever-free,
Without a mark, without a bound...

The man who wrote those lines had surely never crossed an ocean, or he would have learned that a voyage was not freedom, but constraint. Cabined, cribbed, confined to a space no larger than a good-sized parlor, in which three officers and the wife of one of them were expected to live for months: to sleep, to wash and dress, to eat, to read and write and converse. Or, when the sea was wild, coffined in a dark stateroom, strapped to the reeling bunk, alone as a prisoner in an oubliette.

4

She caught herself on the edge of the slough of self-pity. She had, after all, not been crimped aboard; she had come of her own volition and against Jonathan's better judgment. He had warned her: *"You may come to hate it. A ship's not a home. There's no kitchen, no meals to prepare, no garden to tend, no flowers to cut, no visits to pay—"*

But she would not be dissuaded. *"Other captains take their wives along, and you said you would when you had a ship of your own."*

"This will be a long voyage, Amanda. More than a year, for certain. Maybe as much as two."

In the end she had her way. Jonathan gave in, gratefully.

"For my part there's nothing I want more—need more—than to have you with me. It was lonely enough before...before...we..." He reddened around the edges of his dark beard and stopped to clear his throat. Unable to speak of the intimacies of their love, he shifted to pleasures that might compensate her for the discomforts of the voyage. *"There are places I've dreamed of showing you since first I clapped eyes on them—sights and sounds that will have you remembering for the rest of your days."*

Still plagued with guilt about the hardships she would have to endure, he had persuaded the owners to let him remodel the cabin and stateroom, doing much of the work himself and bearing all the expense. There was a new hanging locker for her go-ashore wardrobe, a pulley to raise and lower the hanging lamp, a chair that was bolted down and equipped with gimbals. He had taken her to Boston to select a full set of new and finer china. Even after she had learned to take these conveniences and small luxuries for granted, they still served as reminders of his affection and concern.

And the ports of call were all he had promised. Not only the tropical Edens—Madeira, the Canaries, the Pearl Islands of the Pacific—but the seaside cities of England, Portugal, Brazil, Peru. Like a boy showing off a new possession, he had escorted her along wide avenues and narrow lanes, pointing out the remarkable, the exotic, the beautiful, savoring her appreciation as it confirmed his own. A succession of shared wonders and delights, and there would be more—the wilderness of Canada, the venerable civilizations of Japan and

China and the Indies, perhaps India as well. If only she could survive the infinite stretches of nothingness between.

Not infinite. Come, now. Jonathan said this leg might take as long as a month, and a month was nothing compared to the voyage down to and around the Horn. Even now she shrank from remembering those endless weeks of storm. Buffeting that bruised every part of her body. The sense of imminent, awful catastrophe. Suffering so acute and so prolonged that it blunted the effect of the tragedy that did come—a man lost overboard.

There would never again be such an ordeal to face. It was sinful to let her spirits sink.

Cabin fever was a seagoing form of boredom, nothing more. Idleness was its cause, busyness should be its cure. And there was plenty to busy her: journal to be brought up to date, letters to have ready in case they spoke a ship bound for home, her string bag full of last-minute purchases to be secured against the pitch and roll of the seas to come.

She was fitting the heavy brass lamp into its gimbals over Jonathan's desk when he came down to make another entry in the log.

---

2 P.M.

Makapuu Pt. bearing N, distant 5 miles, from which I take my departure.

157°48' W; 21°13' N.

Wind hauling E and S.

Course, N $^1/_4$ pt W.

Amanda waited till he finished to ask; "What did you have to give for those drunken men who were dumped aboard?"

"More than I should have." Jonathan shook his head. "The worst of them—the one that had to be hoisted over the bulwarks—for him the crimps wanted double. I wouldn't give it, of course. Told them they could row him back ashore. But think of their having the brass to ask it!"

She wanted to keep him, to prolong the intimacy that always flowered ashore, and in the islands even more sweetly. To remind him of days when they had wandered along the beaches, gathering shells; of the morning they had been drenched in a warm downpour at the Pali and dried their clothes on the craggy rocks; of nights when he had given most of the hands shore leave and they had had the ship virtually to themselves....

But Jonathan was already undergoing his sea change, making his log entries, thinking his sea thoughts of speed through the water, directions, and distance. She had lost his attention.

Yet when he passed her on his way back to the quarterdeck, he paused a moment to cup her face in his hand. It was like a kiss. A stolen one, for Jonathan never touched her, seldom even looked directly at her when there was anyone else about, and once the ship was under way, there was always someone about—except when they were behind the closed door of the captain's stateroom. Then there might be others a few feet from where they lay in each other's arms: one of the mates, or the cabin boy, or even one of the hands, coming or going on some errand. But the closed door worked a magic. Behind it they were Jonathan and Amanda. Man and woman, one flesh. When it opened, it was Captain Bright who emerged, a flinty-faced Olympian.

Somewhere she had heard that to impersonate a god an actor of ancient tragedies put on a mask and boots that raised him above the level of ordinary mortals. But this was no impersonation. A captain on his ship, out of sight of land, embodied the law—natural, human, and divine. He must be Moses, Pharaoh, and Jehovah, omniscient and omnipotent. It was a demanding role.

By the time Amanda had finished her securing and stowing, the stays of her corset were savaging her ribs. She undid the fastenings of her go-ashore dress and put it in the locker, where it would hang until they had crossed and recrossed the North Pacific. Slowly she began to unlace, taking a maximum of pleasure in each millimeter of expansion. Like making a landfall, worth all the constriction endured for the bliss of release.

When the corsets were rolled and tied in their laces, she knelt to stow them far back in one of the drawers under the double bunk. From another part of the same drawer she took her oldest cotton dress, a blue one, much faded, that flattered the color of her eyes. She smoothed out the wrinkles, got herself dressed, and was tidying her hair when she heard Jonathan and the first officer come down the aft companionway.

Mr. Smith was reporting on the replacements supplied by the Honolulu crimps. "Them two Kanakas, they're going to shake down fine," he said in his high, tight whine of a voice. "Green hands, but they'll catch on quick enough. It's in the breed."

With the two white crewmen he was not so well pleased. One of them seemed sound enough most ways, but he spoke no language that anyone in the forecastle recognized, which was remarkable, considering what a Tower of Babel it was. There was Heyerman, the bosun, a Hollander who spoke, besides his own language, several German dialects, English, and one of the pidgins used in the Java seas. There was Crank, a Finn who also spoke Russian and German and could make himself understood in English. There was Tono, a Marquesas Islander who had a grasp of all the Polynesian languages, including that spoken in the Sandwich Islands. "King" John, a West African who spoke a difficult pidgin English but good enough Spanish and Portuguese to act as interpreter in the Canaries. And the cockney, Davidson, who had knocked about the oceans of the world long enough to pick up a bit of every tongue known to seagoing humanity.

"Even Davy don't know what this one's talking," Smith said. "But he ain't deaf, nor stupid either. And he'll pull his weight, once we make him understand what's wanted."

The other new hand, the one for whom the crimps asked double, was likely to turn out a right smart troublemaker. One member of the port watch had seen him ashore, roaring and brawling and giving out that he was an ex-officer. "Had a ship of his own, he said, and the bad luck to run her on a reef in the Leewards one night when he was several sheets to the windward."

Amanda noted the play on words and wondered—since it was unlikely that Smith was the author of it—whether it was quoted from the informer's account or was the boaster's own clever turn of phrase.

"The crimps told me he was bosun aboard his last ship," Jonathan said. "Lost his ticket in some gutter."

That could be, but Smith was inclined to believe the man's own story. The crimps would have taken pains to conceal the fact—if it was a fact—that he had once been a member of the quarterdeck elite.

Amanda understood that no captain would knowingly engage such a hand; he would represent too great a threat to the authorities of the ship, being possessed of their priestly secrets and having degraded the priesthood by his fall. Also, when he waked from his alcoholic stupor and found himself imprisoned at hard labor for another stretch of days, he would take a different sort of subduing from the ordinary. She had often heard Jonathan say that a man who came aboard in such a state was not worth the trouble it took to beat him into submission when he sobered up.

"He does speak English, I suppose."

"Aye. He's from the Hebrides, they say. A Scot."

"And what about the Kanakas? They speak pidgin?"

Smith believed that one did, and he could act as interpreter for his mate. Or the Marquesan could help them out. "They'll give no trouble," he said again. "Well, maybe just a bit at the start when they tumble that we've—" He broke off, cleared his throat, and continued in a wheezy whisper that carried just as well as his voice. "I mean to say, about us having—so to speak—a woman aboard."

At that moment the companionway door opened, and a tousled blond head was thrust in. "You asked to be reminded that the log is to be heaved before the watch is changed, sir."

"Thank you, Mr. Martin," Jonathan said.

The ceremony of heaving the chip log involved the bosun and the first mate with the captain standing by. The second officer's presence was not required, and as soon as Jonathan and Smith had ascended the ladder, Amanda called Horace to come down.

"Can I speak to you a moment, Horrie? There's something I want to know."

From the day the Martin brothers had signed on as second mate and cabin boy, they had been "Mr. Martin" and "son" to Jonathan. Discipline had to be maintained as strictly with "ship's cousins" as with any other officers or hands. It was concession enough to invite the first and second officers to take their meals with the captain and his lady. Informality of address would imply an intolerable laxity if not outright favoritism.

Amanda did not dispute this dictum, but she could not accept it for herself. She had no place on the ladder of authority, and such ceremony would have sounded laughable from her. So, rather than flout Jonathan's wishes, she tried to avoid using any form of address at all to either of her cousins. Now and again she forgot herself, as she had just now.

"Mr. Smith was talking to Jonathan about the new hands, the Sandwich Islanders, and he said something about a woman aboard this ship. Do you know what he meant?"

Horace frowned and stroked his chin with one hand. It might have been an imitation of Jonathan, but Horace's puckish face did not lend itself to the expression of gravity. "I haven't a notion. They could hardly have smuggled...wait, now!" His eyes crinkled at the corners. "A woman aboard. That's you, coz! What Smith means is the Kanakas are going to go into a funk when they find out about you. You remember how Tono carried on when he first did?"

Amanda could hardly be expected to remember, since no one had told her at the time, but according to Horace, the Marquesan had looked black for upwards of a month after he discovered her presence on the ship. Polynesians, it seemed, had a taboo against women on any sort of vessel from a canoe up. They considered it an insult to Tangaroa, their god of the sea.

"Are you serious, Horrie, or just teasing?"

"Well, I shouldn't worry about their stealing into the cabin to grab you and pitch you over the side. But you'd do well to have one of us about if you should take it into your head to go for a stroll forward of the mast."

2:30 P.M.   Mustered all hands aft to choose watches.

Port watch (Smith)	*Starboard watch (Martin)*
Tono, A.B.	*Kankkonen, A.B.*
Rory, A.B.	*King John, A.B.*
Kanaka Jim (green hand)	*Kanaka Jerry (green?)*
Davidson, A.B.	*No Name*

Amanda spent the afternoon on a new embroidery, a length of Irish linen she had bought to make a cover for the round table under the cabin skylight. She had already sketched a garland of flowers and leaves to be worked in the center, and this morning in the market she had found some bright cotton threads. With these she outlined the design, all the while turning the tale of the taboo in her mind.

The truth was that a voyage brought bad luck to a woman—not the other way around. The worst of luck. Unless, as was commonly believed, it cured her of barrenness. That was one of the reasons Amanda had wanted to come, one of the reasons (she was almost certain) that Jonathan had been persuaded to let her. But no such miracle had been wrought in her case. At least not yet.

She remembered having heard, when she was very young, that women usually knew the moment they conceived, and a notion had been taking hold in her mind of late that it was her own fault that no such revelation had come to her. Something she was doing—or not doing—or feeling was holding her back.

Was it fear? Fear of the pain of childbirth? But that was nothing to shrink from. She had seen births, helped women, heard their cries, and seen the smiles that came after the cries. If that was what held her back, she was cheating herself. And Jonathan as well.

But perhaps it was something else. Modesty? Carried too far so that it hardened into shame?

Whatever it was, she was determined not to be cheated any longer. Condemned to a shapeless, purposeless, childless existence.

She was twenty-five years old, healthy, of good New England stock whose women, generation after generation, had borne large broods of healthy children. She had a proper mate in Jonathan, who came of the same stock. And they loved each other, truly loved.

The bark had settled into the motion Amanda liked best (or minded least), a slow, controlled pitching forward that ended in a slight roll to leeward. An uneven rhythm, something like a waltz. The wind must be nearly abeam and the swells very long. Nothing could be more auspicious for the beginning of a voyage.

Dip and roll, dip and roll…The words caught a melody and fit themselves around it. Dip and roll, dip and roll.

"Wind of the western sea…"

Her body moved inwardly, in time with the song. She closed her eyes and was lying in Jonathan's arms, as they had lain together those nights in the reef-sheltered harbor-nights so quiet it seemed the power of their love must carry through the timbers of the ship, out across the black and gold water to other ships at anchor, announcing itself to any who lay awake.

Tonight the power would come from outside the ship, from the life force of the sea, carried through the body of the ship to the bodies of the lovers, lending her the strength that would bring fulfillment.

The wind was fair. The sky would be full of stars. The lookout on the bow would stare out over a dark sea wrinkled with silver while she and Jonathan lay together behind the closed door.

4 P.M.	*Course N $^1/_4$ W.*	*Stowed anchors and coiled cables between decks.*
6 P.M.	*" "*	*Wind freshening from ESE, running with all drawing sails set.*
		Est. speed 7 k.
8 P.M.	*" "*	*Same.*
10 P.M.	*" "*	*"*

Amanda lay awake long after Jonathan had withdrawn from her, stretched himself out on his back with one arm under the bend of her neck, and fallen deeply asleep. She never slept like that. He said he depended on it, that those hours counted double and made up for the broken snatches that were all he got most nights. It was she who gave him those hours. All the tensions, conflicts, anxieties that had plagued his day were drawn together and gathered into a great wave that swelled and crested and sank swiftly into peace.

It was a mystery. His mystery. She was its cause, but she did not share in it. Tonight she had believed she would. She had felt the imminence, the gathering wave—like those great waves she and Jonathan had watched the islanders riding.

An acquaintance had taken them to a cliff at the end of a wide-mouthed cove where they could look down on the scene of dozens of young Hawaiians sporting in the sea while a hundred of their elders cheered from the beach. The swimmers had long *papa-he-nalus,* "wave-sliding boards," that they pushed out through the surf to the smooth place where the swells gathered. There they waited, watching over their shoulders for one that seemed to promise.

The trick, their guide explained, was to choose the right wave, to throw oneself onto it at the right moment and paddle furiously till the bottom of the swell struck ground and the top began to curl forward. At that moment the most expert maneuvered their boards so that they slanted forward and down, just in front of the thundering crest, and rode majestically all the way to the cheering crowd on the shore.

Some were too slow to catch the wave. Some were too timid. They made it to the top but held back, let the crest curl and break in front of them, and were caught in the backwash, returned to the smooth place to wait for another chance.

Amanda had assumed that all the wavesliders were men, but their guide said no. One of those who had stood erect, waving arms and shouting exultantly, was a young woman, famous for her daring with the *papa-he-nalu.*

The ship pushed through a swell and dropped on the far side. Through another. Another. Swells as steep as those great waves, that never touched bottom and never broke....

The mystery still eluded her. But she was surer than ever that unless she could grasp it, unless she could ride the comber all the way to shore, she would never bear Jonathan a child. She must find the secret, find the strength, find the courage to abandon herself to the wave...abandon....

Her mind snagged on the word and began to repeat it like a charm, like a warning, like a prayer...*abandoned...abandon... abandoned....*

She played lazily with the sounds, juggling their meaning; dived deeper and brought them up with other words clinging to them like weed...*shameless and abandoned...abandoned sinner...abandon hope....*

Through a thickening mist of sleep she saw a woman with two faces: one, joyous as a bacchante; the other, pitiably deserted, as a house might be deserted...or a child...or a ship.

Abandon ship!

But only if the ship were sinking. Then you were permitted to cast off—which was not the same as *being* cast off. *That* was to be acted upon. To be abandoned was to be forsaken. But to abandon oneself to something—to joy, to grief, to sin—or even, by a supreme effort, to abandon self! And in that moment to act, to be free.

THE SECOND DAY

September 2, 1851
    Spoke ship, Hurricane, *out of San Francisco, bound for Maui.*
12 *midnight*   *N $^1/_2$ W (1 $^1/_4$ Pt easterly variation).*
2 A.M.   "
4 A.M.   "
6 A.M.   "
    Wind SE $^1/_2$ S, a fresh breeze, carrying all sails but
        royals.
8 A.M.   "

Jonathan was at his desk, bringing the log up to the end of the first
sea day, which would come at noon. Amanda was writing another
chapter of the chronicle of the voyage to be sent home as a family
letter whenever the opportunity came. Several chapters had been dispatched from Lahaina, courtesy of a whaler, bound for New Bedford.
This new chapter began with their arrival at Honolulu, where they
had stayed longer than at any port so far...

    ...because replacements had to be found for four members of our
crew.

If you have by this time received my last letter, you know that we lost a man overboard in a terrible storm off Tierra del Fuego. Another—a splendid young fellow—was so weakened by scurvy that he had to be left behind to recover his strength. The others deserted—one in Hilo, one in Lahaina.

This sort of thing is not uncommon in these parts, and captains must avail themselves of the services of native crimps, a peculiarly noxious variety of man that reminds me not a little of the villain of Mr. Dickens's new novel.

About the scurvy, you may remember that Jonathan said I might act as medical officer, and that I prepared myself thoroughly. But I might have spared my pains—all those hours of reading and consulting with Dr. Gough on the proper measures to be taken for sunstroke, cholera morbus, broken limbs, fevers of the brain, and I know not what else! There has been no illness but scurvy, no call for any medicaments but vinegar and lime juice. I must own to being a bit disappointed on my own account, although of course I am happy—

Mr. Smith broke the silence of the cabin by announcing that the time for the noon observation was at hand. Jonathan put away his work more deliberately than usual. He was giving Horace a few moments' grace. Poor Horrie! He would never learn the art—or the science—of punctuality. Amanda could sympathize, for her own nature was no better tuned than his to time's tyrannies. Not those that concerned a sailor, who—as Jonathan was always reminding Horace—dealt with *"sun and moon and planets, which move at their own rates, not waiting for laggards or hurrying to keep an appointment with early arrivals."*

In matters of navigation—the calculation of where on the featureless face of the sea a ship stood at any given moment—time, as precise as fallible man with fallible instruments could measure it, was the key.

Moving like those heavenly timekeepers, he was taking the chronometer from its case to wind it, noting on a card that its hands showed today fourteen minutes and eight seconds less than Greenwich mean time. Both men checked their pocket watches against the chronometer but did not reset them. That would be done when local time was calculated after the observation they were about to make.

The second officer was still missing. No. He was coming now. Amanda heard heavy running steps cross the officers' mess. Horace began speaking as he entered the cabin. "Sorry to be late, sir. There was a devil of—" He checked himself ran a hand through his curls, straightened his back, and amended the phrase to "some trouble about the changing of the watch."

Smith's long ears went back like an angered cat's, but Jonathan gave no sign of having heard. Horace accepted the reprimand and hung his head. There was a portentous pause.

Finally Jonathan nodded to Smith, who returned the nod. Each took his sextant from its case and held it protectively against his right breast pocket. Jonathan led the way on deck. Smith followed, and after him, Horace, who was too chagrined to throw Amanda even a greeting of the eyes.

It was just as well. This ritual, which she had witnessed a hundred times, never ceased to strike her as comic, like the moment in church when the organ struck up the lugubrious anthem known as the offertory, and the gray-haired deacons began passing the collection boxes along the pews. As a child she always had to bite her lips and wriggle her shoulders to suppress laughter at such times. If Horace had caught her eye just now, it would have set her off.

Alone, she was free to laugh all she liked, but that killed the impulse. She went back to her letter writing:

> *The market in Honolulu is not large, but it is very colorful, especially the stalls that display fish and other sea creatures used as food. Some of the merchandise is almost too colorful. The parrot fish, for example, which is every bit as green as the name suggests, or perch—all shapes, sizes, and shades: striped, spotted, or splotched with black, white, yellow, pink, blue, or orange on a ground of bright silver or gold. These are eaten raw, after a soaking in lemon or lime juice and fresh coconut cream.*

I was anxious to sample some of the more exotic shellfish or the sluglike bêche-de-mer, which is said to be delicious, properly prepared, and to have all sorts of health-giving properties. But our cook refused to carry any such creatures back to his galley and was so put out at the suggestion that I thought for a while he too might desert.

Having got his way in this, however, he has turned the sun of his countenance upon me, and we are to be rewarded with a New England fish chowder! One of the hands trailed a line over the stern as we left the harbor and caught a "proper fish," which was presented to Jonathan and me. I asked if the man didn't want it served in his own mess, but Cook said, "No'm, he don't hold with eating of the fish and hope the fish'll do the same by him if it should come to that." This, with a smile that creased his black face like a reefed sail!

Eight bells were struck, first on the quarterback bell above her head, then on the much louder one at the forecastle companionway. In another few minutes Willy would begin to lay the table, but it would be nearly half an hour before Cook carried his tray across the windy expanse of the waist. She had time to finish with Ouwahoo.

My chiefest delight in the islands—a memory I shall always carry with me—was the sight of the native women walking along the wharves or riding horseback through the streets. Hawaiians, as they call themselves, are larger-bodied than we. Fleshy is the word one might use, but it carries an opprobrium that is quite out of place in describing these magnificent beings. There is a savage and commanding beauty about them that puts to shame the prettiest of the haole *ladies. (Haole is a Hawaiian word for a white or other foreign person.)*

Try to picture a tightly corseted British or American female standing five-foot-three in her heels, dressed in muslin to her chin, wrists, and ankles, keeping her complexion safe under rice powder and a black parasol; and beside her, a dark giantess, half a foot taller and weighing half again as much; barefooted, bare-

headed, except for a garland of flowers and fern jammed down on her mane of glistening black hair. Her dress is a loose robe called a holoku. *The neck is open and low; the sleeves, full; the body of the garment, unfitted from yoke to hem. The colors are of an intensity that not even the flowers of this demiparadise can match. They would not flatter a woman of our race, even one with as ruddy a complexion as mine, but they accommodate themselves perfectly to the dark skin, hair, and eyes, and the flashing white teeth of the islanders.*

She looked back over the page.

Abandoned is the word one might use, but it carries an opprobrium....

It was not what she had written, but she thought it. Almost with envy. These galloping, striding, laughing women were not cheated of love by fear or shame or a sense of sin. One had only to look at them to know.

The big tureen was set on the table before Jonathan. He filled the first bowl, and Willy set it before Amanda, holding it for her while she adjusted the little sandbag that leveled it against the heeling of the ship. The next bowl went to Smith, who looked faintly uneasy as the aroma of the chowder rose to his nostrils. Horace was on duty and would eat later, so the last bowl was Jonathan's. He signed for Willy to remove the tureen, pronounced a short and somewhat perfunctory grace, and the meal began.

There was seldom much table conversation aboard the *Maria M.* Amanda had given up striving against the silences. But today the men had something to talk about. Smith had gone forward to investigate the trouble in the starboard watch and had taken those measures he considered appropriate to "shake things down a bit."

The element that needed shaking down was the new hand Rory, who had sobered up to a splitting headache, a heaving stomach, and a smoldering rage. Smith had "concluded to knock the nonsense out of him."

"And did you succeed?" Jonathan asked without irony. Smith

19

thought he had but would not care to wager until the man came to.

It was hard to believe, looking at the mate, that he had the strength in his arm or the violence in his nature to beat a man senseless, not in anger but in a deliberate meting out of coercive brutality. He seemed so unsure of himself, so eager to submit to authority. Amanda had once thought he must resent serving under a captain ten years his junior, but she had come to believe that Smith not only did not aspire to a command of his own but would reject one if it were offered to him. He took pride in being what he called "reliable," but he had no ambition.

Also, he was not in good health. He had grown thinner and paler on the voyage. At the moment he was breathing more deeply than normal and only through his long, narrow nose. His hand, holding a spoonful of chowder, stopped halfway to his mouth, trembled, and let the liquid spill back into the bowl.

"Feeling a bit offish," he apologized. "Have been the whole of the forenoon."

Jonathan suggested that Amanda might dispense a dose of salts from the medicine chest, but Smith looked alarmed. A dose of salts was not at all what was wanted. In fact, one might say, just the other way about. What he would not mind accepting, if the lady would be so kind, was something for headache.

"Headache!" Jonathan's astonishment was understandable. It would hardly have been more out of character if Smith had asked for a remedy for hangnails or a fallen arch.

But the poor fellow was badly flustered by the captain's reaction and mumbled an immediate retraction. What he had meant to say was something for dizziness. A slight bilious attack was what it was, brought on by something he had eaten or drunk ashore.

"I thought you never touched anything stronger than milk." It was said with a smile that blunted the irony, but Smith was impervious to humor.

"That's God's truth," he said earnestly. "But it might just have been the milk. It's got from goats hereabouts."

"Are you feverish?" Amanda asked.

Smith thought he might be, but not— Suddenly he bit down, gagged, rolled his eyes in desperate apology, and dashed for his cabin.

He did not return.

While Willy was clearing for the pudding course, Jonathan went to see what was wrong. He came back looking somber. Smith was coming down with something for certain. He had vomited what little he had eaten and was now in his bunk, under blankets, shaking with a chill.

Amanda had brought along a small library of medical books, and she consulted them all. The chapters on fevers covered a number of types, with lists of symptoms for each. The descriptions did not agree from one book to the other, and none fit Mr. Smith's case in all particulars. Also, and this was most distressing, the remedies prescribed were radically different. For example, in a case of inflammatory fever, *"if the patient be young and strong and of full habit of body, a vein in the arm should be opened and from 16 to 20 ozs. of blood abstracted."* But in the case of a fever of the "low" type, *"great care must be taken not to reduce the patient too much by carrying the bleeding and other depressing measures too far, lest the fever assume the typhoid character."*

She decided to avoid purgatives, emetics, and other depressing measures altogether until her patient's symptoms arranged themselves to conform to one of the orthodox varieties of fever, or until she discovered another disease that produced them. In search of such an alternative, she read all the way through the *Guide and Companion to the Captain's Medical Chest* and, in its final pages, came upon a section entitled *"Child Birth."*

She tried to imagine Jonathan reading these directions: how to tie and cut the cord between mother and child; how to remove the afterbirth if it did not come of itself; how to wash and care for the infant during the week or more that the mother was to be kept quiet; how to dose her with laudanum if she continued to suffer pain. But *"the process being natural, needs but little interference, or assistance.... During the pains, the patient will naturally hold her breath, and at its termination will give vent to it and utter a groan.... Someone of her fe-*

male friends may take hold of her hands." (A strange suggestion in a text designed for use on a merchant ship at sea! One woman aboard was novelty enough; female friends, an impossibility.) "*Or a sheet may be twisted and tied to the foot of the bed, on which she may be allowed to pull.... Toward the close, the pains generally become sharp— she utters a cry and is delivered.*"

If Amanda were to utter a cry and be delivered, there would be no one to hear but Jonathan. He would have it all to do alone, with no guidance but these pages and what she herself could tell him. She could depend on him—they could depend on each other—in such an exigency. But a female friend, a woman to confide in and converse with about those things that did not seem appropriate for or worthy of Jonathan's attention—how grateful she would be for such a blessing.

She looked over to where Jonathan was sitting, staring at the pigeonholes of his desk and tapping his pen on the open logbook. He looked very stern, but by half-closing her eyes Amanda could evoke the face she had first loved, strong as a man's should be, but sensitive as a woman's, open, easy to read—at least for her; the face he had chosen to hide under the beard and mustache. Perhaps one day, when he had no longer any need to make himself look older, when time had caught up with him—or he with it—he would go back to that other loved and loving face.

He felt her eyes on him and spoke. "I wish Mr. Martin had done his lessons with the sextant."

"Was he to have lessons?"

"Unless he means to teach himself. A man who expects to learn navigation ought to be about it before he gets too thick up here." He tapped his forehead sharply and winced as if he had started a pain. "I begin to think he will never make a captain."

Amanda had been thinking the same thing, but she rose to her cousin's defense. "I'm sure he'll pick it up quickly, once he puts his mind to it."

"It's not only the navigation." Jonathan did not elaborate, but Amanda knew well enough in what ways Horace fell short of

Jonathan's expectations. "I'm sorry for it," he said. "Sincerely sorry."

That was true. He was genuinely fond of both the Martin brothers. If his manner to them was formal, demanding, and sometimes downright harsh, that was the way to help a boy become a man, a man become an officer, an officer become master of his own ship. It was The Way—the only way for a Martin or a Bright or any male member of the clans to which they belonged.

But it was not Horace's way. He had never wanted to go to sea. Uncle Matthew had striven to root this "lack of ambition" out of his son's character, but to no avail. Aunt Agatha had taken Horace's part, arguing that he had a bent for the ministry, which was, even for a Martin, an acceptable alternative to a maritime career. In the end she prevailed, and Horace was sent off to Harvard to study.

It was a new world that opened for him in Cambridge, full of wonders he described to Amanda every time he came home: a community of compatible souls, dedicated to the life of the mind, comparing, contrasting, examining experience; reading—to oneself or aloud to a companion or a group—poetry, essays, even novels; discussing what one read, debating viewpoints and insights; attending lectures (Horace was especially keen on those delivered by Mr. Emerson, whose views were frowned upon in orthodox Salem); in short, leading a life whose chief goal was the molding of a philosophy to live by.

If she lived in Boston, Horace assured her, the fact of her being female would not bar her from this Eden. Many ladies, maidens as well as matrons, attended—even participated in!—"reading parties" and symposia. Amanda tried to imagine herself reading aloud to Jonathan when next he was at home. Not the sort of literature Horace was exploring. It would have to be factual—history or accounts of voyages and travels.

It was not till long afterwards that it occurred to Amanda that Horace had never spoken of his studies in theology. Not, in fact, till she learned from Jonathan that he and Willy had signed on for the voyage.

"Horace is leaving college? Why?"

Jonathan shrugged as if to say, "Why not?" It was not often the firm had a ship with berths for two apprentices: a second mate's for Horace and a cabin boy's for young Willy, a splendid opportunity for both the Martin boys to "get the salt in their scalps" with a friendly captain for mentor and their Cousin Amanda to look after Willy, who had just turned fourteen.

Though the brothers resembled each other—the likeness between them was almost comical—they were polar opposites in character. Willy was as delighted with the prospect of the voyage as Horace was dismayed. Some of his tasks the lad disliked, principally those that reduced him to the status of a body servant, but in all that concerned the running of the ship, he was eager and apt. The bosun spoke well of him, and Jonathan was pleased.

But with Horace he was not pleased. A second mate's office carried no authority but what the man could win for himself by his fists and foul language. Horace made use of neither. He did his work well enough, going on deck with his watch in good humor and in all weathers. In the storms of the high latitudes, he had struggled with frozen ropes and canvas aloft or pulled his weight on deck under a constant deluge of icy water, asking no favors, offering no complaints. The men of his watch loved him. But they did not fear him.

Fear—sometimes called "respect"—was what an officer must inspire. The ship's safety depended on that. When Smith took it upon himself to beat the obstreperous Rory, it was because fear had to be instilled as an antidote to the poison he was spreading in the forecastle. Horace had seemed unaware of that necessity. If the mate had not intervened, the captain would have had to. Sooner or later, and better sooner.

All this Amanda understood and accepted (though she had some trouble seeing Jonathan in the role of castigator). Horace and she had talked of it a few weeks ago, on the one occasion during the voyage when they had been able to indulge in one of their old "confidings." He did not dispute the premise, he said, but he did not aspire to a position that required it of him. He had "chosen a different path."

Till now Amanda had been shy of asking why he left that path, but now she sensed that he expected the question. When she asked it, however, he hesitated, flushed, and asked if she would promise to keep his confidence.

"Haven't I always?"

"Of course. But that was before…well, never mind. For all I know, Father told Jonathan before we sailed."

Horace had gone to his father to ask for a position in the family's Boston countinghouse.

"But you were so happy at the college. You made me envious."

"I wanted—I *want!*—to be married. And I must earn a living for myself and my wife."

Amanda was flabbergasted. Not that Horace should have fallen in love but that he should have—could have—concealed it. For how long?

Not long. He had known the lady since the first days of his sojourn in Cambridge. They had been drawn to each other from the start, but only recently had they confessed to each other the depth of their attachment. "We are, in our own minds, husband and wife," he said solemnly. They had planned to be married and settle in a room at Mrs. Clarke's boarding house, "until between us we could save enough for a home of our own. Louisa is a gifted artist. She does copies in oil of famous paintings. Earns her own living with her brush. But she would prefer to copy nature rather than some other painter's view of it. I want to provide her the security that will permit her to create."

Horace's explanation sounded so unlike him, so stiff and defensive that it might have been taken verbatim from his speech to his father, in which case Amanda could well imagine how poorly it had been received.

"There was no opening for you on Long Wharf?"

"I was not answered. Only scourged with words and sentenced to a term in the galleys."

Amanda put her next question even more diffidently. "Did you speak to Aunt Aggie?"

Horace nodded.

"And she agreed with Uncle Matthew?"

Horace shook his head. "Mother's not one to judge a person without having at least set eyes on her."

"You mean to say you didn't take her to meet them? Before you told them your intentions?"

"It was stupid, I suppose. But I was afraid...and right to be, as things turned out. Suppose he had said those things in Louisa's hearing!"

It took some affectionate but persistent probing to dig out the details of Uncle Matthew's objections. It was not only that Horace's young lady was a painter—hardly a respectable profession, even for a man, by Martin standards. Or that she earned her own living, which cast greater doubt on her virtue. She was also a Unitarian.

"A birthright Unitarian, if there is such a thing. And you know Father's views on that 'heresy.' He would have been less displeased if I had proposed to marry a Quaker or a Catholic."

"You haven't told me what Aunt Aggie said."

"It was Mother persuaded me to do as he asked. Or, rather, as he *ordered*. 'If you are constant in your affection,' she said, 'time will not diminish it. And if you are diligent in your effort, if your father has a good report of you, you may find his mind altered on your return. If not—you will at least be better prepared to do without his help.'"

Amanda wondered that Horace had been so easily persuaded to submit. But to his mind there was only one alternative: to go west to seek his fortune in some pioneer community, or still farther west to pan for gold. He had no skills that would serve him in the first instance, no capital with which to equip himself for the latter.

She wondered often in the days that followed that conversation how she and Jonathan would have fared against such opposition. Would he ever have asked her to marry him? Would she even have known she loved him?

In one sense, of course, she had always known. From the time of her earliest memories, Jonathan had been her protector. When he and her brothers reached the age when boys turn tormentor, she became the favorite target of their teasing. More often than not, when it grew too cruel, Jonathan would draw the others away or distract them so she could escape. If he teased her himself, it was so gently that it was more likely to make her laugh than cry.

As they grew older, the teasing turned on him, drove him into exile from her. For years—she remembered them now as the most painful of her growing up—he avoided her, hardly spoke when they met, stopped coming to the house, though he was still her brothers' friend.

Then she heard he had gone to sea. Without even saying good-bye. He had forgotten her. Very well, she would forget him! And she did. Or supposed that she did.

Her brothers brought him home to supper when he returned from that first voyage. They all sat in the parlor afterwards, talking of cargoes and commerce and commands. She took no part in the talk, content to be able to watch him without being watched. He had changed. Grown taller and more imposing. There was a sternness in his jawline that had not been there before and little trace of the shy and tender playmate-protector.

Then he looked her way—before she could turn her eyes—and smiled. She felt as if he had reached out to embrace her. As if everything in his mind and heart were revealed to her: love and longing and the promise of devotion. But he never looked her way again, not even when he said his good-nights.

She met him on the street a week or so later. She thought he meant to stop, to speak or let his eyes speak for him. But he only hesitated an instant, tipped his hat politely, and went on.

The next time—she could bring back the moment by shutting her eyes—was the supper at the town hall. There were long tables set up on sawhorses, smells of Indian pudding and codfish croquettes, a clattering of crockery. Some of the guests were already seated. Others—young men and boys—were maneuvering to find a place beside some particular person. Jonathan pulled out a chair for her and inquired with a tilt of his head if he had permission to take the place to her right. She nodded consent.

But while he was gone to fetch her a glass of cider, someone else took the empty seat, an elderly gentleman whom she felt it unseemly to offend. She was still trying to think what to do when Jonathan returned.

He looked at the gentleman and then at her in hurt amazement, as if he had been rudely and publicly rejected. Amanda started to stutter an explanation, but he did not wait to hear it. He set down the cider and found himself another place. She could have wept for vexation.

She did not see him again for a year. He came once more to call, but when she was not at home. And a few days later he sailed on his second voyage. Again without saying good-bye.

Next time it was her father who brought him to the house. A first officer now, bronzed and bearded, but still handsome—perhaps even more handsome, with an unselfconscious dignity that erased the last vestige of his shyness.

Again he was invited to supper, and this time, when the man-talk was done, somehow (not by accident, she believed, though she had never talked to her parents or her brothers about her love) she and Jonathan were left alone in the parlor. But neither of them could bridge the awesome abyss that opened. They sat a few minutes in uncomfortable silence. Then he excused himself and left.

He confessed, after they were married, that he had come intending to ask her to marry him, believing she would accept his proposal, but he had been struck dumb. "I could have as soon have said what was in my heart in Latin or Greek as in plain English. It's as if the more I feel, the less I can find words for."

His next voyage lasted two years, years during which she lived in hope and fear. Mostly hope. She was sure he loved her; sure she loved him; sure he would come for her—*if* he came back. Not every man who sailed out of Salem did return. What if he were lost at sea? Or stayed away so long that he forgot her? Or found someone else to love, not being bound by any promise?

He did come back, of course. Safe and sound and having done

well for himself. Her father brought the news from the harbor the day his ship came in. "He asked after you, Amanda, and said he would come to call."

She hardly left the house lest she should miss him. When he came at last, it was in the afternoon, and none of the Martin menfolk was at home.

They sat in the parlor, her mother knitting and keeping up a figured bass of small talk. Jonathan said almost nothing, and Amanda hardly heard even that. Her ears were tuned to another voice, calling to her from the prison of his shyness. But she knew no way to answer. At last, so abruptly that it seemed almost rude, Jonathan got to his feet and proposed that Amanda walk to the harbor so she might "have a look at" his ship.

"In this inclement weather?" Mrs. Martin looked up in surprise. Then she smiled and said no more.

They did start toward the harbor, but soon they had turned and were heading toward the shore, beating into an east wind that tore at her shawl and hair, pushed so hard against her that she could not keep up. Jonathan put his arm behind her and propelled her forward so that she seemed to move with a strength not her own.

They stopped in the lee of a great hummock of beach grass. Jonathan was speaking at last. The words were snatched by the wind before they reached her ears, all but the one word "love," which he seemed to be repeating. Over and over. He took her in his arms, the safe harbor in which she would live happily ever after....

"Have you ever thought you might have a go at learning, Amanda?" Jonathan's voice brought her back to the ship, to the cabin, to the present.

"Learning what?"

"Navigation."

Amanda could not believe he was in earnest. She had never heard of a woman being offered such an opportunity: to be inducted into the secret society of mariners, taught the use of its paraphernalia, allowed to interpret the oracle.

"There are wives who use the sextant and do all the computa-
tions." Jonathan had read the astonishment in her face and was de-
fending his proposal. "At least I know of one who does, and I've
heard there are others."

She turned the idea in her mind and found it intriguing. And flattering. But why now? Suddenly? After so many months of voyaging?... Unless it was Jonathan's way of goading Horace into buckling
down.

"Very well," she said. "If you think I'm capable."

"I don't see any reason why not. You've always been good at sums.
If you've a mind to put your mind to it..."

"I've a mind to try.

Jonathan seemed unduly relieved, but all he said was, "It's good
to have a spare spar aboard."

He went to have a look at the sky and came back disappointed.
"It's clouding over. I'd like to have started you out with a lesson on
the sextant, but we'll have to wait till there's a sun for you to shoot."

Second day begins with breeze steady from ESE, 6 + k. Noon observa-
tion of sun (lower limb)

74°25'	*N 15°23'*
12'	*N 7°41'*
74°37'	*N 23°04'*

Remarks aboard:

    The Tropic of Cancer was crossed approx. noon, Sept. 3.

    Smith being indisposed, bosun took charge of port watch.

Latter part:

    Sky overcast, barometer dropping slowly, stands at 30" at dark.

THE THIRD DAY

AMANDA BRIGHT'S JOURNAL

September 3, 1851

Mr. Smith continues sick with high fever and much stomach pain. Jonathan has appointed the ship's carpenter, Flagg, to assist me, as our patient ought not to be left untended for any considerable time. Flagg is of the opinion that this illness resembles what is called autumnal fever at home. If so, he says, it will run its course in a week or so, there being little we can do except make the poor sufferer as comfortable as possible.

Flagg sponged off Smith's body during the night and will again today. We have used a mixture of fresh water and witch hazel for this purpose, but the latter will soon be exhausted if the fever continues, so today we shall try using half fresh, half salt water instead.

This Flagg is well on in years, thin, gray, and tough as a weathered shingle. Better educated than most foremast hands, he has read a good deal and is an interesting conversationalist, when he can conquer his shyness of talking to a female. I wish I had come to know him sooner. Is it not strange that adversity—or rather, is it not strange that it should take adversity to introduce two mortals who have been sharing this confinement for so many

weeks and months without exchanging more than an occasional
greeting?

·◇·

September 3, 1851
  Course N by W, variation 1 pt easterly.
Noon position:
  N 24°10'; W 157°50' (estimated).
  Sky overcast; wind has risen to force 7 or better, still ESE,
    hauling S briefly, then back to ESE.
  Barometer steady just below 30".
  Ship running under triple-reefed topsails.

H orace sat in Smith's place at the noon meal, and the conversation was mostly about the weather, which was warm, wet, and windy. It seemed to Amanda that she had been listening—or half-listening—all her life to these solemn prognostications derived from omens as obscure as the livers of Roman birds: risings and fallings of a column of mercury; circular movements—clockwise and counter-clockwise; temperature gradients, averages, means.

"Neither Heyerman nor Davidson has ever heard of a real tropical hurricane this far above the Line and this late in the fall," Horace was saying.

Neither had Jonathan, but he wanted his second officer to know how to maneuver a ship in one, how to stay clear of the "dangerous semicircle." He was illustrating the strategy by a drawing on the tablecloth made with the point of a clean knife. Amanda did not object to the drawing, but she did wish the lesson could be postponed until after the main course. Cook had served up the last of the fresh meat, nicely roasted and garnished with a vegetable that was like, but certainly was not, an Irish potato. She thought it delicious. Having a better appetite than her companions—and for the second day in a row—made her feel a glutton.

The man-talk went on and on, continuous as the sounds of the rigging and hull. The topic had shifted to the new hand Rory, whose superior knowledge made it possible for him to impose on the credulity of his shipmates—"even the whites." And by implication, more disastrously on black, brown, and yellow.

"It's when the going gets rough that a man like him can be dangerous," Jonathan said. "Times when the work is extra hard, the food bad, the water low. In a storm like that one coming down to the Horn. Or too long a calm. The men will have grievances—some real, some fancied. And given the chance, he'll work on them. At that point, it's too late to deal with him. You must have got the upper hand of him from the start."

Whatever Horace wished to say in answer had to be postponed. Word came down from the quarterdeck that the foretopsail (which Jonathan had been eyeing with apprehension all the morning) had split and must be lowered for repairs. That was work for all hands. Even Willy was included in the call.

"We might as well get on with your navigation lessons," Jonathan said when he and Amanda were alone at table. "Let's see how much you recall of what we went over yesterday."

They had spent nearly an hour, he lecturing and she listening, on the laws that governed those great curling triangles on the surface of the earth that could be made somehow to reveal secrets in the heavens. She had asked a question now and then, questions Jonathan had answered precisely and in meticulous detail. But her mind slipped through the meshes of his words and swam off on some uncharted course of its own. When he quizzed her now, she recalled nothing. Nothing at all.

"Why didn't you stop me, Amanda, and say you were not understanding?"

"I thought I was."

He was frowning, not angry, but puzzled, searching for a way to begin again on the level of her ignorance or stupidity. She could have wept for shame.

"Let me ask you this," he said slowly. "Do you understand why it's so important to know where we are at sea?"

"I think I do."

"Could you put it into words?"

"You need to know where you are so you can tell what way to steer…to…get where you want to go."

"For example?" Jonathan spoke gently, patiently, as if he were encouraging a backward child or a clever dog.

"Well, say you wanted to go to—"

"To San Francisco. From where we are at present." He supplied the destination and laid out the problem. "What course would you have to steer to make landfall there?"

"Northeast—or southeast. Depending."

"Depending on what?"

She saw what answer was expected of her, but she also saw a flaw in the logic that led to it. "Except that we *could* sail straight east till we fell in with the coast, couldn't we? And then sail up or down till we fetched the entrance to the bay."

"How would you know which way to sail when you fell in with the coast?"

She had fallen into a trap any halfway sensible being ought to have seen and avoided. And Jonathan's continuing patience was beginning to exasperate her.

"Are there any other reasons you can think of? Reasons for knowing—as precisely as possible—where the ship stands? Take your time. Think it through."

Amanda dredged the muddy bottom of her mind and came up with offshore dangers—rocks, shoals, and islands. To these Jonathan added the coast itself, approached under conditions of poor visibility, "with a gale at your back, like as not, and fog ahead." For these and other reasons (which he implied were numerous, as well as self-evident) a captain must keep a careful reckoning of his position from "departure" on and must check it constantly against a "fix" obtained from observations of the sun or other bodies that would—if properly manipulated—establish both latitude and longitude.

"Is it clear so far?" he asked.

She said it was, and he looked at her in a way that made her feel like an instrument being read.

"All right, then, let's get to the matter of latitude." He drew a grid of lines on the tablecloth. "Let this be the ship." An X at the center of the grid. "And she is sailing—do you happen to know what course we're making, Amanda?"

"North?"

"By compass it's a point west of north because there's an easterly variation here." He began to move the knife up one of the vertical lines. "We're sailing as close to true north as we can." The knife point crossed one of the horizontals, then another. "And so we go till we reach the 50s." The knife stopped. "There we catch the westerlies," the knife executed a smart right turn, "and ride them all the way to the coast." He looked up to be sure she was paying close enough attention. Then he held up a finger and said, "Now!"

A tingle of irritation ran over her skin, and she had to remonstrate with herself: she must listen humbly and be ready to answer sensibly when questioned, not compounding her original sin of inattention with that of contentiousness.

"Can you tell me how we'll know that we've got to the 50th parallel? That it's time to head east?"

"When we catch the westerlies?"

Jonathan ignored the flippancy. He was waiting for the right answer, holding his breath, his mouth a trifle open like a parent teaching an infant to eat with a spoon.

She tried the obvious alternatives: by keeping a reckoning, working out each day's sailing from the log; by taking observations of sun, moon, or planets. But Jonathan was after a particular answer, and in the end he had to supply it himself. The North Star. Polaris.

"Centuries before we had clocks or compasses, men learned how to use the polestar to point a direction and tell them how far north or south they were." And he launched into a narrative history of navigation from the Vikings to Columbus to Mercator.

There was something peculiar, something not like Jonathan, about all this. Not just that he was wasting words, forgetting his purpose, piling up parentheses. There was something else, the way the words grouped themselves in clumps and spurts instead of orderly ranks…. He was not well! His color was too high. Along the edges of his beard his cheeks were bright.

The tingling sensation ran over the surface of Amanda's skin again, and this time she knew it for what it was. Not irritation, but alarm.

She was doing the lesson he had set for her in *The New American Practical Navigator.* Someone—most likely her father—had told her that everything a man needed to know in a lifetime at sea was contained in that volume, written by Salem's most illustrious citizen, Nathaniel Bowditch. He had opened the secrets of the officer caste to any American seaman who could read and cipher and was willing to apply himself. His book, simply called "the Bowditch," was written in language plain enough for any halfway intelligent Yankee: *"The latitude of a place, being its distance from the equator, is measured by an arc of the meridian contained between the zenith and the equator, hence, if the distance of any heavenly body from the zenith when on the meridian, and the declination of the object be given, the latitude may be found."*

She understood every word except "declination," but she had some trouble fitting them together into meaning. Her mind kept sliding off the curvature of the clauses. She tried reading it aloud: *"Case I. When the object rises and sets…"*

That would do for the sun, but Jonathan had set her the problem of finding latitude by the polestar, which did not rise and set. She must look further, to Case II: *"When the object does not set, but comes to the meridian above the horizon twice in 24 hours."*

Did Polaris do that? Or did it simply brighten and dim as daylight came and went, standing always in the same place, directly over the earth's northern pole? She would have to ask Jonathan about Case II. Meanwhile there was the Rule, which she ought to commit to memory: *"Add the complement of the declination* whatever that might be *to the meridian altitude* which meant the height at noon; *the sum will be the latitude, of the same name as the declination."*

She was running out of wind. It seemed pointless to commit to memory what she didn't understand. Perhaps she was too old to learn—as Jonathan had said, "too thick in the head." Or perhaps it was because she was a woman, good at sums, but neither gifted nor trained for the manipulation of imaginary triangles that curled themselves mysteriously around the globe.

Jonathan seemed more himself at supper, but quiet. Afterward, they sat in the cabin, he at his desk, she at the round table. The ship was wallowing ponderously, and the lamp swung in a long ellipse. It went through her mind that there was some analogy between the movement of the circle it threw on the green baize of the table cover and the movement of the earth around the sun. In both cases, something appeared to move—the lamp in one case, the sun in the other—while in reality it was the other way round. The table, the cabin, the whole ship, moved under the lamp, which was still. The earth moved around the stationary sun.

Jonathan made a sound like a groan. She turned to look. He was hunched over the logbook, and something in the way he held his shoulders told her he was in pain. But he said nothing, did not turn.

She tried to recapture her thought about the lamp and the sun, but it had lost its shape and seemed hardly more than silly.

Jonathan groaned again. This time it seemed to startle him; he looked to see if she had heard him. Amanda came to stand by his chair, putting her hands to his cheeks. They were hot, not burning like Smith's, but certainly hotter than normal.

"Does your head ache, Jonathan?"

He said not, but he let her persuade him to lie down on the sofa beside the desk. She fetched a shawl for his legs and a pillow for his head. He reached for her hand and gave it a playful squeeze. Jonathan always seemed to regard illness as a misdemeanor and found it hard to accept "coddling" except when it was disguised as humoring Amanda's "need to play nurse."

When she had made him easy, she settled herself at the desk, partly to be close to him and partly to look at what he had been writing in the log. She suspected that his "dead"—or deduced—reckoning might be easier to grasp than Bowditch on latitude, and it was.

At noon, the ship's position was estimated at 24°10' north latitude. Jonathan had just written in a new position of 25°, a gain of 50' of latitude in six hours because he had calculated the speed of the ship as slightly more than seven knots. This estimate came from the chip log, which had been heaved at two-hour intervals. The reckoning was unusually simple because the course was due north, so distance traveled could be translated directly into latitude gained.

She leafed back through previous entries to see how they had been constructed. "What does it mean here where you say that we crossed the tropic of Cancer?" she asked aloud.

Instead of answering, Jonathan asked her for an orange and got out his penknife. He began to carve the peel in a pattern like the net of meridians and parallels on a globe. When he was done, he clasped it between his thumb and third finger and made it turn on an axis that ran from stem to blossom end, pointing out that the fruit was slightly flattened at its poles, "and the earth is flattened in the same way.

He was beginning at the very beginning again, with the great circles of longitude and the concentric circles of latitude. Amanda composed herself to hear him out: *"prime meridian," "measurement east or west," "right ascension and departure," "declination," "apparent movement," "Capricorn and Cancer," "equinox," "solstice."* The ponderous Latinisms were laid on her like commandments.

"There are two entirely different movements," Jonathan was insisting, as if she had disputed it. "The best way to understand that is to act it out. Take the orange here."

She did.

"Now hold it at an angle. No, tilted more. Remember—23° off the vertical."

She held the orange as he bade her.

"Now start it spinning. The other way. The sky seems to be moving east to west because the earth is moving west to east."

The other movement was the orbit. The hanging lamp over the table would represent the sun, and she was to walk around it in an oval path, noting how the light fell, how one hemisphere or the other was favored at the far ends of the oval because of the 23° tilt.

Amanda felt like a priestess carrying a sacrificial vessel, commanded by Moses, who had his Commandments from Jehovah and with them the burden of leading his people through the wilderness. Jonathan faced a wilderness of water instead of one of sand.... Moses had been warned he would not live to reach his journey's end, ordered to pass on the burden and the Commandments.

"Jonathan!"

He broke off his exposition in midsentence.

"You're ill!"

She could see his lips forming a denial, but she hurried on, censoring panic from her voice, yet insisting on the truth of her statement. "You're ill, and Mr. Smith is gravely so. We're only three days out of harbor. Why don't we put back?"

THE FOURTH DAY

September 4, 1851

> *Course maintained through 8 A.M. N by W.*
> *Estimated position: 26°30' N; 157°50' W.*
> *Wind continues fresh to strong gale, ESE to SSE, gusting.*
> *Seas high, confused at times; broken clouds and rain squalls.*
> *Barometer fluctuating, mostly above 30".*
> *Ship running under close-reefed topsails.*

AMANDA BRIGHT'S JOURNAL

September 4, 1851

Mr. Smith is very ill. Flagg and I watched by turns and together through the night. His fever is so high that he is quite beside himself, muttering and tossing his head without opening his eyes. It is dreadful to have to watch and be unable to relieve him.

The Guide *advises that in cases of inflammatory fever—which is what we now take this to be—no stimulants should be administered and only the lightest, if any, food should be taken lest the advent of blood to the head of one weakened by fever induce an apoplexy. The patient must, however, be persuaded to drink as much and as often as possible. This has been our office and not an easy one, as Mr. Smith no longer seems to understand what we say or, for that matter, who we are.*

By dawn I was quite worn out and laid myself down on the sofa so as not to disturb Jonathan's sleep by coming to bed. But it was impossible to rest there, as the motion of the ship kept threatening to roll me off. Flagg discovered my predicament and installed me in an improvised chaise lounge, consisting of Jonathan's desk chair, a sea chest padded with blankets, and a number of strategically placed cushions. Thus secured as if in a hammock, I slept for a couple of hours and did not even know when Jonathan woke and passed through the cabin on his way to the quarterdeck.

Flagg has promised to contrive for me today a fiddle board for the sofa so that I can use it as a sleeping place if we have another night of vigil.

I have not yet had a moment to speak with Jonathan, but I take it that he is recovered from his indisposition of yesterday and that it was not—heaven be praised!—the fever after all.

·◇·

At ten o'clock Horace came to fetch both of the sextants.

"The sun is breaking through," he said, "and I'm to use the mate's, to see how it compares with the Old Man's."

Amanda had expected to be called for her postponed lesson if and when the sky cleared, but Horace brought no invitation for her. Of course, if he was buckling down—really buckling down at last—there was no reason.

She was a bit disappointed. Not that she was deeply committed to the subject, but she had looked forward to having a legitimate reason to go on deck. What she ought to be concerned with, rather than problems of longitude and latitude, were those of the laundry: how to wash and dry the bed linens of the sick man. Water was available, thanks to the canvas trough in which they collected what ran off the courses during the rain squalls. It was not fresh enough to drink, but it did very well for washing. The difficulty was drying the sheets after they were clean. Even when the sun shone, the spray that continually washed over the decks would not only dampen anything hung there but impregnate it with salt.

The only place suitable for her purpose was the galley, but it was so small and crowded that she could not ask Cook to make room for a basket of wet linen—unless it could be hung out of his way. If a rack could be fashioned and hung over the stove, in the current of heated air that rose from it...

She was making a rough diagram of such an apparatus when Flagg came out of the sickroom. His gestures conveyed the news that Smith was resting but not much improved. Still without speaking, the old man came to look over her shoulder at the sketch, nodded thoughtfully, inquired whether she would like him to undertake its execution, and, having got a nod of affirmation from Amanda, took the paper and made his way on deck.

AMANDA BRIGHT'S JOURNAL

I have had more converse with Jonah Flagg during our night watches and have learned something of his history—not an extraordinary one, I should think, but one that accounts for his character, which is certainly not ordinary.

He is from the Maine coast, of seafaring folk, and has spent most of his life in ships of one description or another, fishing, whaling, or trading over the water-covered world. He once had a wife and two young children, but they died while he was away on a voyage. He blames himself for having "basked like a black fish" under tropical skies while his loved ones were perishing in the cold of a bad New England winter. I have the impression that he welcomes this opportunity to perform offices of mercy for a man whom he has no reason to love, offices that he could not perform for his dear ones in their hour of need.

·✧·

She stopped to reflect how little she welcomed the same opportunity. She had a sense of obligation, but not the natural turn for nursing a woman was supposed to have. Was it because she was not yet a mother? not yet wholly—truly—a woman?

·✧·

I still believe it would be better if Jonathan were to order the ship headed back to Honolulu. His reasons for not doing so are several, but they do not impress me as sound.

First, there are financial reasons: expenses and losses to the owners. The worst of these would be fees for replacing our replacements, who would surely desert the moment their feet touched the wharf. The sums already paid to the Honolulu crimps would be forfeit, and they would charge new and possibly higher sums next time.

Also there would be some loss of perishable cargo, in which our own money is invested. Jonathan's hope is to sell these commodities at a large profit in the settlements on Vancouver Island and reinvest that amount in furs, which can be sold at an even greater profit in China, or bartered for tea and silk, which can be sold at a profit back at home. Thus he hopes to work ourselves free of the necessity to make many more such voyages as this. (To which I say amen!)

But against these considerations must be weighed the health and safety of those aboard. We cannot care properly for Mr. Smith; and inflammatory fevers, neglected, sometimes prove fatal. Also the disease may spread! Even if Jonathan has escaped it, other cases may develop. Each man who falls sick will throw an added burden of labor on the rest, and if this storm continues, exposure to the elements and lack of sleep will lower all hands' resistance.

The owners of the Maria M. *are men of commerce, but they are also Christians who would never hesitate to choose the welfare of their fellow beings over the turning of a profit. Besides, in this instance four of those beings are their own kin.*

When we talked of this last evening, Jonathan was not ready to admit that there was any real danger, but I mean to speak to him again. We are still only four days out of port. Our destination is at least twenty days distant. And Mr. Smith is no better, may be worse.

·✧·

She planned to speak to Jonathan about this at the noon meal, but she was not at table for it. There had been another crisis in Smith's condition. Both she and Flagg were needed to restrain him while his body was sponged and to force liquid down his throat. When at last she could be spared, she was too tired to eat. She went straight to her stateroom, lay down on the bunk, and fell asleep.

Her dreaming was troubled. The ship rolled, and she had to strain to keep from rolling with it across the wide double bunk. The strain carried into the dream as a nagging voice that said she ought to get up and move to the chairbed in the cabin. She was arguing that there was too much light, that she would be in the way of Jonathan working at his desk, that she would be disturbed by the voices—many voices—mingling with the sounds of the storm. Some of them were giving orders, others were muttering complaints. She couldn't make out what they were saying, but now and then there was a snatch she could recognize: a phrase or two from the *Guide and Companion*, parts of Jonathan's lecture on trigonometry, a halloo from the cross-trees and an answer from the deck. There were songs, some of them familiar but most not so. And through it all a heavy sense of effort. She was trying hard, as hard as ever she could, not giving up, answering all the demands put upon her—or at least about to answer, once she had climbed this long hill, dropped this weight, pulled herself over this obstacle. But it was hard. Her limbs were leaden. It was hot and airless…dark…impossible to breathe….

Slow to come awake to what was happening, she fought the assault as if it were part of a dream, with a dream effort, expecting every moment that the nightmare would begin to dissolve.

The man's hands were running roughly over her, feeling through the fabric of her skirt for her legs to spread them, pushing her hands away as they moved to defend her. His face was pressing so close that she could get no air but what he had breathed out. He was grunting like a boar in rut, close to the opening of her ear, lowering himself onto her, crushing her rib cage. Death by pressing—Salem's old punishment for witchcraft.

Terror gave her strength. She freed her hands and clawed at the soft part of his neck under his beard. He cursed and muttered.

"…not play the fine lady with me, Sal!"

The voice was hollow and breathy, but she knew it.

"Jonathan!"

He slapped her hard across the mouth.

After that she did not struggle. She stood outside the body that was being violated and regarded it as if the nightmare were being dreamed by someone else. The dreamer felt many things: pain from the stinging bruise on her lips, horror and humiliation, and a strangely perverse excitement as the hard lump pressed against her groin and the grunting grew to a groaning. She was helpless. And not entirely sorry for it.

Jonathan was cursing again. His hands jerked and trembled like a palsy victim's. The hard lump no longer obtruded. He was blaming her for his impotence, and in foul language.

The ship fetched a sudden lurch. He rolled away from her. Amanda slipped out of the bunk, crossed the three steps to the door, wrenched it open, and was free.

As she crossed the cabin, she saw Horace coming down from the afterdeck. He called to her, but she did not answer. Nor stop, not till she was safe in the sanctuary of the sickroom.

Flagg was not at the bedside. Smith was strapped to his bunk, unconscious, quiet except for a low moaning breath that came and went like a pulse. She crouched on the sea chest, doubled over, holding her knees, letting the whirl of images slow and settle in her mind.

Rape! Jonathan had done his best to rape her! That was reality— unbelievable, but unarguable. She remembered an engraving—was it in a book or framed and hanging on a wall? "Rape of the Sabine Women." It was the first time—perhaps the only time—she had ever encountered the word. A classic work of art, a thing she had looked at a hundred times without seeing anything but the baroque beauty of its composition, till one day her eye rested on it for a longer than usual moment, and it unraveled into images of repellent violence. But never till now had she understood its true meaning.

Some things were coming clear now, but they did little to console her. The fever had struck Jonathan as it had Smith. He had held his own against it longer because he was younger and stronger. Even in delirium he was strong and desired strongly. But he did not desire *her!*

"*....not play the fine lady with me, Sal!*"

Or did he say "gal"?

Who was Sal? Some woman whose body he had rented along with the bed on which he entered her? When? Had all this happened before they were married? Afterwards? Was it perhaps just now, while they were in port in Honolulu? Was Sal one of those abandoned native women who knew how to give and receive love, how to stir passions in a man that she, poor, pitiable Amanda, could never hope to equal? This was his other violation! He had made her jealous of a prostitute. Stripped her of self-respect, besmirched her pride.

"It doesn't matter! Doesn't matter! Doesn't—" she hissed into her fists.

All that mattered now was that she could not forgive Jonathan, not now, not ever. She wanted never to see him again. Never to feel his touch. If she could, she would run from him as far as the other side of the world. She could run no farther than the confines of the cabin. But she could build a wall around her shattered self.

Some time later Horace came looking for her.

"Jonathan's out of his head, Amanda. You've got to give him something to quiet him."

But she would not stir.

"Flagg and I have had a time to get him tied down. He fights like a maniac. He'll do himself harm."

The words reached her ears but did not penetrate the wall.

"What's wrong between you?"

She felt no need to answer.

"If he said something that— Look, Amanda, he isn't himself. He said things to us you wouldn't...I never would have...I mean to say..." Horace's distress and embarrassment made breaks in his voice. "You can't hold it against him. He isn't himself."

But he was! One of his selves! This man had lived inside the man she loved and married. Still lived....

Horace was begging her to help him, to resume her proper role and free him to resume his. His role—she realized—was the command of the ship. If Jonathan was incapacitated, Horace was the ranking officer. He had a right to any help she could give.

"Don't you have something that'll bring down the fever so he can get some rest?"

"There's Dover's powder." She spoke in the voice he had been hoping for—calm, comforting, dependable.

Horace relaxed with an audible sigh. "Flagg said he thought it would be that. But we don't know the dosage."

She stood up and waited a moment for her knees to steady themselves. "It hasn't done Mr. Smith much good that I can see," she said. "But the *Guide* says most fever patients respond to it."

She made her way to the table under the skylight, opened the medicine chest, and began pulling out the bottles from which to measure the ingredients.

"Will you give him the draught, or shall I?" Horace asked.

"Flagg and I can manage," she said.

Horace kissed her on the cheek and went on deck.

2

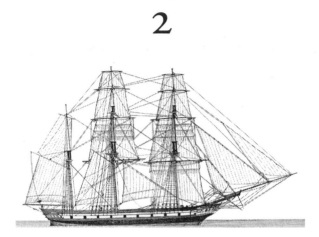

Horace Martin,
Master

THE FIFTH DAY

The storm had grown worse. The sky was mottled with dark splotches that looked like the marks on the bodies of the two sick men. The wind was brutal; the sea, outraged.

Amanda wrote no journal that morning. It was a time for covering up, not for recording, what was in her mind. She was tired—physically weary of the struggle to move from one sickroom to the other, to stand upright without holding on while she mixed or administered a dose of medicine. But she was not ready to risk sleep.

When Horace came down at noon, he found her embroidering. "Setting us an example? Like old Captain Corcoran's wife?"

"Who was she?"

"Father used to tell about her. When he was a boy, on his first whaling voyage, the captain's wife used to take out her tatting whenever the wind blew up, just to show it she was not to be intimidated."

Amanda smiled and felt the strain between her shoulders ease, but she went on with her work, bracing herself against the shuddering downhill plunge, waiting till the wave passed under the hull and the keel leveled, hurrying to draw a colored stitch through the white linen, setting her needle for the next stitch, and bracing again.

"Manna?"

It was the name he had called her when he was too small to say

Amanda, and it carried her back, far back, to a time when she had played mother to this child, rehearsing for the day she would play the role in another setting.

She looked up. Horace was waiting with his question.

"Some of the men want us to turn around."

"Jonathan won't hear of it."

"I know. But..."

Amanda repeated what she could remember of Jonathan's roster of reasons for not turning back, to each of which Horace nodded agreement. Then he added one of his own.

"And if we beat into this all the way back to Honolulu, we'd have hell's own time getting into harbor, with the wind throwing surf on the reef. There's no decent holding ground on the outside. But that's not what I've been thinking of. As things stand now—"

Flagg came out of Smith's stateroom, where he had been on watch since midmorning, and Horace interrupted himself to ask advice about the chip log. It seemed not to be giving a reliable account of the ship's speed. Was there any thing to be done about it?

Flagg thought not. Most captains didn't bother to heave the log while the ship was scudding. Overtaking seas sometimes set it spinning backwards, and there was more drifting weed and flotsam than usual to foul the line.

They talked across her as if she were not present, and she ceased to listen. It was no affair of hers. She had her own concerns. She must steady her hand so the needle would enter the linen just one thread away from where it had entered last time, pull the stitch tight, but no tighter than the last, and repeat. Around her—above, below, on all sides—chaos pressed. But here at the round table, seated securely in a chair bolted to the timbers of the deck, she was protected—as in a womb.

Flagg had gone, and Horace was talking again. But not to her. He could speak his thoughts aloud because she was there; that was all. It was about the reckoning.

"...already so far off as to be no use. Heyerman thinks so, too. He says all we can do is ride this out and wait till the sky clears for a shot of the sun."

(So Horace *had* learned to shoot the sun. Good.)

She would have liked to ask some questions about the lesson that had been offered and then denied her: Was it difficult to use the sextant? How long had it taken to get the hang of it? But Horace had gone on to talk of something else.

"...wouldn't have thought I'd take to this sort of thing. But it's heady as strong drink. Especially when you feel you're doing well." And he did feel that. He had been commended by the two men aboard whose opinions he valued—Heyerman and Davidson.

"Davy's taken over the starboard watch," he added parenthetically, "and is having his troubles with Rory. Which reminds me. I don't think I told you: he's offered to help out with the navigating. Says he has a sextant of his own at the bottom of his seabag."

"Davy or Rory?"

"Rory."

"You're not going to let him?"

"Why not? I wouldn't trust him with the helm. He'd have us headed for the nearest grogshop—wherever he supposes that to be. But if he can measure a meridian angle and knows what to do with it when he's got it, what's there to be lost?"

Did that mean he had not learned to use the sextant after all? She asked the question casually, without looking up from her needlework. Horace hedged. He had found the sun and brought it down to the horizon. But the deck was unsteady and the sky clear only for a moment. His angle was not the same as Jonathan's. Not by considerable.

When Amanda was alone again, she looked at Horace's last entry in the logbook.

September 5, 1851

> *Day commences with wind from ESE to SE, very heavy seas. Barometer 29.5". Heyerman says this means we are within 150 miles of the center of a hurricane.*

That was all!

No rate of speed recorded. No position estimated.

The ship was lost! Running before a gale, under a cover of cloud that hid the heavens. There was nothing in the way for a thousand miles, so the danger was not immediate. The ship could hold her own against the forces that assailed her till they wore themselves out, as they would; till the sky cleared at last, as it must.

But what then? When the heavens revealed themselves, there would be no one to read them. Horace had not mastered the mystery. And he had given up on the reckoning, so there was no way to compute, even roughly, how far they had been blown or in what direction. No one to assume the priestly function. No one but Rory. If he knew what he claimed to know, he was master of the ship. And if he did not know, the ship was without a master.

Chaos burst the shell of her sanctuary and knocked the needle from her hand. Fear flooded the cabin. She would have to swim hard to stay afloat, but her body was terror bound. Her mind raced backwards instead of ahead. If only the clouds had held off on the day Jonathan offered to teach her, or if he had offered sooner, in time to vest her with the knowledge that was power—power to act, instead of to be acted upon.

She went to the bookcase over the desk, took down the volume of Bowditch and the sextant case, and unlatched the lid. The instrument was appalling, a jumbled jigsaw of bright brass, black wood, and ivory. But Bowditch would sort it out.

"A sextant of reflection is constructed on the same principle and may be used for the measuring of altitudes in the same manner as a quadrant."

On the page facing that passage was an engraving of both instruments, each part lettered and explained in a key below. Amanda read and decided that she would not bother with the quadrant. The sextant was the vessel in which Jonathan caught and contained the magical power.

When she thought she understood the function of all its parts, she took up the instrument carefully, as if it were eggshell. There was the ring into which the sight tube was to be inserted. There was the horizon glass on which it was to be trained. Through the clear pane one could look to the horizon. The other, the silvered pane, reflected an image of the sun, transmitted by a movable mirror mounted on top of the sextant, which was connected to an arm that pointed to the calibrated arc at the bottom of the instrument.

"Move the index the arm till you bring the image of the sun's lower limb to touch the horizon.... The degrees and minutes pointed out by the index on the arc will be the observed altitude."

So far she understood. In theory. Now she must practice. To do that she would need a false horizon and a mock sun: a horizontal line above which stood some round object.

The steps of the companion ladder in the officers' mess were bound with brass, and the hanging lamp above the dining table had a round brass base. By standing back as far aft as possible, backed against the partition, she could find the bright line of the third step, but the image of the lamp eluded her. The sextant was heavy and awkward to hold at eye level. Twice she lost her balance, and it struck her cheekbone. She wedged herself against the table so that she was supported back and side, and tried again. And again.

She swept the index back and forward along the 120° of arc, without ever catching a glimpse of her "sun," till her arm ached. finally, just when she was ready to give up, there was a sudden flare of daylight. Bare feet, ankles, and frayed trouser legs came into her field of vision. Someone had opened the companionway door.

Lowering the sextant, she saw one of the Sandwich Islanders staring at her, his mouth open so that his teeth were a ring of white, his eyes making similar rings of white around their dark irises—a mask of comic incredulity. He dropped the pail he was carrying and fled the way he had come. Water and wet rags spilled over the floor.

Amanda had sopped up the worst of it by the time Davidson appeared with another pail of rainwater, much amused by the contretemps.

"Shaking like a cabbage palm, he was. And jabbering about a devil face."

"That would be me with the sextant, I suppose."

Davy shook his head. Wouldn't you think a chap who'd made more than a single voyage would have recognized the instrument? But then, there was no telling what went on in a Kanaka's head. First-rate hands, they were. Had more heart for work aloft in a gale than most whites. But unpredictable. Something would set them off, and there they'd be, carrying on like a bunch of scared old— He caught himself in time to amend the figure of speech he had intended to "like a bunch of scared sheep."

They divided the water between the two pails, and Davy carried one into each of the sickrooms. When he returned, Amanda was try-ing to insert the sight tube into the sextant's ring.

"You don't happen to know how this is done?" she asked.

Davy couldn't say that he did. He'd often had a hankering to use one of them things, but mathematics was needed, so he'd heard, and he'd never gone past simple sums. He did think, however, that what she was doing would come easier if she was to loosen the setscrew of the ring.

He performed that act for her, and the tube slipped into place. Then he helped her adjust it so that it was parallel to the plane of the instrument, as Bowditch instructed. Finally he showed her a bet-ter way of holding the sextant in the viewing position.

"If you grab on a bit higher, ma'am. Like that. See if that don't keep it from bounding about."

It did. But now there was another difficulty. With the sight tube in place there was not enough light to find even her false horizon, much less her false sun.

"I must be doing something wrong." Amanda offered him the in-strument. "Why don't you have a try?"

Davy smiled an odd, snarl-shaped smile and mumbled something about having to get back to work on a storm sail, but it was clear that he could be persuaded. Amanda was beginning to prevail when Horace came down, looking for his sou'wester. Another rain squall was in the offing.

"I'm glad to find you," he said to Davidson. "It was you mended the fore-topsail yesterday, wasn't it?"

Davidson said it was.

"She's pulling fine, and we're steadier for it."

"Aye, you want a lofty sail in a wind like this here."

"But will she take the strain? It's an old canvas.

Davidson considered before answering. "Well, sir, she'll hold for a while. But an off sail might ease her some."

Amanda had begun putting the sextant away, loosening the sight tube, slipping it out of its ring, fitting it into the slot in the cover of the case. Horace glanced over at her and interrupted his consultation with Davidson to say, "Be sure you latch the lid, coz. We can't have anything happen to the instrument."

She was rebuked. Like a child caught playing with objects belonging to her elders instead of with her own proper toys.

Jonathan's fever was on the rise again, but he was not delirious. Dark red blotches showed everywhere on his body. His abdomen was distended and painful. Amanda kept administering doses of Dover's powder because doing something was better than doing nothing. Also, it was part of her charade: the punctilious performance of duty, caring for Jonathan as if her feeling for him were what it had been before all feeling had been numbed, all feeling but the memory of anger.

When Jonathan was awake, his eyes followed her around the stateroom as if he had asked a question and was awaiting her answer. Once, when she had helped him drink and eased him back on to his pillow, he reached out a hot, shaky hand to detain her. Amanda braced herself for the words that would come now and those she must speak in response. But all he said was her name. After a moment, his hand dropped, his eyes closed, and his breathing sounded as if he were dozing.

Willy was also beginning to follow her with anxious eyes. It was to reassure him, more than Jonathan, that she forced herself to chatter as the old Amanda might have, relaying news from above decks like family gossip: how well Mr. Martin was doing, how "cheerfully and promptly" the men obeyed him (that being Jonathan's measure of good forecastle morale), the force and direction of the wind, the behavior of the barometer, the astonishing mildness of the air.

Jonathan drank his medicine and lay back, listening with his eyes half-closed, nodding or shaking his head if a response was required, smiling sometimes, until he dozed.

"Cousin Amanda?"

"Yes, Willy?"

"Is he...do you think?..." It was so thin a whisper that she had to read his lips to know that the lad was asking, "Is he going to get better?"

"I don't know."

Yesterday she would have said, "Of course!" Then she had thought Jonathan immortal, able to perform the labors of a Hercules, to suffer the insufferable, survive the unbearable, come unscathed through any ordeal. She had also thought him faithful, chaste. Today she knew that no one was immortal or deserved to be. They were all flawed, all doomed, adrift on a hostile ocean, watched over by no kindly Providence, given the illusion of controlling their fate but not the means.

All day—for many days it seemed—she had been thirsting for air. She had not gone on deck lest she make a nuisance of herself, but that no longer seemed so heinous an offense. She wrapped herself in her cloak and climbed the after companion ladder.

The first gulp of wind was too big for her lungs and set her coughing, but the second made everything right. Lifting her face, she could feel the sun, hidden under a thin layer of cloud, burning softly. The men working on the deck forward had stripped to their trousers. She envied them. Her cloak was heavy and hot, and when she threw back the hood, the wind caught the short hairs that framed her face and turned them into whips. The only way to stand was facing into it, looking aft, past the taffrail to where the great overtaking waves were building—up and up, into towering crags that threatened to topple.

The ship would be swamped! Unable to bear the weight of water that was curling over, its crest already breaking into foam. Then, at the last possible instant, with a movement that was almost indecent, the vessel heaved up her stern and let the wave slide under, hissing along the bulwarks as it passed. Already another sea was gathering.

Horace touched her on the arm. "You'd better come below, coz." And when she resisted, he whispered, "Please. Don't make things worse.

He looked in the direction of the wheel, and she noticed for the first time that the helmsman of the watch was Tono, the tattooed Marquesan, and the man who stood lee helm, one of the Sandwich Islanders. Two dark, savage giants, who were glaring at her as if she had committed, or was about to commit, some outrage.

"I need to talk to you," Horace said as they started down the companionway. "I don't want to exaggerate the problem, but…"

"Do they blame me for the storm?" Amanda asked.

"The Kanakas? I don't think so. Or maybe they do. It doesn't matter. They don't cut any ice with the old hands, and it's they who're…" Horace scowled and wiped the back of his hand across his mouth. She saw him again as a gangly, tow-haired stripling, using that gesture to preface the confession of some minor misdemeanor for which he hoped to be granted absolution. "It's a question of authority. Yesterday I was the ship's dog. Today I'm the Old Man. That's too big a jump. Especially an order they don't like."

"What order don't they like?"

"They don't like this heading, not even Heyerman."

"Heyerman wants to put back?"

"Not put back. Head into it. He says it's the only way to ride out a storm like this. The Old Man said to keep her running before the wind, but that was two days ago. It's blown up considerable since." Horace was arguing with himself. "I've heard it all my life: 'Keep her bows to the big ones!' When you've got more wind than you can handle, douse sail and head into it."

Amanda remembered the waves at the stern and was sick at the thought of breasting them. Also she thought she remembered Jonathan saying something quite different, something like *"Keep her stern to the seas."* But Horace was not asking that sort of advice from her. Hers was a different office.

"It's a hard decision," she told him. "Especially since you can't get any help from Jonathan or Mr. Smith. It can't hurt to talk things over with Heyerman. And maybe some of the other old hands like Davidson. But when you've heard them out, you must make up your own mind." Horace was listening to her with the same expression Willy wore when he asked if Jonathan would die. As if she were an oracle. It was enough to scare her into silence, but her voice went on, clear and sure, repeating the articles of faith on which they had both been raised.

"You are the captain. No matter what you were yesterday or the day before that. Make up your mind and hold to it as if there were no other way. You give the orders; they carry them out. You're master of the ship, and her safety—the safety of all aboard her—depends on you."

As Horace went back to the quarterdeck, he seemed to walk more slowly, with his shoulders slightly hunched, as if carrying a weight newly laid upon him.

Amanda began to light the cabin lamps. First, the gimbaled one over the desk. It shed light on the logbook, which was open; the volume of Bowditch, which was closed; and the polished lid of the sextant case, which was latched. Next, the hanging lamp over the round table. It swung in its usual slow arc around the sphere that was her own: the green baize world, bounded and divided by the fiddle so that it could hold, in separate compartments, her journal and writing materials, the medical books and chest, and her embroidery basket, in which the folds of white linen and skeins of bright threads bloomed like an arrangement of flowers.

THE SIXTH DAY

AMANDA BRIGHT'S JOURNAL

September 6, 1851

 Both patients continue very ill. Neither sponging nor powders seems to affect their fevers, which are as high this morning as they were last night. Their faces are flushed, their eyes abnormally bright, their lips dry and cracking, tongues the same.

 Jonathan is delirious at times, but not violently. Mr. Smith seems to be sinking into a sort of coma. Occasionally he rallies and takes fluids, but he is very weak.

 The blotches on the bodies of both have spread and deepened in color. In Mr. Smith's case, they now cover every part but his hands. Jonathan has none on his face, but the marks on his abdomen and chest are vivid and somewhat raised. He refuses all food but has taken this morning almost a cupful of weak tea.

·✧·

Amanda finished her morning entry, looked in on each of her patients again, then came back to the table. Flagg and Willy were busy on deck. She was on sick watch, and she must stay awake, but her eyes were too tired for embroidery, so she decided to write an installment of the family letter:

All of you would be proud of Horace and Willy. However much one loves a brother—and that is how I view them both—one is likely to underestimate his capacities, to think him always a little younger, weaker, less endowed with the powers of mature manhood than is the case.

With Horace I was not the only one; Jonathan also underestimated him. Under these very trying circumstances, he is showing his true colors. The burdens so suddenly thrust on his shoulders have caused to be revealed a talent for command that lay dormant till now. He is as surprised at its emergence as anyone else.

It was true. Already Horace was reaping the reward she had hoped for. His authority was established in his own mind, and he could turn his attention to other matters, make decisions involving more complex and unpredictable interactions than those of sun, moon, and planets. He was on the way to "making a captain."

With Willy the change is of a different sort. He has been diligent, though not good-humored, from the start. Determined not to accept any mothering from me or fathering from Horace, he kept his distance so rigidly that he seemed at times almost surly. (Not toward Jonathan, whom he admires, nor toward our first officer, Mr. Smith, to whom he is respectfully polite.) His one real friend has been our bosun, who undertook to tutor him in all sorts of nautical arts and with whom he has been bunking since we left the Azores.

But now the lad's natural warmth of heart has reasserted itself. He has volunteered to help with the nursing, not, I think, entirely out of devotion to Jonathan. Without being in the least demonstrative, he has seemed genuinely concerned to relieve me of as much labor as he can, even those distasteful chores that are traditionally left to us of the distaff-encumbered sex. I know he would far rather be on deck, making fast, belaying, scrambling up the ratlines—doing a man's work. I see his eyes light when the call for "all hands" rings out. But at all other times, he is at Jonathan's sickbed, urging me to rest.

His manner toward Horace is also changed. They are more like brothers than I have seen them before; yet Willy is as respectful to him as to the captain he signed on to serve. It must be deeply flattering to Horrie if he has time and mind to be aware....

Horace came down to make some notations in his log. Although he could not see what she was writing, Amanda felt uncomfortable and put the letter away with the pages of her journal on Ouwahoo. She was considering another visit to the sickrooms when Horace spoke.

"Heyerman is sure we'll be able to get a noon shot today. Can you work out the position if we do?"

"I? Certainly not!"

Horace swiveled around, surprised at the ill-natured vehemence of her answer. "I thought the Old Man was teaching you."

"I thought he was teaching *you.*"

"We only got as far as the observed angle. But you've been reading in the Bowditch, haven't you?"

Amanda nodded.

"Couldn't you at least have a try?"

"Why don't you ask Rory? You said you meant to."

"I was a fool. The man's a menace. We'd be better off with him overboard or in irons."

Amanda had never heard this sort of verbal violence from Horace, but he assured her that he meant what he said. One day—perhaps today—he might take Heyerman's advice and knock the fellow into the scuppers.

"What has he done?"

"Nothing. And that's what he proposes to do for the rest of the voyage by the looks of it." Horace sounded like the captain he was replacing, working up a tirade of indignation against the idler, who not only failed to pull his own weight but provoked others to follow his example. "He has them all grumbling and groaning. They go through the motions, but the yard doesn't move, or the sail's not sheeted home. We could have been caught in a trough and broached to this morning. And he'd have drowned as deep as anyone else. The damned fool!"

She let Horace's anger burn down a little before she asked what he had in mind to do—"besides knock him into the scuppers, which might be a bit difficult, considering the size of him."

Horace's outrage dissolved, leaving only a wry grin. "You're right, I couldn't do it. But you told me to make up my mind and hold to it, and I can do that. I've given the orders: north by west, with as much sail as it's safe to slap on. There's no way they can change that—short of mutiny, which they've not the stomach for." He seemed to be listening to himself, judging whether this statement was convincing—and deciding after a moment that it was not. "What it comes to is, I must prove myself."

"Prove yourself what?"

"Fit. And that means able to navigate. In these circumstances the logical thing would be for the command to pass to the man who's the most of a sailor. That's Heyerman. But he defers to me. I'm the master of the ship, and it's mine to give the orders; his to see them carried out. Why? Because he thinks any officer—even a ship's cousin like me—knows more than he does about navigation. I'm afraid—ashamed, really—to have him find out."

Horace's candor melted her resistance. Amanda promised to re-read the relevant parts of the Bowditch and be ready to help with the observation if the sky did clear at noon.

She began the task bravely. Her eyes kept going out of focus, and she had to slap herself awake twice before she was satisfied she could manage the simplest of the operations: finding the ship's latitude from an observation taken precisely at noon. But it was more than likely the sun would not show itself at noon. The sky was a patch-work of small blue and large gray shapes. Bowditch offered for such cases an alternative procedure—using an observation taken near, but not precisely at, noon.

She read it aloud: *"The latitude of a place may be accurately deter-mined by observing the sun's altitude when near the meridian, and not-*

ing the time by a watch regulated the preceding morning or following evening, by either of the methods given in this work."

That sent her to the index to look up methods of regulating a watch, and she learned that to do so at sea one must know the sun's altitude and the ship's latitude. But it was because she didn't know the latitude that she needed the time. It was like one of those maddening dictionary definitions that, to avoid embarrassing subject matter, send the reader in circles of *cf above* and *cf below.*

Nevertheless, she was beginning to grasp the essence of the procedure. Three quantities were involved: the altitude of some celestial body, the time, and the observer's latitude. If any two were known, the third could be found. Since what she wanted was the latitude, she must know the sun's altitude and the time at which it was taken. For that she would have to carry Jonathan's watch on deck along with the sextant. The watch had run down, of course, but she could rewind it and set it by the chronometer—which had not been wound since Jonathan was stricken! The face of the instrument read twenty minutes past six. It had stopped hours ago. For the moment she could not recall why this constituted a catastrophe, only that it did; that the balance between knowledge and ignorance—between power and impotence—was altered for the worse.

As penance (though the fault was not of her committing) she tried to reason it out: Why did a ship carry Greenwich time like a coal of Promethean Fire? To light what beacon in the dark? Why should a captain in the North Pacific need to know the hour at the Royal Observatory on the other side of the world?

Time, she recalled (had she learned it from Jonathan or read it in the Bowditch?), was the measure of distance east or west. So many hours along the sun's path (which was not really the sun's but the earth's) equaled so many degrees of longitude—east longitude or west longitude, measured from Greenwich because there had to be some line, arbitrarily chosen, from which to begin. The British had fixed on the meridian of their great observatory and made the other maritime nations acknowledge it as "prime." So Greenwich mean time was the standard against which all other times were measured.

For longitude. That was the point. The difference between time at Greenwich and time at ship was longitude. Without a chronometer set to Greenwich time and carefully rated for error, there was no way to know how far east or west the ship stood.

She told Horace about the chronometer when he came down to eat. He looked so tired, so vulnerable, and so determined to be neither that she wanted to throw her arms about him and tell him not to worry; she would put all to rights.

"It doesn't matter so much, Horrie. It's only longitude we can't get without the time. Latitude is what we need most, and I can show you how to find that."

"How? We're not going to get our noon shot, it seems."

"You'll get a noon shot some time. And by then you'll have learned how to work it. I'll help you."

"All right. We'll have a go. As soon as I've had a bite." He was trying to sound optimistic. "But I have to warn you, coz, I'm apt to start nodding once I've given my stomach something to stop its growling."

They had settled at the round table under the skylight. Amanda was reading Bowditch aloud: *"If the distance of any heavenly body from the zenith when on the meridian…"*

Horace frowned. "That means the altitude at noon?"

"Not exactly. The altitude is the distance above the horizon. Distance from the zenith is the rest of the way up."

"I see. The right angle minus the altitude."

"Yes. Now: *'If the distance from the zenith and the declination be given…'"*

"Declination?" Horace's face was a sky full of scudding cloud.

"Declination has to do with how high the sun rises on any given day. We say it 'comes north' in summer, meaning it rises higher in the sky, gets closer to the zenith. And the other way round in winter. It 'goes south,' or rises lower."

Horace shook his head. "I don't know that I make sense of that, but maybe I needn't. Can I just do it all by rote?"

"You can, but—wait, Horrie. If we use the polestar instead of the sun, it's easier to understand." Her eye was caught by the bowl of oranges wedged into one of the compartments of the fiddle. "I'll show you the way Jonathan showed me."

She took one of the fruits and began to cut a girdle around its circumference, talking as she worked, partly to hold her pupil's interest and partly to keep her mind's grasp firm. "All you need for the moment is to see how the sun's light strikes the earth. We won't bother with the meridians and parallels. This is the equator. These are the poles. The lamp will be the sun. Now, the polestar is much, much farther away than the sun, as you know. Imagine it's up at the tip of the mizzenmast. If it were dark, you could see it through the skylight there."

Horace nodded his acceptance of these assumptions. Amanda took the "earth" in hand, began the stately dance, walking the elliptical path around the hanging lamp, holding the orange at the right inclination, spinning it counterclockwise around its stem-axis.

"If you imagine yourself somewhere on the top half of the orange peel, say, at that nick where my knife slipped, you'll see how the spinning motion makes our day and night, or what appears to be the rising and the setting of the sun. Now: think about the star up there at the tip of the mast. Does it also seem to rise and set?"

"I suppose it...no, it doesn't." Horace spoke in incomplete phrases, as if he were deciphering an inscription. "It doesn't because...because it's too far...no, because it's straight up...directly above the...above the earth's axis."

"That's right."

"But does that help us? I can see why it's a star to steer by. So long as you're heading north. Toward the pole. But I don't see...wait, maybe...no, I really don't. How does it give one the latitude?"

A moment ago Amanda had known. Now she did not. A moment ago she had seen it all, whole and in motion. But to transmit that knowledge, she had to arrest the motion, had to break the whole into its component parts. To do that she had loosed her hold—and lost it.

But she did not confess. "Let's take it step-by-step," she said. "First, let's imagine that we're standing right at the pole." It was coming back, was almost within her grasp.

If she could catch even a trailing end, pull gently but steadily, she might bring the rest of it. "Where would we see the star in our night sky?"

Horace took the orange from her hand, touched the stem end, and squinted up at the skylight. "Well, I should think...oh, of course." He laughed aloud. "What a dolt I am. Straight up."

"At 90°. Now." (She was using the same didactic expletive she had found so hard to tolerate from Jonathan.) "Let's say you're on the equator. Where would you see the star?"

"I'm not sure you'd see it. But if you did, it would be...right on the horizon, wouldn't it?"

"And what if you were halfway between?"

"The star would be halfway up?"

"Exactly. The altitude of Polaris is the same as your latitude. At the pole it's 90°. On the equator it's 0°. On the 45th parallel, it's 45°, and so on.

"That's all there is to it?"

"There are some corrections. But Jonathan says you can forget about them and still come within two or three degrees."

"Not close enough for making port, I don't suppose," Horace said, "but good enough for now, eh, coz?"

They beamed at each other in a euphoria of victory. "All we need is a clear sky in the north sometime between dark and dawn."

The stateroom ports had been covered with deadlights to keep out the wind-driven water, and it was so dark that Amanda had to stand for a moment, blinking her eyes to accustom them. The small gimbaled lamp on the partition swung with the roll of the ship so that the light fell square on Jonathan's face. He was lying on his back, his mouth sagging open, the skin stretched taut over the skull bones, his eyes staring. She touched his arm. It was cold, but there was a quivering under her fingers. Bending closer, she saw that he was lying in a mire of blood. Her mind snapped shut like a frightened shellfish.

Water rushed and the ship wrestled. Sails pulled, ropes strained. But she stood doing nothing, thinking nothing, holding to the edge of the double bunk.

Slowly, faintly, as if from some place or time so remote that it had no substance, came a voice reminding her that a person at the point of death could be revived by brandy. But it must be administered quickly. Quickly!

Her brain turned slowly and brought up from darkness the image of a decanter. Where? In the sideboard of the captain's cabin? No. Then where? Slowly, another image: the pantry of the officers' mess.

She made the journey at a dream pace, effortful but snail slow. Found the bottle. Unstoppered it. Poured an inch of the liquor into a glass and started back. It was hard to keep from spilling as the ship rolled, lurched, and pitched. She would have done better to bring the decanter to the bedside. What if she lost her balance and fell and had to go back? Every instant of lost time meant loss of blood, life draining away.

An eternity later she was standing beside the bunk, trying to open Jonathan's jaw with the fingers of one hand while the other held the glass, ready to pour. Some of the liquor ran down his neck, but some of it got into his mouth. Jonathan gagged, swallowed, and coughed. She waited till he had stopped, then quickly and more deftly poured in another dollop. This time he swallowed without gagging, but he locked his jaw against another intrusion.

After a moment he shuddered and sighed. The rhythm of his breathing seemed stronger, more regular, but slow. very slow.

To find where the blood was coming from and stanch it, she must turn him over. It was like trying to move a stranded skiff. Beyond her strength. But to get help she would have to leave him and go on deck. And it seemed to her that if she left—even for an instant—Jonathan would die.

The ship rolled heavily, and his body shifted a little. It struck her that it might be possible to make the storm her ally by pushing him on the leeward roll and bracing against the countermovement. She strained till her head pounded and her arms trembled. Jonathan was trying to help her. Weak as he was, he was trying, straining, willing himself to move. There! They had gained. She had him almost on one hip, and he was resisting the movement that would have rolled him back. Perhaps the next big swell—no, perhaps the next—or the next?

Now, with all her strength! The ship lurched. Jonathan grunted. And it was done.

The rest was horrendous, but not hard. He had bled from his intestines, and the hemorrhage had stopped of itself. His linens would have to be changed, his body cleansed.

Someone spoke.

She turned and saw Flagg. He came closer, and blackness came with him, swallowing his face. She could hear his voice, but the words were carried away like a hail from a storm-driven ship. She was falling. She could stop herself if she made the effort—a great effort. But why should she? In blackness there was rest.

THE SEVENTH DAY

Amanda was ashamed. Everyone made excuses for her. Flagg assumed that she was expecting. Women who had never fainted
in their lives often had the vapors when they were expecting for the
first time. His dear wife had been like that. As strong and healthy a
young woman as Amanda, cool-headed too, not one to flinch at the
sight of blood. Could bandage the worst hurt ever, without changing color. And endure pain. Take that time she twisted her ankle,
missing a step on the way down cellar; she lay there calling, but so
quiet it was goodness knew how long before he could hear her out
to the shed where he happened to be working at the time.

On and on the old man rambled, offering his memories for her
comfort.

Before their boy came, she—Mrs. Flagg—had been sick to her
stomach and like to faint the whole of most days. Went for weeks
like that. Though not so bad with the second child. Some said that
was because it was a girl. Not so hard, girls weren't. But then again,
some said it was always easier the second time. The main thing was:
fainting came natural to a woman who was expecting. No reason for
her to be embarrassed or alarmed.

Horace assumed that she was coming down with the fever. "For
heaven's sake, coz—for all our sakes—do what you can to ward it off.

Go to bed for the day. We'll manage the sickroom chores between us, Flagg and Willy and I."

But Amanda was not coming down with the fever, nor was she pregnant. She had fainted because, at that moment, she had no wish to live. When she looked on Jonathan, dying, she was ready to follow him into oblivion. Like a Hindu wife, an incomplete being with no hold on life except through her lord.

She could hardly believe it of herself. She had been enduring the ordeal of proximity, of tending and touching this man she once loved, convinced that his betrayal of that love had cut it at the root, killed it, left her feeling nothing. Not pity nor anger nor even resentment.

But she had been deceived. What she had taken for absence of feeling was a balance—the terrible opposites of love and hate held in equilibrium. Yesterday the balance had tipped and brought love to the surface; now hate was in the ascendant. And shame. For Jonathan's sin against her was not only the act he had committed—or tried to commit—and what it had revealed about him. He had also showed her something in herself that she could not accept. Something she could not name. Or would not. But she could and would root it out.

Horace reported that his Polaris shot had not gone well.

"The sky was clear in that quarter from midnight on. But there was no horizon. I kept trying, thinking I would still be able to find the star as it came on to dawn if I knew where to look. And I did get an altitude. 40°. But of course that's out of the question."

"Why?"

"Because that would put us nearly five hundred miles ahead of where my reckoning has us."

Amanda wondered when he had begun this reckoning, but all she said was, "It's clear now. We could try for a shot."

"It's past noon."

"There's a way to use an altitude taken either before or after noon. It's more complicated, but I think we could manage."

Horace was willing to try. "But not just now. I've got the fore-topsail to bend on."

"Did it split again?"

"It did. We rigged a staysail to hold while it was being repaired. Now that has to come down and the old one go up. And if the wind doesn't kick up hard again, we ought to shake the reefs out of the courses. At least Heyerman thinks so, and Jonathan said I was to listen to him in anything that has to do with the setting of the sails."

Horace spoke as if he expected her to challenge this authority. When she didn't, he went on, in a different voice.

"I know what's behind all the grumbling. Work. Hard, punishing work. Going aloft to make more sail and hardly down on deck when you're ordered up to douse it. A man begins to wonder why the mate can't make up his damned mind. But what they haven't the brains to see," his tone sharpening, "is that it's the wind that's changeable, and one must trim sail to suit it, no matter who's discomfited. I'd like to see one of these self-appointed sailmasters make a better—"

He stopped.

"I've changed, haven't I, coz?"

"Not for the worse."

"I wish I were sure of that."

Remembering what he had once said about rejecting the role of mastery, Amanda found it difficult to describe the changes she saw without giving offense. She spoke of "competence," of being "the most of a sailor," of "responsibility shouldered," and "the common good."

Horace listened with an expression she could not read, and when she was done, he heaved a sigh. "It's true. It's as heady as wine, the feeling that you're master not only of men, but of the elements. That you can pit your wit and your will against even the sea. But that's *hubris,* coz. The darker side."

"What is *hubris?*"

"The old Greeks' tragic flaw. We can talk about it when we tackle the latitude shot. The fore-topsail can't wait."

The next time she saw him he was standing in a knot of men at the foot of the foremast. The two dark Hawaiians were already making

73

their way up the ratlines, clinging like monkeys when the mast whipped, alternately swinging them out over the sea or hard against the shrouds. And now someone was starting up after them. Horace! He had reverted to his old role, setting an example instead of issuing orders. Jonathan would say he was not going to make a captain after all.

Amanda was trying to put the time to use, working in the Bowditch so that she would be ready for the lesson when Horace was ready. But her mind was drunk with weariness and reeled from one thought to another without grasping any of them.

"Add together the log. cosine... Was that some sort of pun?.. *of the latitude by account...* What had Horace meant about his reckoning? He had kept no log, had not even heaved the chip log... *the log. cosine of the declination, the logarithm in the column of rising...* She liked the sound of that, declining and rising, like waves. Waves of five-digit numbers called, for no apparent reason, logs... *Reject 20 in the index...* Why have an index of integers if one could reject them at will?... *The sum will be the natural cosine...* What sum? Had she been told to add something to something else? She could not recall... *from which the latitude may be obtained by the common rule."*

Perhaps. But not by her. Not till she had slept. If she could get as much as a half hour's nap, she would make a fresh start and force her way through those senseless clauses. But where could she sleep? The sofa was no good. The fiddle Flagg made her had been misplaced, and without it there would be no rest. What she needed was a narrow bunk, running fore and aft like the mates'. And there was such a space on the floor of the stateroom, alongside the double bunk. Jonathan was sleeping so heavily that he would not even know she was there.

By doubling her heavy cloak under her, she made a mattress, and then wrapped herself in a warm shawl. It was as snug as a cradle. Stretched out full-length, letting go with muscles that had been tensed for days, she let herself sink deliciously into nothingness.

Creation crashed around her.

There was a whoosh of water, like a cataract, a sound of splintering timbers, shrieks, thuds, a dreadful scraping and tearing of fabric. She and Jonathan were caught in a snarl of straps, linens, and clothing, tangled like two shrouded bodies in a common grave. The weight of his body bore down on her as cruelly as it had the other time. This time he was trying to help, not hurt, her. But he was too weak and the force pressing them too strong.

Then, without warning, the pressure eased. The cabin righted itself. A glass rolled noisily along the floor.

"She's come up, bless her! I thought she…" Jonathan said and then ran out of breath. It took all his strength and hers to get him back into the bunk, and when he was there, he fainted.

The noises from the deck were louder. Men were running, shouting, stamping, dragging what sounded like a tree. The motion of the ship was strange, as if it wallowed in a calm swell. She would have to tie Jonathan in before she could go up to look. Her impatience made her awkward and slow. Willy opened the door. His blond hair, wet and wind-tangled, showed like an aureole in the light from behind him.

"Horrie's overboard! And they won't put out a boat!"

"Jonathan! Did you hear that?"

But of course he had not.

"Come and make them, Cousin Amanda. Or he'll be…" Willy choked on the word and started away.

The debris of disaster was everywhere on deck. Spars and rigging hung in a ghastly jumble around the foremast. Kegs rolled crazily on the water-swept waist as the ship rocked between the huge seas. One of the Hawaiians was trying to help the other to his feet. The fallen one was bleeding from a wound on the side of his head. Close by, another man, whose face was turned away from her, lay against the bulwarks in a sculptured pose of agony.

Someone shouted to her to take care as she began to fight her way aft. The quarter alley was almost blocked by remnants of sail that hung from the spencer mast. King John was struggling to cut it away.

"Where's the bosun? Where's Heyerman?" she asked.

The black man dismissed her question with a quick shake of his head.

"I want him to lower a boat."

Still without looking in her direction, he moved one of his arms in a gesture that took the place of words he had no time to search for: Heyerman had been swept into the sea with Horace. There was nothing to be done for them.

The vessel was disabled, and the men left uninjured would have all they could do to save her. There was no time for grief.

Davidson was at the wheel; Tono, the Marquesan, his bush of hair drenched flat, stood beside him. Neither looked her way as she struggled, hand over hand, toward the stern. Holding to the taffrail and staring out over the shifting mountain range of water, she searched for the lost men and dreaded to find them. If she should—if she saw them and they her—if they called out or raised an arm to beg help and she could do nothing...?

A splintered yard rose on a crest and sank again. She watched, but the sea never cast it up. At least not while the ship was up. It must be there, tossing as the ship tossed, as the lost men might still be tossing. But she never had another glimpse of it. Or of them.

"One of the hands has hurt hisself, ma'am." Flagg stood close beside her and spoke loud enough to be heard over the roaring. "Broke his leg by the look of things. Would you want me to see to a splint?"

"I'll come," she said.

Would she want the man carried to the carpenter shop? The workbench could be cleared. Amanda said that would be fine and then remembered the Hawaiian with the head wound.

"Let *him* be carried down to the officers' mess. I'll bandage his hurt while you're getting the splint ready for the other."

As she passed the wheel, Davy acknowledged her presence with a jerk of his head, without taking his eyes from the sea and the spanker boom.

"How much damage is there?" she asked.

"She took on some water, but the pumps'll clear her out once we've got enough hands to man them."

"What about all that rigging and the yards?"

"We lost the fore-t'gallant mast. And the tip of the jib-boom. But she can run without headsails and royals. We can jury-rig something later on."

76

The two Kanakas were waiting for her in the officers' mess, whose floor was awash. It made her think of the incident of the spilled water pail, and she tried to recognize the man she had frightened. Probably it was the wounded one, but she was not sure and did not like to ask. The other, who said his name was Jim, translated for her, persuading his companion (whose name, he said, was Jerry) to accept laudanum for the pain and to submit to her cleaning and dressing the bruise-wound, keeping close watch all the while to see that she did not perpetrate some evil magic.

She worked quickly and—considering the difficulties—skillfully. But the instant she was done, both men fled without a word of thanks, leaving her with the ambivalent emotions of one who has ministered to a wild bird and been pecked for one s pains.

The man with the broken leg was Rory.

It was the first time Amanda had seen him close up, and she was surprised by his face. It was not handsome, but it was likable—very wide at the cheekbones, so that his eyes looked small, but blue and bright. His hair and beard were reddish and curly, his eyebrows and the backs of his hands a tangle of fine wires of red gold. Not at all what she would have expected in a man of the Hebrides.

Rory asked for and got a dram of rum, which loosened his tongue and roughened his burr. He talked continuously through the operation, but Amanda shut herself off from the sound, struggling to match the directions in the *Guide* with the notes on setting a fracture taken from her sessions with Dr. Gough.

As far as she could determine, the break was not a bad one. The bone fragments were not perceptibly separated and did not have to be realigned. But she and Flagg were inexpert, and there was much wasted motion and time before they were sure the leg was ready to be bound to the barrel stave that Flagg had planed smooth.

Only when they were nearly through wrapping it did Amanda let her patient's voice filter through. He was making jokes. And in quite a pleasant baritone voice. But there was something…the intonation, the musical pattern?…as if…

The fellow was flirting! Amanda looked to see if Flagg was aware of the impertinence, but his face told her nothing. Her own face was turning hot.

"You're to keep this leg elevated," she told Rory sternly. "And send me word if it begins to swell so I can loosen the wrapping."

He said he would do that, thanked her, and then—with only a slight shift of tone—launched into a speech of condolence. He was sure all the men joined him in sympathy for her loss. For his own part, if there was aught he could do to relieve the present difficulty, he would welcome the chance. It was not particularly well put and perhaps not sincere, but it came near to melting her to perilous tears.

She went alone to Horace's cabin.

How much smaller it was than the first mate's. With the door closed, there was hardly space enough to pull open the stowage drawer below the narrow bunk. She tugged at the handles; they resisted. She tugged harder. The ship rolled; the drawer slid out; she was thrown back against the door. Horace's sou'wester fell from its peg. Still wet.

"He's not lost after all! He wasn't on deck when the wave washed over. He's been here and left his rain gear and gone forward to see about something...."

Amanda clenched her fists and pressed them against her head till the lying voice inside it was stilled. Then she began to empty the drawer. It was stuffed tight with all manner of possessions: gloves, socks, an extra belt, a wallet, bars of soap, shirts of different weights, a knitted watch cap. That was a gift from Aunt Aggie; she had used up all the odds and ends of yarn in her workbasket, working them in no particular pattern but achieving an effect of concentric circles that was not unpleasing. Horrie had worn it often in the cold high latitudes.

How was she to tell Aunt Aggie and Uncle Matthew? In a letter that would be carried to them by strangers? Or wait and tell them herself when the *Maria M.* came home? They would be standing in a crowd of others on the wharf—Salem's wharf, not Boston's. News

78

of the ship would have been carried when she was sighted off Marblehead. Everyone would be there waiting: Mother and Father and Grandfather and the parents of the two Martin brothers, of whom only one was coming home.

She bit down hard till that pain had stilled the other. Then she began to empty the drawers, making two separate piles of their contents: one of personal things, the other of clothing, remembering what Jonathan had done with the gear of the man lost off the Horn.

"We'll try to see that the valuables and keepsakes get back to his family. But the clothing might as well be used. It's a long time between ports where a man can replace what wears out on a voyage as long as this one. Some captains auction off whatever is valuable. I prefer to let the bosun make a division."

Willy would want Horace's fine pair of hairbrushes, the unsmoked meerschaum pipe. But none of the clothing, except the socks, would fit the lad. Horrie was three inches taller and at least that much broader in the shoulders and chest.

Her head was beginning to pound. Or was it the pumps in the hold? She straightened up and saw the books, crammed into a rack alongside the bunk. A copy of Lever's *Young Sea Officer's Sheet Anchor* (that, Willy would want), Emerson's *Poems,* and a copy of the *New Testament* inscribed: "With the abiding affection of your mother."

As she took them down, something slipped out of the volume of Emerson, a folded paper on which was written in a graceful feminine hand:

> *As loving Hind that (Hartless) wants her Deer,*
> *Scuds through the woods and ferns with harkening ear,*
> *Perplext, in every bush & nook doth pry*
> *Her dearest Deer might answer ear or eye:*
> *So doth my anxious soul, which now doth miss*
> *A dearer Dear (far dearer Heart) than this,*
> *Still wait with doubts, & hopes, and failing eye*
> *His voice to hear or person to discry.*

At the bottom of the page a note, written in different ink but in the same hand:

> From Mistress Anne Bradstreet's 'A Letter to her
> Husband, absent upon Publick Employment.' How I
> wish that my own dear husband were absent on
> employment of so short a term.
>> Your ever-loving wife,
>> Louisa

Amanda let herself fall forward against the bunk, pressed her face into the blankets, and screamed.

Sometime later, Willy pushed open the door. They stared at each other like criminals caught in the same guilty act.

"What do you want to do with—"

They spoke the same words at the same moment and broke off at the same point: when Willy saw what lay on the bunk and Amanda saw that he was carrying a seabag, lumpy with Heyerman's possessions.

It dawned on her that Willy had suffered not one bereavement but two, the second perhaps even harder to bear up under. For he and the bosun had lived together in their tiny cell in closer proximity than many married couples; had cohabited in the pure, original sense of the word. Now Heyerman was gone. Without forewarning or farewell. One moment he was there—solid and strong and dependable. The next moment the fabric of reality had disintegrated, leaving—nothing.

She reached out to take the boy in her arms, but he flinched and drew away. The pain must be like having the skin of one's soul burned away, she thought. He needed to be comforted, helped to heal, but how, if he would not let her touch him?

"There, now! Let yourself cry! It'll do you good." One could say such things to a woman. Not to a man. But perhaps if a woman were to show the way.... Tears did not come to her as easily as the scream, but she would try. She stared at the egg-and-dart pattern on the lamp stand till her eyes smarted, and forced out a sound something like a sob.

"There, now," Willy said. "There, now, Cousin Amanda. Don't take on." His voice was gentle, and his arm went around her shoulders, cautiously, as if she were a bramble. "You know it's no use. It won't...bring them back."

He was weeping now, but she could pretend not to know, pretend not to hear him say, "I could see them...for a long time...in the smooth after the wave broke."

She could have screamed again at that, but she continued her quiet sobbing. Willy was rocking her, repeating his "there, now" like a lullaby. How strange that the only way to comfort this man-child in anguish was to make herself a child....

It was evening before she had a chance to talk with Flagg, to ask him to explain to her precisely what had happened to the ship.

"It's hard to know rightly," he said, hesitant and—she thought— evasive. "Most likely she was...just brought to by the lee."

"What does it mean to be brought to by the lee?"

"Well, now. You mind how she was sailing? With the wind large? Sometimes a ship'll fly off so's to bring it on the other side. So the sails all catch aback, and there she hangs, at the mercy of any big one that breaks on her beam."

"She just flies off of herself?"

Flagg was not willing to commit himself on the point. It might have been the result of a mistake in judgment. "If the helm was ordered put about, say, and she got caught on the way round, missing stays."

"Did Horace—did Mr. Martin give the order to put the helm about?" Had he weakened and given in to the pressures after all?

Flagg could not rightly say. There had been some talk, he believed, of heading her up into the wind. And Mr. Martin was on deck at the time but forward, as he recalled.

"Who else could have given such an order? The bosun?"

Flagg could not rightly say.

"Who was at the wheel?"

Flagg claimed not to know. Amanda was sure he did. But the harder she pressed, the more pervasive his ignorance. One thing he would say, and that was, "There's little use worrying what's past mending."

This man was her friend, and wise in his way. So perhaps it was best to let it go at that.

"What course are we making?" she asked.

Flagg sighed relief. He was just coming to that. The helm had sent to ask if she was to be held on the same heading as before the accident. Due north.

"North by west, I think it was." She forced Jonathan's exact words from deep in her memory. "North by one point west. There's an easterly variation here."

When Flagg had gone to carry her order to the helm, she realized that she had no idea what an easterly variation might be and went to the Bowditch to look it up.

3

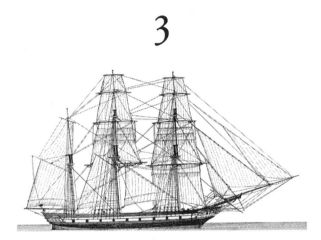

The Interregnum

The Eighth Day

The ship sailed herself, as if the men responded to some imperative communicated without words, through a process as organized and compelling as the circulation of blood. Amanda had appointed the Finn, Kankkonen, to replace Heyerman as bosun, but the work seemed to go forward without his intervention. In less than twenty-four hours most of the tangled rope, wire, and wood had been cut away; debris cleared, jettisoned, or lashed down. If everything was not yet shipshape and Bristol fashion, it was only a matter of time, a little more time.

She was trying to bring the same degree of order into the after-cabin, sorting out books, papers, instruments, dishes, embroidery stuffs; drying what had been dampened; washing inkblots from the desk and logbook (Horace had neglected to screw down the cap of the inkwell, and the last entries were all but obliterated), when Willy came to tell her that Rory's leg was swollen and paining him greatly.

"Where is he now? In the carpenter shop?"

"In...*his* bunk."

Then she remembered. Her permission had been asked to move Rory into Heyerman's cabin in the deckhouse. Even as she gave it, she had wondered how this would affect Willy, who would otherwise have been bunking there alone. Observing him now, she thought it had done some good. There was still a stricken look about his eyes, but they were no longer glazed with grief. It was better to have a companion, someone from whom he could evoke a response, something he could not get from either of the sick men he tended, both of whom were inert as corpses most of the time he was in their presence.

Rory's greeting to her was cheerful, which did credit to his spirit, for the injured leg was bulging above and below the linen wrapping. He asked if he was not to have rum this time but took her refusal in good humor, keeping up a monologue of mock complaint, which seemed to serve as a substitute anaesthetic, until she had completely freed the leg. Then, as she prepared to wrap it again, *"keeping in mind that the alignment of the bone is to be maintained, and the limb prevented from moving, with out undue constriction of the surrounding flesh,"* his tone changed, becoming at once more serious and more flirtatious. He was suggesting—recommending!—that she appoint him to succeed Heyerman.

"I've already chosen a bosun."

"Have ye now?" A silence of expectation, as if she owed him more answer than that. "And who, if ye dinna object to me asking?"

"Kankkonen." And she almost added, "Of course."

"Kank? Och! The Finn!"

Rory's red eyebrows shot up, then pulled together and down. He seemed to fall into a brooding over how she could have come to commit such an appalling error of judgment.

"You're going to have to stay off this leg for quite some time," Amanda said.

"Aye. I'm afeart so. And that's why I thought to take over the bosun's post. I'm no' fit for work aloft, but I can free others. And do what the others canna."

She looked up and met his eyes. Rory trimmed sail slightly and continued on course.

"What ye maun have for your bosun is a man of experience. A stout heart and cool head, they're all to the good. But experience. That's the main thing." He waited for her to agree.

Amanda went on with her bandaging, her mind sniffing out a trail that would lead to decision—the right decision—unaffected by emotion, vanity, or whim. For here was a man who had served as bosun on more than one voyage, if the crimps' account was true. As mate or as master, by his own account. Yet she had not even considered him to fill Heyerman's place. Why?

The reason that came easiest to mind was that his injury unfitted him for work. He was saying he should be used to direct the work of others. But only a captain ordered others to perform tasks he did not set his own hand to. Did the fellow mean to insinuate himself into Jonathan's place?

Her indignation flared, and then died.

There was after all some logic to the proposal. When Horace considered letting Rory take over the navigation, she had been opposed. And later Horace himself had opposed it. But now the case was different, and a different decision might be required. But she was afraid to make it. Afraid on the one hand of trusting this boasting brawler and on the other of trying the impossible herself and failing because she was afraid.

"Tell me," she said, "is it true, as I've heard, that you once had a ship of your own?"

There was a moment of indecision. Rory had to choose between denying past glories and admitting to ignominious fall. He chose to brazen it out.

Yes, he had once had his own ship, and a damned fine old brig she was. No such beauty as the *Maria M.* (this in a tone of perfunctory flattery) but likely to have outsailed her on some points for all that.

"What happened?"

He repeated word for word the pun about running onto a reef in the Leewards while "sheets to the windward." But not, he would have her understand, through any fault of navigation. He knew where he was, knew the dangers, should have posted a lookout in the crosstrees.

"I'll not deceive ye, ma'am. I've a weakness for John Barleycorn. And when I've a drop too many ta'en, I'm the Bull of Bashan. Ravening and roaring. It's a terrible affliction."

With the abandon of one who knows the value of confession, he excoriated himself for having failed to root this flaw from his character while young, wallowed in the shame of his recent past, and predicted a future of retributive punishment. Amanda had a sense of being maneuvered into a position where she would be vulnerable to attack.

Rory was veering round to the subject of his skill as a navigator, claiming that he had—when sober—no peer with sextant, quadrant, or circle of reflection. He could pick the Dog Star or Aldebaran out of the dawn or twilight sky, find the line of the horizon in the dark of a moonless night, bring down any celestial body to meet it in any weather, however the deck might reel underfoot. There was a closing cannonade of terms: time sights and lunars, azimuths and equations.

At last he paused. He was giving her the chance to speak, to accept the opportunity to be rescued from her unconfessed but obvious ignorance. But Amanda went stubbornly on, tying off the ends of the linen strips and tucking them into place.

"Wait a bit!" he said, as if the notion had only this instant surfaced in his mind. "Why wouldn't that be a thing I could do for ye? The navigating."

"There's no necessity," she said curtly. "And besides, I'm afraid you'd find it difficult to manage the instrument when you can't put weight on both your legs."

Back in the cabin, copying what she could from the blotted logbook, she was distracted by the memory of Rory's lifting eyebrows and the tone in which he had said, "Och! The Finn!" So insolently disapproving her choice—the choice that had seemed so indisputable for reasons she could no longer recall.

Why Kankkonen rather than Davidson or King John or even Flagg? Had she picked the Finn because he resembled the Dutchman? Both were portly. Both had heavy voices and accents. Both were respectful of and presumably loyal to her as Jonathan's surrogate. But what other qualifications did Kankkonen have? He was not popular with his mates nor in any sense a natural leader. He was not the sailmaster Heyerman had been. Davidson had taken over that function and, now that she thought of it, without being ordered to do so. Naturally—as so much had been taken over. Different men had assumed different facets of the authority Jonathan once asserted. Each to his own bent; all together when all hands were required; nothing left undone or neglected.

Except for her part. They had turned to her to set the course: to establish the ship's position, determine the destination, the distance and the heading. That task was hers "naturally," and she was neglecting it.

She turned the blotted page and began a clean one:

September 8, 1851

10 A.M.   The estimated position of the ship was

She had no way of estimating a position. Horace's last entries had been little more than guesses, but even they were lost—blotted. Unless she could reconstruct them from what she remembered of their talk.

He had made one rough observation of Polaris, but he had not entered it in the log. (*"It's out of the question...would put us five hundred miles ahead of where my reckoning has us...."*) If the star stood at 40° above the horizon that night, the ship was on the 40th parallel. But Horace's reckoning had put it five hundred miles to the south. Dividing 500 by 60 (each degree of latitude being equal to 60 miles—that much she had learned), his estimated position must have been on, or close to, the 32nd parallel. They had been traveling north steadily for a day and a half since then. But at what rate of speed she had no way of knowing. The best she could do was make an arbitrary assumption that could be corrected later: choose a latitude somewhere between 40° and 32°—say, halfway between.

---

10 A.M.   The estimated position of the ship was 36° N, from which
I take my departure.

She wrote the word *departure* and looked into the void—an enormous, echoing emptiness in which she stood, alone, on a small, un-

89

steady platform of planks, holding in one hand an awkward instrument of brass and glass, in the other a volume of words and symbols, most of them indecipherable.

She dropped her head onto her arms, and slowly there came into her mind a tale—read or told to her as a child—a fable of the East, in which a wise man was condemned to death by a vengeful potentate.

"...unless your great wisdom can teach you how to eat—at one sitting and alive—an elephant!"

The court was assembled: the turbaned nobles, the scimitar-bearing eunuchs, the caliph and his victim, and last, as the cream of the cruel jest, the great lumbering beast, led in by its keeper.

"Are you ready?" asked the potentate.

The wise man called for a knife, a fork, and a napkin. They were brought. In silence, he seated himself spread the napkin, and took up the cutlery.

"I am ready now," he said.

"You are going to eat the elephant?"

"Yes, sire, since I must."

"But how?"

The wise man smiled and shrugged. "One bite at a time," he said.

That was the wisdom that must save her from the void: one, small, doable task at a time. She opened the Bowditch, but not to the directions for finding latitude by observation. That was too big a bite. She would try instead *"Method of Keeping a Ship's Reckoning or Journal at Sea."*

The old navigator had provided a sample page of seven columns, below each heading a set of squares to be filled in at the end of a day:

Course	Dist.	Diff. Lat.	Dep.	Lat. D.R.	Lat. Obs.	Diff. Long.	Longitude by		
							D.R.	Lunar	Chr.

Her course was north, the compass heading having been corrected for variation. Distance she couldn't compute till she knew the rate of speed through the water. Difference in latitude would have to wait till she had the distance. Latitude by dead reckoning: there was the place to write her assumption of 36° north. Latitude by observation she would be able to fill in at noon—given a clear sky. Longitude by dead reckoning: there she would write Horace's assumption that the ship was sailing straight up the 157th meridian. Longitude by chronometer would have to remain blank until and unless she learned how to ascertain the time and reset the instrument. Longitude by lunar—she didn't even know what was meant by that.

Seven bells struck. Half an hour till noon. And the sky was sternly, imperatively clear.

She stationed herself where she had seen Jonathan stand for this observation, at the foot of the mizzenmast. Davidson was making some repairs to the gaff above her head. If she had trouble with the sight tube, she could call on him. She made one last inspection of the instrument to be sure everything was properly tight or loose or level. As she started to raise it to her eye, she was conscious of a sudden movement aloft. She looked up and saw Davy clamp his elbow against his side. She took the prompting gratefully.

Even so, it was difficult to hold the heavy object to her eye and steady despite the ship's movement. It took patience and persistence to master the trick, and when she had, all she could see was a blur that changed from blue to gray and back to blue as she moved the instrument or its index arm. Davy motioned for her to stand away from the mast, closer to the rail. She did, and found the horizon, lost it, and found it again: a line of dark against the lighter blue. But no sun! She swept the index arm from 0° to 90° and back, over and over. But there was only that canting, careening line.

She kept at it till her knees were shaking and there was a knotting in her abdomen. She had not been seasick since she was a child, not even on the stormy passage around the Horn. She moved to the rail and leaned against it, drawing strength from its solidity, her eyes closed, her breath coming and going deeply. Slowly the knot loosened, but she dared not try again this day.

As she turned to go, she became aware of eyes. Davy was watching from the rigging, and the two Kanakas, who had been assisting him, hung motionless in the shrouds. Forward in the waist: Willy, Cook, and the Marquesan, all staring, their so-different faces united in some emotion that was not hostile—nor friendly either. She felt a pressure forcing up her arms. It was as if they were willing her to find the sun and bring it to rest on the restless horizon. The collective will. She was its instrument, as the sextant was hers. She was not permitted the luxury of failing.

This time her stomach cramped before she found the horizon. She knew she would vomit if she persisted. Shutting both eyes and controlling her breathing, she fought down the nausea, and as it retreated she began—without any conscious decision to practice deception—to go through the motions she had seen Jonathan go through: the facing into the sun, the slow sweep of the index arm, the abrupt halt, the short sweep back, the set of the screw that held the arm to the arc, the final delicate adjustment of the vernier screw, and the reading of the angle. All this with tight-closed eyes.

Jonathan always took a number of such observations, comparing his readings against Smith's till one or the other noted that the sun was beginning to drop. But she could not hold together for another performance, mock or real. She was on her way to the ladder when she saw Rory in the door of the forecastle companionway. He was not close enough for her to tell from his expression whether or not he had been deceived.

Cook was hobbling toward her, calling to her to wait. He had narrowly escaped being drowned in his galley, where he was pinned under the wreckage for an hour. But once freed, he had bound his wrenched knee with his headkerchief and set about reconstructing his workplace. As soon as someone could be spared to bear a hand with the stove, he promised hot drinks if not hot meals. Meanwhile, he was distributing rations of salted beef, ship's biscuits, and dried apples. What he wanted of Amanda now was permission to break open one of the crates of oranges in the hold for "something to tempt the captain's appetite."

"Share them out with all hands," she said, "one apiece for as long as they go around."

It was hardly a largesse, but it was received with cheers.

Smith was too weak to peel the fruit, but he sucked at it when it was held to his lips. Jonathan could not be roused even for that.

"Has he been awake at all?" Amanda asked Willy.

"Not while I was by."

He had not been truly conscious since the broaching. Since he could do nothing to undo the tragedy, perhaps it was a blessing. *"Where ignorance is bliss...."* But men like Jonathan did not choose bliss on such terms. He would have despised himself.

From habit, she seated herself at the round table, where her embroidery basket had once stood. That was stored now in the sideboard. She considered getting it out and starting on a new flower, to be busy at something that took no thought and might prevent thought on other matters, like her failure to find the sun at noon— and her pantomime of pretense.

She could not understand why she had done such a thing. She longed for someone to whom she could confess it—not to obtain absolution, but only to put her transgression into words so that she could examine and explain it to herself. That was one of the ways in which she had been useful to Horace and, before him, Jonathan: by listening to the recounting of their failures as well as their victories, their hopes, and their doubts.

Who would be her listener? Willy was too young and, for the present at least, too vulnerable. Flagg? It would be hard to make him understand how she had got into the position. The one who would understand was Davy.

Davy already knew! He had shown her how to hold the sextant that first day and had conspired in the deception on deck—indeed, had all but suggested such a thing by his prompting. He had known from the first and might already have told others about it, thinking it too good a joke to keep to himself. If he let drop so much as a hint—by accident or deliberately—word would run from mouth to mouth in the forecastle, starting laughter that would rob her of what little authority she had achieved.

She paced the narrow cabin, securing a latch here, a book there, winding the deck watch, trying to find something on which to fix her mind till the shame burned itself out. She began turning the pages of the logbook, backwards, retreating into the past, back, back, to the pages where Jonathan's rounded hand alternated with Smith's angular scrawl. Days when the world had been ordered and safe.

There were the meridian altitudes of the sun and the latitudes by observation, labeled S and decreasing steadily until, on July 6, they had crossed the equator at a little after noon; then, marked N and increasing till the day they had made port at Hilo. And in the margin opposite each entry there was a small clump of figures, three lines each, unlabeled except for the designation N or S. Some of them seemed to be additions; others, subtractions. In either case the last line gave the ship's latitude:

$$S\ 22°37'16''$$
$$\underline{N\ 22°35'08''}$$
$$S\ 00°02'08''$$

Something subtracted from something else gave their position at noon on July 6. But what? And why subtracted, not added? On the day they came into Hilo the first two lines had been added:

$$N\ \ \ 0°46'$$
$$\underline{N\ 18°44'}$$
$$N\ 19°30'$$

which was the latitude of Hilo. But how was it derived from the two unlabeled lines?

On a sheet of foolscap, Amanda copied all the little clumps of figures from July 6 to September 3, the last entry in Jonathan's hand. There was a discernible pattern in the second lines. The readings recorded there changed steadily and in one direction whether the ship stood at anchor or ran before a gale. So it must refer to something unrelated to the ship's position but essential to the calculation that established it.

She stared at the figures till they moved on the page like MENE, MENE, TEKEL on Belshazzar's wall, but there was no Daniel to interpret for her.

She went back to the log entries, looking for some other pattern that might give her a clue to the meaning of this one. There was the meridian altitude, increasing steadily—no, not so. It increased till they made port on July 17. After that it declined....

Declination!

Her mind leaped a gap and landed safely.

The second line was the sun's declination on a given day. Declining from 23° at the time of the summer solstice to 0° at the time of the equinox. Marked N till then; S, thereafter.

She held fast to the second line and pulled herself up to the first. What did it record? Not the meridian altitude on a given day but...the difference between that and 90°. Zenith distance. What she had been trying to help Horace understand.

At Hilo on July 17 when the sun was nearly straight overhead at noon, the first line of the clump read N 0°46'. It was marked N because on that day the sun, going south, had passed over the ship. She consulted the Bowditch for confirmation.

"If the object [the sun in this case] *bear south when on the meridian, mark the zenith distance north."*

She went back over other entries to confirm this new insight and to fix it indelibly. Another illumination was flickering. She made herself quiet to receive it. Something to do with working backwards, from the bottom line up.

Her mind made another leap. Working backward from latitude, through declination to zenith distance, she could predict the meridian angle. If she knew—even approximately—what her latitude ought to be, she could preset the sextant and make it easy to find the sun. She could do that tomorrow if the sky was clear at noon. Better yet, she could do it tonight! With the polestar.

The best place for an observation of Polaris was in the bluff curve of the forecastlehead, territory into which Amanda had never ventured. *"You'd do well to have one of us about if you should take a notion to go for a stroll forward…"*

But there were no loungers on deck when she went up. And the man on the bow watch was the one who spoke no known language, with whom no conversation was possible. All to the good.

Her eyes accustomed themselves to the darkness, and she made out the star, directly forward of the bowsprit. The helmsman could steer by it and forget the compass if he chose. But through the sight tube of the sextant she could see nothing.

She waited awhile. The star brightened as the darkness deepened. But when she looked through the tube again, she still could not find it. By now it was night, and the horizon was lost in a blending of black sky and black sea. There would be no line from which to measure the altitude, even if she found the star. But she went on searching, sweeping the index up and down, the instrument right and left.

With the naked eye she could see Polaris clearly, and it occurred to her at last that the sight tube might be a hindrance. Removing it, she squinted through the empty ring and caught and held the point of light. Straight ahead and a little less than halfway up in the sky. There it was, and there it would be in civil twilight tomorrow or in the first light of day when the horizon was given back.

Tucking the sextant under her arm, she started for the quarterdeck. Davy detached himself from the shadows at the foot of the foremast and came to offer her a hand with the ladder leading to the main deck. He had been watching—watching over—her all this time.

"Not yet," she said as if he had asked a question. "But I know how to go about it. Tomorrow—"

He raised a hand in a gesture she took as a warning not to say more, lest she be overheard.

THE NINTH DAY

She was holding Horace by both hands, talking. She, asking; he, answering. Their speech was slow, quiet, effortful, soaked with regret. Horace's voice was unaltered except in its clarity, which was muffled. He said very little, and that in explanation of his part in the disaster; he was at fault, he had misjudged.

She wanted to know precisely what it was he had misjudged, but she wanted even more to spare him, so she spoke of her own part: where she had been at the moment of the broaching, why she had not come up on deck at once, why no boat had been lowered. He was shaking his head as she finished, but she couldn't tell whether he meant that it would have been wrong to launch a boat in such a sea, or wrong not to. She wanted to ask but felt the question might breach some code of conduct—be discourteous or disloyal.

While she hesitated, Horace spoke again but so low she could not make out the words. He was slipping away. She had let go of his hands, and it was impossible to catch them again. Currents were forcing them apart.... She had to use her own hands to bring herself up through the water, holding her breath till she broke the shimmering surface overhead....

And came awake.

She did not open her eyes, but she was awake and knew—after a moment—where she was. She had come to Horace's cabin after midnight, thinking she might rest better in a bunk than on the sofa. She had slept deeply. Outside the porthole the sky was bright.

Footsteps crossing the deck overhead told her that the helm watch was changing. She ought to be on deck. But there was something she must finish, something left over from the dream that was already dissolving. Horace's face lingered, quiet and full of regret, but nothing of his voice. The memory of the living man was receding like the dream. Already hull-down on the horizon, it would sink and lie like the ruins of Atlantis, as layer after layer of silt and sand—the detritus of living—covered and concealed it.

Grief flooded like a spring tide and overflowed the dike she had thrown up against it. Tears ran from her closed eyes. She must not let them wash away the task the dream had laid on her. She must remember.... But already she had forgotten. Maybe it would come back if she kept in motion, kept swimming till her feet touched bottom or her hand grasped a spar.

It was late in the forenoon watch. The sky was clear. With the noon observation she would finish off the first full sea day of which she had kept a log. The course was—and had been—north by west. Winds had been southerly, at times southwesterly, slackening, but still fresh. Under "Transactions" she had recorded the sails carried: topsails on main- and foremast, a fore-topmast staysail, the spanker, and, since early this morning, a main-topmast staysail as well. Also since early this morning, the seas had been much reduced.

For her longitude she must still assume that the ship had not deviated from 157° west. For latitude, she would add a day's running to her assumed 36° north. But to compute a day's running, she must know the ship's speed.

An experienced hand was supposed to be able to guess within a knot the speed his vessel was making, but the new bosun seemed stunned when she put the question to him. He scratched slowly at his chin, grunted deep in his belly, and fell into a brown study.

"Just roughly," Amanda prompted. "The average speed over the past twenty-four hours."

Kankkonen scratched higher along his cheek and said that no one had heaved the chip log, but if she wanted, he would do so now.

"I thought it was no use in such a heavy sea."

Kankkonen shrugged. He had known captains to heave the log regular in worse water than this here. It was up to the missis. He stood ready to oblige.

And so, in a few minutes, a trio assembled at the rail on the starboard quarter: the fat Finn, with the wooden quadrant cradled in his arms; the tall African, with the spool of marked line; and Willy, with the half-minute glass.

"Hunh!"

The grunt was an order to himself. The bosun's thick body swung out like a discus thrower's. The chip log arced up and then down out of sight. Amanda saw a flash of red as the rag that marked the end of the "stray" line went over the rail.

"Turn!" shouted Kankkonen.

"Done!" Willy upended the glass, which he had been holding as if it were the Grail.

Grains of black sand dropped through the narrow neck. The reel hummed; knot after knot ran over the rail. Willy's eyes never left the glass; King John's never left the reel. Amanda had the sense of being witness to an ancient, pagan rite, the propitiation of some demonic force, in which even an unbeliever had no choice but to join because the demon was unappeasable by other means.

"Stop!" Willy spoke as the last grain of sand fell. King John slapped his hand down to stop the line. The bosun reached over the rail and brought up the last of the numbered knots, counted with his fingers the smaller knots of the marking cord, and finally measured the distance between that mark and John's hand.

"Seffen knot, tree faddom," he reported.

"Isn't that quite good?"

It was. Very. Considering that she was running without her foret'gallant and her jibs.

"Would you say she's been making this speed the whole time since noon yesterday?"

99

Kankkonen thought five knots would be more like the average. King John dissented; he would say more. Maybe six. Amanda decided to use the helmsman's rather than the bosun's guess. It was only for a rough reckoning, something to compare against the more precise position she would establish at noon.

As she went below, she heard music from before the mast, Rory with his concertina, entertaining the watch.

AMANDA BRIGHT'S JOURNAL

September 9, 1851

Our patients are no better, perhaps weaker. The spots on their bodies seem paler but are still prominent. Both men pass thin stools with signs of blood in them. Their faces are heavy; their lips, dry; and their tongues, which were covered yesterday with a white, fuzzy substance, are now turned brown.

We give them oranges to suck, or drip the juice into their mouths when they are too languid to make the effort. Cook has got a small fire going, over which he is drawing some tea. Later he may be able to brew barley gruel.

·✧·

She sat for a moment looking back over the entry, permitting herself to look again in memory at Jonathan's face as it was now—drawn, pale, and vulnerable, with hardly a trace of the other Jonathans, the one she had loved or the one who had *"unpacked his lust with words."* She could pity this man without forgiving the other.

When she went on deck again, Rory had been moved to the foot of the mainmast, his splinted leg made comfortable on a cushion of folded canvas. She ignored him, but as she raised the sextant, she heard him call a warning.

"Have a care there, missis!"

Too late! Light exploded in the cavity of her head. She had forgotten to replace the filter glasses last night after her search for Polaris. The pain was dreadful, and through it she could hear Rory's voice continuing: "Ye can burn yerself blind on a sun like today's."

She wanted to blind him in revenge. To blame and punish him

for her agony. She would not suffer the added outrage of his sympathy. She closed her will around the pain and strangled it.

While it was dying, her fingers moved, first to find and pull into place the dark, colored panes that should have protected her, then to make a small adjustment of the vernier screw. The instrument was preset, and the observation would have been easy if she could have forced open the injured eye. But it was tearing so that she had to blink out fluid every few seconds, praying that no one stood close enough to see the drops fall.

There was silence all around her till she brought the sextant down. Then Rory spoke.

"And where wad that put us, ma'am, if ye dinna mind me asking?"

"I can't say till I've worked the shot," she said, hoping he did not suspect that she had no altitude to work.

His eyebrows rose and fell. "But maybe ye could hazard a guess if we're aboon or below…say, the bay of San Francisco?"

"Not without working the shot. And I'll have to look up the latitude of San Francisco."

"Aye, do that," he said softly.

Amanda stood over the chart, running her eye along the 38th parallel of latitude to where it intersected the landmass of North America, just above the break in the coastline that opened into the great natural harbor of San Francisco; a long, easy reach. "What he wants is to head for the nearest grogshop," she told herself, fighting the temptation of that long, alluring curve. "Horace said so from the first."

But there were other, better reasons for heading east. Some of the hands, like Rory, might abuse the freedom they would win when their feet touched the planks of San Francisco's wharves; some would not. Some might be shanghaied aboard another ship; some might sign on—voluntarily and sober—a ship bound home. That was what she would do if she had a choice.

She had determined she would begin the letter today.

September 9, 1851
My dear ones:

She waited, her pen at the ready, for the words—simple, truthful, and spare, like the lines of a hymn. And as she waited, she summoned the faces her words must reach: Horace's parents and hers, and all the others. The tribe scattered over New England and even farther, but still bound by a cord of affection, which her words would draw tighter when and if they struck the solemn note of requiem.

Her hand began, at last, to move.

My dear ones:
I have meant for too long to include in this letter a dramatis personae. Some of the characters you already know, but others—and some of the most interesting—are new.

This was not the message she had summoned them to hear. But it was a way of holding them close and clear in her mind till she could gather strength.

I shall begin with those who, for reasons I shall explain, must be minor players in my narrative—the four black men (or to be more exact, three dark brown and one truly black). They are all fine, strapping fellows, tall and physically powerful. The two Sandwich Islanders (who have been rechristened Jim and Jerry) were almost indistinguishable until one of them injured himself and was forced to wear a bandage. Tono, a Marquesas Islander, is covered with blue tattoo marks that make his face even grimmer than nature has made it. His hair is bushy and matted and bound with thongs so that it looks like baled hemp. The West African, who is called King John (presumably because of his noble bearing), is blue-black of skin, taller than the Polynesians, with a frame one might call willowy if it were not so strong. All of these men are splendid sailors, and John is (I am told) a truly superior helmsman. But there are insuperable barriers to any real communication between them and me: barriers of language, barriers of understanding and respect.

I have discovered in myself a prejudice that persuades me that persons of a darker color have different—lesser—capacities. And the dark-skinned foremast hands harbor a similar opinion of, or prejudice against, me. It is not only a matter of the Polynesian taboo against a woman on shipboard. The African, who believes in no such superstition, clearly assumes different and lesser capacities on my part in all but one function—the nursing of the sick and injured, which is allowed to be within my competence. In that, he and all the rest defer to me without question. And are quite wrong to do so, for I am ignorant and without any natural aptitude for medicine.

Now for the roster of principal players—five men about whom I shall have more to report as the voyage continues: Davidson, a cockney, whom the men call Davy; Flagg, the carpenter; Kankkonen, a Finn, whose nickname is Crank; and the two whites who were brought aboard in Honolulu (drunk or drugged or both). The most valuable, all round, is Davy, who is now

She intended to write "acting as sailmaster," but that would have led to the explanation she was not yet prepared to make. So she changed the last letter of the last word:

not particularly impressive to look at, of average height, hard muscled, but narrow of shoulder and hip. He is balding (not at the crown like Jonathan), and to shield his forehead from the sun he wears a cap, peaked at an angle that matches his sharp, thin nose. As that feature also dominates his voice, he is in a sense "all nose." Born in Liverpool, he went to sea "as soon as he could be trusted in trousers," has at least a quarter of a century of experience, and knows about as much as there is to know of the seaman's trade.

Of the same vintage, but quite different in all other ways, is Crank. As thick as Davidson is thin, he moves slowly, setting his great feet so firmly on the deck that it is obliged to hold steady under him. An exception to the rule that fat men are merry, he never laughs, almost never smiles. Perhaps because his jowls are too heavy to be lifted. His eyes are a watery blue. His voice is just what one would expect from that barrel of a chest, and he uses it so seldom that it carries considerable authority.

One of the men brought aboard in Honolulu presents a most intriguing puzzle. He speaks no language anyone aboard understands, and understands none that is spoken to him. For a while our bosun believed him deaf and dumb, since he did not use his voice but set about establishing a set of signals. The work required of him he has learned by watching and imitating others. He is quick and willing, but so much of the gear and its handling was clearly unfamiliar to him that some of the men concluded he had never been to sea. Others say he could not have caught on as quickly without previous experience, but that it must have been in a vessel of a quite different sort.

Flagg says one of his watchmates believes the man to be an Egyptian who served his apprenticeship on the type of scow that carries freight on the river Nile. But he does not fit my imagined concept of an Egyptian, being lighter in complexion, with a rounder, flatter face than one would expect in a son of the Pharaohs. I prefer to believe him the child of a mating between some modern Marco Polo and a native mother in the remote northern wilderness where Russia and China meet. If so, it may be that when we drop anchor at Nootka, No-Name will find someone with whom he can communicate, for Russian traders who intermarried with Esquimaux have left many descendants in that region. Meanwhile he gets on wonderfully well without words. (By the by, he is neither deaf nor dumb. He can utter sounds as well as the next man but has given up doing so, I believe, because he found them inadequate to his purposes—long before he came aboard our ship.)

The man who was put aboard with him is a Scot, from the Hebrides, named Rory. The two are neither old shipmates nor friends. In fact, the only exception to No-Name's generally equable temper is his violent aversion to Rory. I have the impression that he blames him for his capture by the crimps, but Rory swears that he never laid eyes on the fellow till he woke up in our forecastle, and he feigns surprise at being assured they were delivered to us in the same jolly boat. He does, however, allow the possibility that they both got drunk in the same native bar on the same powerful okolehau to which our Scotsman ascribes his latest fall.

Amanda stopped. It was easy—almost too easy—to write about Rory but hard to place him in the cast of characters. She was not yet sure of his role.

She went on deck at dusk for a last inspection of the sky. It was clear, but something made her doubt it would be clear tomorrow.

Forward on the forecastlehead, Rory was singing a tune that was familiar, with verses she had never heard before and could only partially make out. Some sort of sentimental lament for a love lost or left behind. More interesting than the song was the accompaniment. King John was playing on a small instrument like a shepherd's pipe a sweet, shrill obligato that made her think of snakes. No-Name was squatting on his haunches, his back against the weather bulwark, drumming on the deck with a pair of belaying pins. The Kanakas were tapping on the sides or tops of kegs. And over it all, the harp of the wind.

Her face was burned, her mouth chapped, but her body carried a richness drawn from the depths of the day. The silkiness of the south wind curled around her, soothingly, seductively, speaking of sleep.

She settled herself again in Horace's bunk. It was just the right length and width for her. How could he manage, with his much greater height? How could he *have* managed? She must learn not to think of Horace in the present.

Perhaps it was a mistake to sleep here. She would be vulnerable to dreams, dreams of sorrow and loss, dreams that would split the thin skin that had grown over the wound of grief.

But the prospect did not appall her. If the choice was between forgetting and grieving, she would choose to grieve.

THE TENTH DAY

AMANDA BRIGHT'S JOURNAL

September 10, 1851

I shall not try to determine whether our patients are better or worse. The changes in their condition—if any—are so small and so quickly reversible as to be without significance.

Mr. Smith bled from his intestines during the night. Flagg was with him and, having profited by my experience, was less shaken than I. But even Flagg is no longer optimistic. Until today he has insisted that things would soon begin to improve, with the fever subsiding and real recovery commencing at the end of the second week. All this he made bold to predict because he once suffered (at home in New England) a similar complaint. But he now enter-tains the same gloomy forebodings that I do: that despite all our efforts—

There is simply not enough air or light or clean water or soap or sun or leisure to care for them!

·✧·

*Coarse N by W   Wind SSW, fresh. Barometer just below 30".
Sky overcast.*

The sun was obscured all morning, but several times it seemed about to burn through. Amanda had the skylight opened so as to be alert to any change at the zenith. She sat beneath it, reading in the Bowditch about the cause of variation of the compass and how to measure it.

An argument was going on somewhere on the quarterdeck or in the rigging of the mizzen. The voices were blown away by the wind, and she had little interest in what was being said, but it began to make her uneasy because it was the first time she had heard the men s voices raised in anger. A sign of the slackening of the discipline Jonathan had established and Horace maintained—Horace and Heyerman between them. The old bosun would not have tolerated such an altercation as this; the new one was participating in it.

He was under attack by Rory, who was complaining that the Finn didn't know a joke when he tripped and fell on it. Kankkonen replied in a booming basso that obscured all but one recognizable word: "adwice." Something about "bad adwice."

Now everyone was joining in, taking sides. They were arguing about the broaching and who was responsible for it. Amanda felt heat run through the trunks and branches of her nerves. Kankkonen was blaming Rory and his "bad adwice." Was it Rory who had persuaded Horace to alter course? But would Horace have taken the advice of a man he called a menace who ought to be put in irons?

There seemed to be as many versions of what had happened as there were men on deck. King John was blaming one of the Kanakas, who had been at the helm. Tono was blaming Heyerman, whom he had never liked. The Kanakas were jabbering angrily in their own tongue. There was a babble of more specific accusations. Someone said that Rory had persuaded the helmsman to fall off and that Horace was coming aft to correct this mutinous change of course when a rogue wave caught the stern.

"The de'il he was! The poor lad didna know his ass from an anchor. It was Heyerman ga'e the order to the helm, and our Miss Nancy was comin' aft to find out the reason."

Amanda covered her ears, although the roaring in them would

have drowned out the rest in any case.

Was it possible Horace had *not* been at fault? He had blamed himself in her dream. But the dream was *hers*. And she dreamed it after Flagg planted the notion in her mind. Or at least permitted her to jump to that conclusion. Horace's tirade against Rory came back to her like a verdict: *"We could have been caught in a trough and broached to...dismasted...."*

And so they had been, but that did not tell her how or why.

Rory might be accusing Heyerman and ridiculing Horace to cover his own guilt. But "might" was not proof. Nor were the Finn's suspicions. She would have to have other evidence, more reliable testimony, before she...before she could...what? Even if she could establish guilt, what could she do?

Horace had not carried out his threat to put Rory in irons. She was in a far weaker position than he, with the crew reduced by two deaths and two debilitating fevers. Flagg said it was better not to worry what was past mending. Perhaps what he meant was not to know what would force you to act.

But she had to know. She would begin by making inquiries—only of those men she could fully trust—and taking into account all that might bias their witness. She must be just, even if she were unable to administer justice.

She had found Jonathan's azimuth compass in one of his locked drawers and consulted Bowditch on its use—measuring the variation of the magnetic compass. After her struggle with the sextant this instrument seemed childishly simple. When sunset came, at the end of the first dogwatch, she carried it on deck and set it on an arrangement devised for her by Flagg, consisting of a hatch cover, a molasses keg, and a barrel-top, toenailed into place just abaft the jeer capstan.

The sky was spectacular: clear to the north and west, with clouds banked south and east of the place where the sun would go under, their tops showing orange, fading to rose, to purple, and finally to ultramarine.

She had preset the sight vanes for Jonathan's old estimate of a variation of 12°. Now, as the orange-red circle slipped into the place she had assigned it, she could see that the vanes would have to be adjusted. The variation was still easterly but greater.

The sun flattened along its lower edge. Amanda set her eye to the tiny slit, swung it one degree to the right, then another. Another. The final reading must be taken at the instant the circle of the sun was halved by the horizon. A swell lifted the ship. As it dropped again, she had a clear view of the burning center of the sun resting on the sea. She caught it in the vanes, pushed the stop on the compass, and straightened up to read it.

Sixteen degrees!

It was no longer possible to assume that the ship had been traveling straight north, up along the 157th meridian. Unless leeway (a gift of the wind) or some current (a gift of the sea) had compensated for the lie of the needle, the ship had been steering east of true north and might be closer to land than she had supposed.

Flagg came by see how his "contraption" was working, and she showed him what she had learned, partly to reward him and partly to firm her own grasp on the procedure.

The old man listened, smiled, and asked if she had brothers.

"Three."

He seemed genuinely surprised. He would have sworn she was raised by "a dad who didn't have no son. But then maybe you come first, before the boys?"

"No. Two of my brothers are older than I. Why did you think different?"

It was a hard thing to put words to, he said. But there was something more like a boy about her "taking hold like you expected to be able to do whatever's at hand."

"It's more like a boy to take hold?"

That depended, of course, on the sort of thing taken hold of. There were things a girl would naturally take to. Flagg had so vague a notion of what these might be that he left the item blank. A boy, however, was disposed by nature to take hold of *this* sort of thing.

This, meaning "urgent," or "technical," or, possibly, "nautical."

There was no one within earshot, and it seemed a perfect opportunity to begin her probing of the accident. She began by saying, with a sigh that did not have to be feigned, that she was having a hard time writing to Horace's parents. Flagg was instantly—effusively—sympathetic. It would be hard in any case, and being related...knowing the parents and all and how the blow would fall...a young man of such promise...

"Promise he did not live to fulfill," she said. "That's what makes it so bitter."

Flagg could not go along with that. "If he'd been taken before, like the other poor fellow—you mind the one?—then I'd have to agree. But he'd come into his own, had young Mr. Martin. You can ask any man of the crew, and he'll say the same." It was, Flagg claimed, a joy to obey his orders. "Brave as a lion, he was, with a heart of gold. Tender gold."

With that last she had no quarrel, but on the matter of being obeyed, Flagg's account didn't square with what Horace had told her nor what she had gathered from her eavesdropping.

"What did Heyerman think of Horace? As captain?"

Flagg found the question obscure. Perhaps if the lady would explain what she was after...

She was after the identity of the man or men responsible for the broaching, but she was mindful that Flagg had evaded her earlier questions. Perhaps she should begin by stating her premise. "The ship broached to because the heading was altered. Isn't that so?"

But Flagg saw her drift and cut himself loose. It was time for him to be looking in on his patients. Past time, in fact.

She had bungled it again, forgetting the division between the forecastle and the quarterdeck. Whatever one might think of one's fellow members of either faction, one knew where one's loyalty lay.

Amanda packed up her apparatus and stood a few minutes, staring at the darkness into which the bow pointed. If the ship was on course, Polaris should be showing at any moment. If she could find the star before she lost the horizon, she could measure the angle and establish the position at last.

She went to get the sextant and return the azimuth compass to its case. By the time she was back, a few stars were showing overhead, but the sky to the north was still dark. There might be horizon clouds in that quarter. Or it might be that light from the deckhouse was blinding her to the pinprick of light.

She made her way forward along the weather rail. Rory was giving his evening concert to his usual audience. As she passed the galley, she could hear Cook rattling utensils and humming an obligato to Rory's song, which came to a long, wheezing close just as she reached the forward corner of the deckhouse.

"Won't be many such fine evenings as this where we're bound," Rory said. "If we've the good luck to make port. Or, ye might say, the bad."

Someone asked a question, and Rory's answer to it was a snort of laughter. Did he know the Canada coast? Why, he could chart it. He had dropped a hook in every one of the fur-trading harbors from the mouth of the Columbia to Sitka and Petersburg. He would have fought twenty devils to keep from having to spend an hour in any of them again. But of the lot, Nootka was the worst. And by a good deal.

She could not hear whether there was another question or whether he continued without prompting. His voice dropped—not in volume but in pitch—a trick that imparted significance to what was to follow and implied a need to keep it secret. She strained to hear and was angry at herself for taking the bait and for not being able to catch every word.

He had shifted into his appalling pidgin for the benefit of some part of his audience and was explaining that the inhabitants of Vancouver Island's wild west coast were cannibals, whose insatiable bloodlust was barely concealed under a feigned interest in trading. The great Captain Cook had come near being boarded by a murderous party of warriors in a cove misnamed Friendly. Being Scottish and nobody's fool, Cook had slipped anchor, drifted with the flooding tide, and moored at a safe distance, lingering in the vicinity only as long as necessary to make some repairs to his vessel and keeping an armed watch around the clock.

Amanda knew none of this history, but it was possible. She was almost—but not quite—sure that Cook was not Scottish, but even that was possible. And it was possible that Rory had visited these trading posts, though it seemed odd he had not mentioned it to her.

Someone asked in pidgin what was meant by the word "cannibal."

"Say them like for eat'um people," said Rory.

This was translated into Hawaiian, and the response was a murmur of polite amusement and one bray of laughter that was anything but polite. Amanda guessed that the laugher was the same as the one who had asked the question: the Marquesan, Tono.

"Did I say summat comical?" asked Rory.

Tono controlled his mirth and began to explain that although Kanakas were not eaters of long pig by custom or preference, they were not forbidden by strong taboos like the *haoles*. For his own part he had a decided partiality for the dish, preferring it to goat or sheep.

It took a long while for the Scot to get a definition of "long pig." Amanda could judge when it penetrated—and how deeply—by the profundity of the silence that fell.

This gave Tono an opportunity to "seize the word," and he did. Addressing the Kanakas in their own, or perhaps his own language, shifting now and again into pidgin for Rory's benefit, he delivered what could have been a parody of one of the latter's boasts: a battle in which he, Tono, had performed feats of valor and violence, an account of the enemies he had disposed of, with details—for instance, how in a hand-to-hand encounter of recent date he had bitten off and swallowed the ear of his antagonist.

Rory interrupted with a feeble oath. He had heard enough! God must be punishing him for sins blacker than he recalled having committed, to shut him up in a forecastle full of bloody savages.

There was a mocking comment from the African.

"Aye," said Rory, righteously, "but that was when I'd a skinful. And I'll say this: I've yet to suffer such a drought as would drive me to lickin' up the blood I spilled, like this heathen dog."

That was translated, and again there was laughter led by Tono.

Eight bells. The evening watch was called.

The men moving past Amanda did not notice her. One stopped to urinate over the side a few yards from where she stood. She had been afraid to move lest she betray her presence, but she might as well not have bothered. She had faded into nonbeing. Was she of so little importance that no one cared what she saw or heard?

The Eleventh Day

She woke before dawn from a dream that had comforted her. She could remember nothing of it except two older women, her mother and, perhaps, Aunt Aggie; and that she had been cradled in their affection, lulled, loved....

There was no going back to it. Sleep would not come, and the thoughts that came instead led in other directions. She got up, tidied her hair, and went on deck.

The wind had dropped, but it was chilly. To starboard the sky was perceptibly lighter. There were still some stars at the zenith. On the horizon a bank of clouds lay across the path of the coming sun. King John was at the wheel; he greeted her with a ceremonious bow and a question about the captain's health. Amanda said it was no worse, though the truth was she had forgotten to look in on the sick men and was reluctant to do so now. Facing east, with the coolness of the breeze striking one cheek so gently that it barely stirred her hair, she was suspended in a peace like that of the dream she had lost.

Bare feet thumped on the deck. It had been a long time since there was quiet enough for such a sound to be heard. Voices came faintly to her—Davy's nasal twang over the others. Someone was starting up the ratlines. There was to be a change of sail.

Color was seeping into the eastern sky: blue-green and pink and lavender iridescence, like the belly of the dying mahimahi on its bed of leaves in the Honolulu market, like the shimmering aurora veils that flushed and faded in the southern polar sky. Beauty seeped into her mood with the color and made her sad. They were linked, beauty and grief. One reminded her of the other, and the impulse to share reminded her that there was no one with whom she could. She was bereaved and exiled—cut off from the dream love of mothers, from the child love of brothers, from the woman love of a man. All the comforting presences of her life were dissolved. Loneliness wrapped her like a furled sail.

She moved forward along the quarter alley to a place where she could watch the silhouettes of the men on watch take shape with the coming of light. There was an odor of coffee, wafted by some trick of the wind. Cook came out of his galley with a steaming pot in his hand, saw her, ducked back, and came out with a mug.

The brew was weak and hot and tasted better than she would have believed possible. Her mood was warming with the sun yellowing the east. In a golden haze, the day was beginning: the eleventh day out of Honolulu; the seventh since Jonathan was taken sick; the fourth since the accident. What had happened to the days since? They blurred into each other like sea and sky in this light. She must make sure to set everything down, or she would forget.

AMANDA BRIGHT'S JOURNAL

September 11, 1851

They are no worse. Mr. Smith's fever may even have abated a little; Jonathan's has not. But they are both exhausted—emaciated, dull-eyed, dreadful to look at. I find it hard to force myself to visit them.

·⟡·

September 11, 1851

The day commenced with fresh winds; log heaved; showed 5 k, 2 fathoms; wind from SW to S. Overcast.

Middle part, wind dropping. Speed logged: 3k, 3f. Temperature dropping. Barometer steady.

Ends with light winds, still SW to S. Hazy.

She was not hungry and did not want to sit alone at the table, but Willy had set her place as usual. There was something if not hostile, at least unfeeling in the lad's strict observance of the old, now-empty, forms; he served her in silent, lonely—almost ludicrous—state. Grief, she knew, expressed itself in many ways. It was even possible that the lad resented her assumption of his lost brother's place. She must be patient, must trust that time would set things to rights between them.

Willy followed her into the aftercabin when the meal was done, and while she worked at her reckoning, he busied himself shelving books and latching instrument cases as if he was reproaching her for untidiness. One day soon she ought to begin to teach the lad as Jonathan had taught her, and for the same reasons. But not just yet. Not while he was so hard to reach and she had so much to learn. Still, when she saw him studying the big chart she had left spread out on the desk, she decided to make a start.

"Would you like to see our track? How far we have come and how far there is still to go?"

But Willy looked away the moment she approached and refused to follow her pointing finger. It seemed a deliberate impudence.

"Run along then. I've work to do." She spoke as if he were a child, saw the flush on his cheek as the words hit, and did not ask pardon. He made no move to obey her, but she did not insist. Let him do as he liked. It was all one to her.

Several minutes later, long enough for her to have forgotten both him and her annoyance, Willy spoke. Standing poker stiff, fists and lips tight, he was delivered slowly, in painful contractions: "Cousin Amanda…you said yourself…he might not get well…and anyways he's not…he can't…someone else has got to…got to be…"

"Be captain? Is that what you're saying?"

Willy did not answer directly but began a long, evasive explanation. It was impossible to finish the voyage without replacements. There would be no way to recruit them in Nootka. Also, it was not likely that both sick men could continue—if they survived—without weeks of rest. The Canadian wilderness was no place for them.

The sooner the ship was headed for San Francisco or Honolulu, the better. "And I don't think Cousin Jonathan would be for going on if he knew," Willy finished with less than complete conviction.

"I'll ask him," Amanda said in a voice that she tried to keep cold and even. "But in the meantime, I don't propose to go against his wishes. I'm surprised that you would listen to anyone who suggested such a course."

She gave Willy a chance to deny the implied accusation, but he ignored it. "That's the reason there has to be a captain," he said. "*You* can't go against his wishes. But a real captain could."

"And who is it you would have for real captain?"

Willy flushed, scowled at his toes, and swallowed. Amanda waited, refusing to prompt him or lower her eyes or look away.

The lad bolted.

She was left shaking with something between fear and fury. It was Rory who had put him up to this. She had not the slightest doubt of it. Rory, who might be responsible for his brother's death. And Heyerman's.

Nevertheless, what Willy said was true—some of it. Unless there was a real improvement in Jonathan's condition, there would have to be a captain appointed. She could not serve as surrogate much longer. Not because she could not change the course Jonathan had laid out for his ship—though she would not, without his express permission—but because she was not "the most of a sailor."

Horace believed Heyerman fulfilled the requirements, but he was gone. Who else was there? She would not for one moment consider Rory, not until and unless her suspicions of him were disproved. The Finn barely managed to function as bosun. Flagg was too old and too humble. Neither Tono nor King John would be acceptable to the white crewmen, she was sure. Davy?

It was not an impossible choice, but fortunately she did not have to make it just now. Perhaps by morning Jonathan would be so much improved that the whole question would be moot. Meanwhile there was work to do. For whoever took command—whether Jonathan or some surrogate—would need to know, and could learn only from her, the position of the ship.

She reached for the Bowditch and let it fall open at random, the way her grandmother let the *New Testament* fall open, trusting the All-Knowing to guide her to the chapter and verse that would meet her needs: *"To Find the Latitude by Observation."*

It was a passage already worn smooth by too much reading. She turned a page. Another. The next was filled with examples: back observations, as well as fore, observations with a quadrant, observations taken with a sextant...

"Example VII. Suppose that on January 1, 1831, an observer seventeen feet above the water finds by a fore observation that the altitude of Sirius is 53°33' when passing the meridian...."

Stars! There were other stars besides dim Polaris. A whole skyful of bright bodies that rose and set and, between rising and setting, must cross a meridian. They could be measured.

She read through the rest of Example VII, marveling at how simple the procedure was. There were fewer corrections to be made than on an altitude of the sun.

*"To find what star will come upon the meridian at any given time...add the time from noon to the right ascension of the sun...*Which, according to the *Ephemeris,* was eleven hours, sixteen minutes, on this day in September...*with which enter the table (VIII) and find what star's right ascension agrees with, or comes nearest to it."*

She turned pages, ran her finger down long columns, and found three stars that would reach their meridians in the hour of civil twilight. The first was a star of the third magnitude, *beta,* in the constellation of Ophiuchus. Next came a star called Etanin, in Draco. And finally Vega, a first magnitude star that would cross the meridian at 7:15, a little over an hour after sunset, just as the last light would be fading.

She went on deck at six o'clock. The watch had just changed. Flagg and Cook were seated on kegs in the lee of the galley. Willy stood near them listening to the talk. Crank was stumping along on his way aft. All the men of both watches, except for the helm, were having a last smoke or breath of air before turning in or turning to.

The subject under discussion was rival systems of navigation: the book versus any combination of signs, portents, and intuitions. One of the Kanakas claimed, in intelligible pidgin, that his uncle could smell land a day's sail away.

Someone laughed mockingly. "Them islands stink of rancid coconuts, that's why. In white man's waters you got to go by the book."

But Flagg spoke to the Kanaka's point as he understood it. It was true that a man could navigate by the seat of his pants, providing he wore such, and by senses other than smell. He himself could find the entrance to his home cove off Penobscot in a blind fog by shouting and listening for his voice to bounce off the rocky cliffs. "But out here in the middle of nothing and nowhere, a body's got to go by the stars and the sun, by the book and the charts. You got to know what you know and how to find out what you don't."

"All a mon needs is to haul the log mornings and shoot the sun at midday." That was Rory.

He was prepared to say more but was hushed by a warning cough. Amanda's presence on deck had been noticed. To defend herself against any suspicion of spying, she raised the sextant and began to search the sky to the south. It was too early, and without knowing the bearing of the stars she wanted, her chance of finding them was slim. But she tried.

A few minutes later Davy came to join her. And a minute or so later, Flagg. She asked if they knew the location of any of the navigational stars. Indeed they did, and the planets as well. But *Beta Ophiuchus* conveyed nothing to either of them. Was there, perhaps, a common name for the star?

Amanda did not know it if there was. "What about Etanin? It comes up a bit later."

They still looked blank. Perhaps she was not pronouncing it properly, but changing the vowel sounds brought no results.

Davy suggested she "have a go" at the evening star, which hung like a lantern in the green zone above the sunset colors. "So's to make sure the telescope sight is working like it ought."

This was harder to use than the sight tube. Amanda could find the horizon easily enough, but not, even for an instant, the planet. Davy offered to try. He had the same trouble, but he went about overcoming it in a way that would not have occurred to her. Instead of training the instrument on the horizon and manipulating the index mirror to find the star, he reversed the process: he raised the telescope sight to the star and, once he found it, slowly moved the index arm along the arc, keeping the star in view, till he had brought the line of the horizon into the clear half of the split pane.

He handed the instrument back to Amanda for a second try. It required a delicate coordination of two different movements, like patting one's stomach and rubbing one's head at the same time. But at last she had the planet burning on—or just to one side of—the line of black and crimson where water and sky met.

"I can do it!" She turned the vernier screw slightly and made the planet jump, first up, then down. "I'll have to practice before I can do it easily. But I can do it."

She happened to glance in Flagg's direction. He was watching with the expression of a child who has no hope of, but cannot conquer his longing for, a sweet or a toy just out of reach. In a lifetime at sea this man had never once held in his hands the key to power over the elements that shaped his life.

"Here," she said. "You have a look."

Flagg took the sextant reverently. Davy offered a hint or two, but they were hardly needed. Flagg was quicker to catch on than Amanda had been. It nettled her slightly to admit it, but his pleasure was so intense that watching him was like intruding on a sacrament.

"I won't be able to work out the latitude from a planet," she said to Davy. "At least not without doing more reading. So if neither of my first two stars will serve, I'll have to wait for Vega."

Both men knew Vega. It was in the Lyre and would be showing any minute now.

"But I have to measure it at the meridian, and it'll be quite dark by then. So the horizon will be hard to find."

That did not daunt her companions. The way to manage was the same as what Davy had done: find the star and keep track of it as the light faded, being careful to shield their eyes from artificial light so they would not lose it.

Davy was the first to make out Vega. Flagg confirmed it. Both men had sharper sight than she. Amanda found the star on the third try and brought the horizon to meet it. The altitude was 82°30'.

"But it'll go higher."

The men nodded gravely. They were entirely caught up in the effort, linked with her and with each other in a comradeship like none she had ever known. It comforted her in a way that recalled the lost dream of her mother and aunt.

Flagg took another reading and found that the star had risen to 83°. "Just like you said it would!"—as if that were the ninth wonder of his world.

They urged each other to be patient, to let at least five minutes pass before anyone tried again.

Amanda got 83°41'. Davy waited as long again and got 83°34'.

"It's dropping, or I mistook the horizon," he said and gave the sextant to Flagg, who got 83°33'. The star had passed its zenith. Amanda tried one more observation to be sure. 83°30'!

The highest reading was 83°41', and it was hers.

Seated at the desk under the gimbaled lamp, she worked out the shot. The men stood behind her, one on either side, looking over her shoulders:

Observed height	83°41'
Dip & refraction	5'
True height	83°36'
Subtract from 90° for zenith distance	6°24' (N)
Declination	38°38'
	45°02' (N)

"Forty-five degrees, two minutes, north latitude," she said triumphantly. "We've crossed the 45th parallel. That means we're halfway."

"Halfway to Nootka?"

"Halfway between the equator and the pole."

Flagg shook his head. Mrs. Bright was certainly a remarkable woman. He had heard tell of skippers' wives who could do the navigating but never expected to meet up with one, much less ship with her. A credit to her husband, she was. "All the same, and no disrespect, ma'am, you're a mite off the mark. We're not so far north as that."

She felt the crown of victory slipping from her. Both men avoided her eyes. Flagg decided to turn in and advised Amanda to do the same. Get a good night's sleep and wake up fresh and ready to solve her problem. Any problem at all.

"But I'm sure of the position," she protested. "We all measured the altitude, so there can be no mistake there.

And here are the tables for corrections: dip and refraction and declination. Look them up yourselves."

Flagg demurred politely. She appealed to Davy, who was choosing to blame the instrument. Most likely the telescope sight was out of adjustment.

"Then you adjust it!" She opened the Bowditch, found the directions for aligning the index and horizon glasses, and laid it before him. "Adjust it and we'll try again. The next star to cross the meridian is Altair, as I remember."

Flagg said that Altair lay too low in the sky at this season. "If there's clouds in that quarter, you won't see it." And there were horizon clouds everywhere except in the northwest.

"The next after Altair is Deneb," Amanda said. A star of the first magnitude, easy to find. She looked up its declination—45°10'—did the reckoning, and found that it would stand at the zenith, directly overhead, at nineteen minutes after nine.

Flagg had left the cabin while she was working. Davy was staring at the open book, his face screwed into a pained, lopsided smile. It took her a moment to understand: the fellow could not read.

Amanda took up the book and read the instructions aloud. Davy recovered himself and began to carry them out. Little by little the tension eased. The sense of comradeship returned. But not as it had been. This man, whom she had thought of choosing to captain the ship, was on the far side of some dividing line, set apart by something as difficult to overcome as a difference in skin color.

There was nothing wrong with the telescope sight, as she—and perhaps Davy—had suspected, but there was still an hour before the meridian passage of Deneb. Davy seemed as eager as she to make the test—for *her* to make the test. Unlike Flagg, he had not lost faith in her.

"If you want to catch forty winks, I'll call you in good time, missis. Unless it clouds over."

Amanda went to her bunk and slept.

She woke before the hour and lay quiet, going over in her mind each of the actions to be performed when she rose: she would grope her way across the dark cabin, lighting no lamp lest it dull her night sight; she would find the sextant and preset it by feel. (A pity she had not thought to do that before she put it away!)

Hour	K.	F.	Course	Wind	L'way	Transactions & Remarks Abd. 12.
6			N	SW		Hazy, no noon observation.
4	4	2	N	SW by W		Wind dropping.
6	4		N	SW-SSW		Clear to north.
9	Est.4		N	SSW		Lat by obs. 45°12' (ƒVega & Deneb).
10	"		"	"		Running with all drawing sails set ex'pt royals & fore-t'gallant & headsails; lower studding sails.

Course	Dist.	Diff. Lat.	Dep.	Lat. D.R.	Lat. Obs.	Diff. Long.	Longitude by		
							D.R.	Lunar	Chr.
N	113	1°53'			45°12" N		157° W		

It came to her that if the latitude had indeed been 45°02' at seven o'clock, two hours later it must be nearly 45°10', which was Deneb's declination! The mast of the *Maria M.* would point to the star. Sweeping across the sky like a gigantic sextant, it would touch it at the top of each swing.

When Davy came to call her, she was already on her way up, anxious about the condition of the sky. Had clouds blown in while she slept? Was the moon too bright? It was already flooding the eastern darkness with light that obliterated all the stars in that quarter. At the zenith, however, there was one brilliant star.

"Is that Deneb?"

"Aye."

"Watch it! Without using the sextant. If I'm right about the position, the tip of the mast will touch the star."

"You'll want the mizzen in that case." Davy had caught her excitement and the concept that sparked it. "The mainmast is raked. You'll want one that points straight up.

Amanda set her back against the foot of the mizzen and tipped her head till she sighted up along the leading edge of the great timber. Its top was lost in darkness, but as she watched and the ship rolled, the star winked out, then burned again. Winked out. Burned.

She had brought along the sextant. Davy, who could still make out the horizon, measured the angle of the star's elevation. He had to face south to find it; it had passed over by two minutes. Their latitude was now 45°12' north. She had been right all along. Deneb was her witness. It had fallen into place like the last piece of a jigsaw puzzle. She was exalted by the power and the glory of it.

What she wanted now—all she wanted—was someone with whom to share her triumph, someone to praise her, but not as Flagg had praised her—for the wrong reasons and in the wrong degree. She wanted the accolade bestowed by one of the anointed. By Jonathan.

"You got it right," Davy said softly. "We're where you put us. It's like you was an angel, sent on purpose just to bring us in safe."

The Twelfth Day

AMANDA BRIGHT'S JOURNAL

September 12, 1851

The weather has turned exquisitely fair, which is remarkable, considering how far north we have come. The change is welcome, as it gives us an opportunity to wash and air the linens of both sick-rooms. Our patients are improved in the sense that their fevers are somewhat abated. Whether other improvements will follow, we shall know soon enough. Flagg believes there will be a real turn for the better today or tomorrow, but he has been predicting something of the sort for so long that he has lost all credit as a prophet.

⬧

I n the hour before the noon observation, Amanda sat at her desk to write.

My dear ones:

It was my intention to write some pages of this letter every day so that I might not forget too many of the details of this life—those that are generally left out of the accounts one hears after a voyage is done. One would think, listening to men spin yarns of such an adventure, that it was all emergencies and alarms, disasters narrowly averted or bravely borne. But tedium is the principal feature of life at sea, unless one breaks it by attention to what might be consid-

ered—under different circumstances—trivial and childish pursuits.

Most of yesterday was lost to letter writing, and most of this forenoon as well, because of the weather. Not the bad weather of which I so often complain but weather so benign—so blessed— that it seemed a sin to waste it belowdecks. It is the first time I have seen reason why the Pacific should be so called. There is a soft, steady wind from the south. Deep blue swells roll by in such hypnotic rhythm that one must fight to stay awake. The sky is brilliant overhead, fading into gray blue haze that erases the border between sky and sea. The eye loses its way in this luminous world.

We are at least a thousand miles from the nearest land, but birds of many kinds are in the air and water. Some, like the majestic albatross, seem to follow us, though they accept none of our offerings of food. Others cross our bows without deigning to acknowledge our existence. Today a whole flock of dark birds, the size of starlings or martins, crossed and recrossed our wake, darting and dipping like swallows in pursuit of flying insects. The sailors call them petrels, but they are not marked like the storm petrels of the Atlantic. I should have discounted the nomenclature entirely but for a display of the "walking on water" from which the name petrel is derived. (It is supposed that, like St. Peter, they attempt to imitate Jesus in this respect.) It is really a remarkable feat they perform, settling with wings spread and upraised, touching both feet to the surface of the swells and moving in hops or jumps, watching all the while for some small fish or sea creature close beneath the surface. I have yet to see one settle to rest.

Also, this morning I was given my first lessons in the use of the marlinespike. I had been watching our Chips work a knot into the end of a lanyard, which was to be used on a newly carved deadeye.

That would lead her into explaining the need for the new deadeye and other repairs resulting from the broaching. She could not put off the telling forever, but neither could she approach it in this oblique fashion. When she was ready, she would begin straightforwardly. She crossed out the last clause and made a full stop.

The knot is called a matthew walker, though no one seems to know who Matthew Walker was or why he is so memorialized. Flagg proposed to show me how it is tied, and before long I was surrounded by tutors, each with his own notion of how I should begin to master the arts of knotting and bending, hitching and splicing. But my fingers proved feeble and awkward compared to the callused digits of my teachers, and, despite their great patience, it was soon clear that matthew walker is, for the present at least, beyond my powers. I was offered instead the task of "worming" some lengths of line that is to be "parceled and served." A sort of five-finger exercise like those to which I was condemned as a child at the pianoforte.

My practice was interrupted (to my great relief) by a call to come to the rail. The ship had entered into what appeared to be a sea of soap bubbles. Looking straight down, one could see that each bubble was actually a small, whitish fin, attached to some invisible body. These fins were all aligned in one direction, like a fleet of ships hove to. Their number was—and still is—legion.

Everyone tried to capture and bring up one of the creatures. In the end it was Cook who triumphed (though he risked the loss of one of our remaining buckets and was scolded by me for it). There were three small blue jellyfish in his catch, two of them undamaged and quite marvelous to examine.

The body of the creature is invisible in the water because its azure exactly matches the hue of the sea. Its form is a flat oval, with short, fringing tentacles below and an opaque wind vane above. Within its soft blue arms lives an even smaller animalcule—a lavender—tinted snail so delicate one cannot pick it up in one's fingers without crushing it.

Now, nearly an hour later, we are still sailing through the bubble fleet, although our sails, which are set to catch the wind theirs are set to escape, push us past them at a brisk rate.

The letter was interrupted by a call from Jonathan, who was distinctly improved since her last visit. He asked for water and held the glass himself, staring fixedly at it as if the task required all his powers of concentration. While Amanda waited for him to finish sipping, she considered whether this was, perhaps, the moment to consult him on the proposal to change course, as she had told Willy she would. But as she was turning in her mind how much else she would have to tell him and how much disastrous news he could bear, his eyes closed and he drifted back into sleep.

There has been an interruption of some duration, and before continuing, I have reread what I wrote three days ago (it seems much longer) on the subject of prejudice and the barriers that separate the races and the genders. I must have been thinking more deeply on the question without being aware of it, for I find that my mind is much changed.

I do not believe it right to prejudge a man's capacities on the basis of his color. But I am still prone to assume that a man who cannot read and write is inferior to one who can. Just as one assumes a slave inferior to a free man.

In the case of slaves, we are told that in ancient Greece and Biblical Palestine, men were not born into slavery but captured and enslaved. If their faculties were not too badly stunted by the life they led thereafter, they might become the equals of their captors. Freed, they might become their betters. But I am not convinced that it is the same with an illiterate, grown to manhood, any more than it is the same with most women.

Even in New England we—most of us—are condemned by our early education to an ignorance no less crippling for being concealed under a fancy dress of Moral Philosophy, Music, and French. We are truly inferior, like slaves who do not even aspire to freedom. For endowed by our Creator with rights, we cannot enjoy them because we are deprived of

Searching her mind for precisely what it was she felt deprived of, she realized that she was writing only to herself. None of those to whom her letter was addressed would be interested in her views on such matters. And they would disapprove of them. Reading over what she had written, Amanda was startled by the boldness of her denunciation of what she had accepted as given until—when was it she had changed? When Horace talked to her about the glories of Cambridge philosophy? Or when his Louisa had taken shape in her imagination as a priestess in that temple?

How clearly this surrogate sister-confidante-companion had taken shape. In appearance, a younger, fairer, improved-upon Amanda. In character, more generous, more open, more lovable. But vulnerable—impressionable and impulsive, lacking Amanda's knowledge of the world, for all her greater store of the wisdom to be got from reading. Louisa listened with eager interest to all Amanda had to say, agreeing with the conclusions she drew or at least offering no objections. If only Louisa could speak. If only there were a female friend to hold Amanda's hand through the ordeals of this voyage, to sympathize and pity, admire and encourage her.

One of those ordeals was the letter she must compose to Louisa, as well as the one to Uncle Matthew and Aunt Aggie. They could not be expected to convey news of their loss to one they had refused to know. But how was she to address her imagined sister? Horace had not told her Louisa's family name or said precisely where she lived. Perhaps in his journal or other papers there would be a clue.

Meanwhile, rather than destroy the pages on which she had struggled—and failed—to bring her ideas into form, she lifted them out of the letter, tearing in half the one on which the passage began, and slipped them into the leaves of her own journal. One day there would be time to read, consider, and begin again.

On deck, she was awaited.

Amidships was a small group, in the center of which stood Rory, propped on a crutch he had fashioned for himself. They exchanged greetings—from Amanda a compliment on how well he seemed to be coming along, from him an expression of gratitude for her efforts on his behalf. During the few moments this occupied, she tried to absorb the scene: the disposition of the hands about the deck, bodily attitudes, facial expressions, anything that might carry meaning if properly interpreted.

The regal African was at the pinrail of the foremast, back to her. To avoid witnessing what was about to transpire? No-Name was at the helm, aft. Flagg and Cook were just inside the door of the galley. Neutrals? Crank and Davy stood shoulder to shoulder against the bulwarks, their fists lightly clenched. In the group around and behind Rory were the Kanakas and the Marquesan.

"If ye've a moment to spare, ma'am, the crew here would like a word wi' ye."

It was the opening of every tale of mutiny she had ever heard—spoken with a burr that blurred the words but not the menace. She could have taken up the tale and carried it forward from these courteous opening hypocrisies to the violent climax. The details might differ (sometimes there were touches of humor; sometimes, pathos), depending on the character of the protagonist, the hero who mastered the rebels and showed them his might and his right and possibly his mercy. But this was real. And utterly unexpected. It should not have been. The signs had been plain, if only she had had the wit to read them.

Rory was still talking, and she must listen, must begin to think what to say when he stopped. But her mind kept shooting off on tangents, going back over portents she had ignored or misread. He was finishing his long peroration on the hands' appreciation of her devoted care for the sick, her well-meant attempt to establish the ship's position, and so forth. She commanded her mind to return to the present, to pull in tight, squeeze out all feeling, all fear. Her fists were clenching like those of the two men on whom she believed she could count for help.

"...the health of our captain and mate. So 'tis for that reason chiefly that the lads have concluded to make for San Francisco, where better care can be had."

She looked straight at him, directing the force of her in-gathered energy, bearing down from the greater height of the quarterdeck, commanding his will to submit to hers, commanding him to move back.

It had no perceptible effect except that Rory seemed unwilling to bring his speech to the end he had planned for it, as if he feared to let hers begin. On and on he went till the last, silly circumlocution had unwound itself and lay like a frayed rope on the deck.

She had heard him out. She let a silence underline that fact. What she had to say would gain power by having been so long contained.

"I'll convey your good wishes to the captain and with them your suggestion about the course."

In the gap between her uttering of the words and their penetrating the minds of her hearers, she turned, raised the sextant—making sure the filter panes were in place—and brought the sight tube to her eye. She was not looking *through* it; she was using the index mirror to see what was happening amidships. Or at least trying to, for it was hard to find the angle.

She lowered it and looked in Rory's direction, acting on impulse, without having planned a strategy to follow.

"You, there! You say you're handy with a sextant. Would you like to try mine?"

Rory was so taken aback that she was afraid he might refuse. But already one of the Kanakas was coming to convey the instrument from her to him. To refuse without giving a reason would have been to lose face. His uneasiness made her bold—and canny. She moved the index arm to the end of its arc as she handed the instrument over. Let him find his own altitude.

Rory received the instrument, examined it carefully, changed the angle of the mirror, rearranged the filters, and looked for a place to stand. One of the Kanakas helped him hobble to the stern of the long-boat, where he could steady himself against the motion of the ship without having to use his hands. He faced into the sun and raised the instrument.

Amanda had often watched Jonathan measure the angle of the sun, but with the eyes of ignorance, learning nothing. Now she was able to isolate and admire refinements: tricks of balance and stance, the position of arms, elbows, hands, and most of all the smooth, rocking motion of Rory's final testing of the sight.

("By this motion the sun will appear to sweep the horizon and must be made to touch it at the lowest part of the arc.")

"Forty-seven degrees, ten minutes. Is that what you made it, ma'am?"

She had taken no reading as yet, but she did not think he knew that, so she lied boldly. "I was lower, but the sun is still rising. So, if I may have the instrument..."

The Kanaka brought it to her, and she had only to move the arm slightly to bring the filtered image to rest on the horizon. She had passed her first test! Measured the altitude of the sun—47°33'. Her dead reckoning prophesied that it would go as high as 48°07'. Now that she knew she could manage the procedure, she could be patient and wait.

But Rory could not. He flung the gauntlet. The men were of a mind to head east, he said. Due east. No insubordination was to be imputed, for there was no officer able to assume command. In such circumstances it was legal—under God and the maritime codes of all nations—for men to look out for their own welfare.

"...and yours and the skipper's as well."

Out of the corner of her eye, Amanda saw Crank and Davy shift position, readying themselves for attack. But they were outnumbered. Unless No-Name abandoned the helm and King John, his neutrality—or Cook and Flagg, theirs. But the latter were no match for the mutinous four....

"You offered once to do the navigating," Amanda said to Rory, as if no new topic of discussion had been introduced. "I've been thinking of accepting your offer."

Rory's face went into smiles too quickly. He was already celebrating his victory by launching into one of his grand brags when she cut him short.

"But before I do, would you tell me from the observation you just made, where you would put the ship?"

Everyone froze in place. Even the Kanakas seemed to recognize the challenge: Rory was being put to the test. If he was to take command of the ship, he must be able to wield the divining rods of the priesthood.

"Well," he said uneasily, "only roughly—"

"Of course. You would need pen and paper to do it properly, as I was reminding you the other day when you asked me to do the same thing. Roughly will do for now."

Rory writhed on the pin, going through an extravagant pantomime of indecision—scowling, pursing his lips, cocking his head, shifting his weight on and off the splinted leg. The Polynesians observed him intently, drawing closer as if they needed each other's support to sustain the suspense.

"A mite north, I'd say, if I had to...a mite north of 38."

"Thirty-eight degrees north latitude?" She repeated the figure with slow, judicial emphasis. "That would be close to the latitude of San Francisco?"

"Close enough."

"I'm afraid your navigation is not sound enough to be relied upon. We're a little below 47°. Nearer to the latitude of Nootka Sound than that of San Francisco Bay."

There was a rippling echo of her pronouncement, translated and passed from nearer to more distant listeners. Rory was reddening. But he was too dangerous a fish to be played. He must be netted and gaffed at once.

"About your suggestion that we head east, it happens I intend doing so. Perhaps this afternoon. Perhaps tomorrow. If our new course brings us up with the coast of California, you will have the laugh of me. But in the meantime, we will continue under the orders of Captain Bright."

That needed no translation. Amanda raised the sextant once more—in pure bravado, for she could not have managed a shot with her whole body atremble. Then, with her head high and her back erect, she went below without a glance at her adversary.

She got out her journal to record her triumph while it was still fresh in her mind, but her hand was still shaky, so she contented herself for the moment with drawing up a list of the able-bodied hands. Ten in all. Two had stood loyally with her; four had stood on the brink of mutiny; four had not committed themselves at the moment when the issue seemed to hang in the balance. It was the neutrals who distressed her. Rory and the Polynesians she understood. But men she had counted as friends had deserted her. Perhaps loyalty was not founded on friendship in such circumstances as these. Jonathan believed it rested on fear and respect. Fear of punishment and respect for the competence of the captain. One aspect of this incident bore out his contention. It was by showing Rory incompetent that she had defeated him.

But the problem she had faced before the rebellion had not been resolved. Unless Jonathan was on the mend, unless he would soon—very soon!—be able to assume some responsibility, unless she made good on her promise-threat to ask his opinion about the course to be steered, she could not hope to hold the advantage she had won.

Willy came to announce that the noon meal was served.

She ate alone and in silence and had time to wonder for the first time where Willy had stood in the scene on the deck. She had not missed him at the time, but she was sure she would have noted his presence.

What a mistake to have let Rory move in with Willy. The lad was so young, so easily gulled; the man, so plausible. Her mind ground to a halt at the edge of the sequitur: Willy's bunkmate was the ringleader, so Willy must have heard the discussions that led to the confrontation. He had absented himself so as not to be counted. And he had not warned her. Worse yet, he had tried to persuade her to appoint as captain a man who was conspiring to seize that post by force. And he, a Martin, raised in a tradition that viewed mutiny as more heinous than murder. It was unforgivable.

Willy had twice cleared his throat. He was asking permission to speak. To make excuses? To cover his shame with fig leaves of explanation—that he had not been privy to the plan, that he had been deceived, that he had been busy in the sickrooms until everything was over? But there was nothing he could say that she would believe now, and she could not trust herself to listen.

4

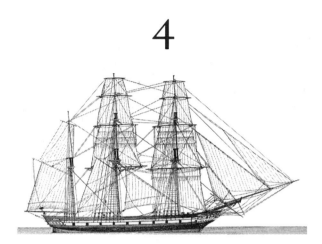

The Surrogate

THE THIRTEENTH DAY

She had stayed at the desk till very late, pretending to work because she was afraid to sleep, obsessed by the notion that as soon as her vigilance relaxed, the helm would be put over. With every footfall she heard above her head, she suspended breath to listen, to follow in her mind the man who was moving there in the darkness to meet with other men, to whisper, to plot, to join in a conspiracy against the surrogate whose authority derived from a commander no longer able to command.

Once, when the wind dropped, she was sure from the motion of the ship that the course had been altered, but when she went on deck, the compass still pointed north by west, and all was as it should be.

The Hawaiian who spoke pidgin was at the wheel and seemed less hostile, more respectful, than he had been. Tono, who was also on watch, actually greeted her and predicted a change of wind. That was good news or would be if the wind hauled to the west. For the westerlies lay in wait, in benign ambush, just above the 50th parallel. The sooner they swooped down, the sooner her victory over Rory would be secured.

The more she thought back over the way that victory had been won, the more inconclusive it appeared. The error he committed could not have resulted from ignorance. The man knew how to handle a sextant. The altitude he read off was close to hers; but the conclusion he drew from it was nearly 10°—600 miles—off. So it came down to this: either he knew how to shoot the sun, but not how to use the result, or he knew and had given a false answer.

In either case he had lost face and followers. But he might win them back. He might fabricate an explanation that would convince his followers he had been trying to trick her. He was capable of persuasiveness, and the Polynesians were disposed to be persuaded. So the mutiny was not put down. Driven below ground, it would travel along paths—loyalties and antipathies, bonds and beliefs—of which she knew nothing. She could not foresee in what quarter it might break out again. But a change of wind—to the west—would be some insurance against it.

When she woke a little after one, stiff in her shoulders and the forearms that had been her pillow, she went up to try for a Polaris shot. The northern sky was blank. The waning moon showed through the overcast that covered the zenith, but there were no stars.

King John was at the wheel. When she came to look at the compass, he asked his usual question about the captain's health. Was this all he knew of English? Or was he reminding her of her place?

Next time she woke it was light. The wind had died. The ship ghosted along through fog so silently that only by watching the wake could one know that she moved.

Amanda used the silence of her solitary breakfast to get her thoughts in order for the twice-postponed consultation with Jonathan. It would be wise, she decided, to have Willy as witness so that the report could be carried to his faction in the forecastle. She thought of him now as a foot soldier of the enemy. When she had finished eating, she inquired whether Jonathan was awake.

"He was when I took him his tea."

But when she went into the stateroom, Jonathan lay with eyes closed. She was not sure he was asleep. Sometimes she thought he feigned sleep so as not to have to acknowledge her presence and the new, strained relationship between them. Or perhaps it was because it took all his strength simply to keep his lungs filling and emptying. In any case, though she was reluctant to wake him, she was unwilling to postpone the interview again. She decided to wait half an hour and use the time to bathe and change her clothes.

In the tiny cubicle of the bath, she stripped, soaped, and rinsed herself from ears to toes in a basin of half-fresh, half-salt water, then rubbed dry with a towel gritty with salt. Dressed in fresh underclothes and a wool skirt and shirtwaist (it was perceptibly colder on deck even when there was sun), she hung her head down and brushed her hair till it bristled and was slow to fall when she straightened.

Standing at the side of Jonathan's bunk, she felt electric energy emanate from inside her in waves like heat shimmer, strong enough to penetrate the deepest of defenses. It took nearly a minute to penetrate Jonathan's, but his breathing changed, his eyes blinked open, focused on her till he recognized her, then closed, leaving a vague smile on his face.

"Jonathan!"

His eyes opened again, and she began crisply.

"I have to talk to you. You needn't answer if you're not up to speaking. Just nod or give me some sort of sign." She looked to make sure the door was open, that Willy was on the other side and listening. "We're almost at the 50th parallel. We may already have crossed it."

Jonathan nodded as if to say, "Good."

"What I want you to tell me is, when do you want the ship put over to an easterly course? Now? Or shall I wait till I can get another latitude shot and be sure of the position?"

Jonathan took breath and expelled it in five audible words: "When you have northing enough."

She wanted to know how much was enough, but he had spent himself. She would have to come back with her question another time. But meanwhile, Willy could carry his tattle to the forecastle, where it would reinforce her status as surrogate.

———

The barometer stood lower than she had ever seen it. How strange that the lightening of pressure on the column of mercury should be felt by a human body as weight, an added, unwanted burden. The sea was ugly, gray, and oily; the surface, contorted as if it reflected some monstrous birth anguish in the depths. Staring straight down over the rail, she could see mist-colored ghosts of dead sea wrack. The sails sagged and snapped. Yards creaked. Water sucking away from the ship's sides sounded like retching.

Amanda longed for the snug harbor of the cabin, but she had a sense of holding back some evil by her presence on deck. So she waited, watching the kittiwakes flapping in slow circles around the slowly flapping sails. Seen from below, the gulls' breasts were whiter than the sky. The black of their wing tips, the yellow of their bills, and the red of their folded feet stood out with artificial clarity as they came back again and again, screaming harshly, making a mutiny in the air.

One of them settled on the surface, ducked its head, and came up with a fish. The whole flock converged on him—or was it her?—and the screaming became more furious. The diver ignored it, stubbornly beating his wings, up, up, till he was on a level with the quarterdeck. Something fell from overhead like a meteor. Amanda caught a glimpse of gray body and a tail from which two, very long, twisted feathers trailed.

"It's a skua!" Flagg was at her elbow.

The gull opened its beak. The fish dropped. The plunging skua caught it before it hit the water, lifted itself with two beats of its great wings, wheeled, and flew off across the bow. Screams of outrage followed its flight, but no pursuers.

"Them skuas are that nervy. They'll plunder any bird up to the albatross," Flagg said admiringly. This put him in mind that for some days now he had not seen the albatross family that had been following the ship.

"Was there a family of them?"

Flagg believed so. At least, there were three birds of the right sizes to be father, mother, and fledgling. They showed up morning and evening, but never all at once, so of course it might not be the same three, or they might bear no relationship to one another.

He was chattering on to no purpose—unless perhaps it was to mend fences. Had he changed sides after all? If so, this might be an opportunity to explore the state of mind and morale before the mast. But Amanda remembered his reaction to her last attempt to question him and could not bring herself to hazard another rebuff.

The gulls were gone, and in the silence the air weighed more oppressively than ever. Then, quite suddenly, it lifted.

It happened first within her, as if some cramped muscle had let go. Then the air around her stirred. A surge of it pushed weakly at the topsails and expired. Another surge and the topsails bellied, sagged, bellied again. The ship rose and settled back. Slap, gurgle. Creak, luff.

The gulls returned, circling and screaming. There was a spatter of rain. Another lift of wind. Then rain, more determined than before.

"Kittiwake! Kittiwake! Hear them? That's where the name come from, you see."

Squawk and scream from the birds. Creak and slap from the burdened yards. The wind made a circle, imitating the gulls, and rain was flung in a spiral across the deck from starboard to port.

"She's coming on to rain, ma'am. You'd best go below."

"The wind's veering."

"Aye. I thought it might," Flagg said smugly. "Said to myself this morning, we'll pick up the westerlies sometime before nightfall."

Dark clouds let down shawls of rain that the wind caught and swirled. Waves were lifting and pressing. Men strained at the lee braces. Davy was coming toward them, his head ducked against the rain. They'd want to sail her full and by, he said, unless there was some thought of changing course?

"These *are* the westerlies?" Amanda asked. "Not just a squall?"

"Aye, ma'am."

"For sure, ma'am."

The men spoke in unison and smiled, first at each other, then at her.

Her wind! That would discredit and disarm her adversary. Let Rory take his sails out of her wind, her wind that would carry them to Nootka.

"Bring her on to a course of east by north, one half north," she said.

Davy conveyed her order to the helm. The ship had but little way, and it took time for the rudder to bite. But as the bow swung round, the great square sails began to pull, one after the other. The vessel lurched forward like a horse that catches the scent of its own stable. The cacophony of the kittiwakes grew fainter as they were left behind. An albatross overtook the ship, gliding so low under the pelting rain that it seemed to fly through the wave tops without breaking them.

Kankkonen came to ask Amanda if she had given the order for a change of course. She said yes. He made no comment, but it was clear that the order should have been conveyed through him in his capacity of officer of the watch. His glumness took the edge off her elation.

September 13, 1851

> *Day commenced in calm; at 2 P.M. wind sprang up, westerly.*
> *Assumed lat. 50°N.*
> *Assumed long. 157° W.*
> *Course E by N ¹/₂ N.*
> *(If the assumed latitude proves less, it may be necessary to steer ENE.)*
> *Log heaved: 6+ k.*

THE FOURTEENTH DAY

AMANDA BRIGHT'S JOURNAL

September 14, 1851

I have been changed by the life I am leading, both for the better and for the worse. For example, I have developed senses I hardly knew existed, including a sense of weather—a consciousness of subtle changes that signify greater ones to come. I remember how we used to make fun (behind his back) of Grandfather Hodges when he claimed he could tell by a feeling in his joints that the glass was about to rise or to fall. I have acquired such a feeling, but it is not localized in my joints. Nor in any other particular part. It is a diffuse, but not unpleasant, uneasiness, a sort of inward straining to restore a threatened balance. I have come to recognize it as the first sign of an imminent shift of wind or temperature or pressure. I cannot account for it but rely on it, nevertheless, and think myself as good a weather prophet as any of the foremasthands.

So much for gains; losses are harder to define. I fear I am less aware than formerly of the human beings around me, what they are thinking and feeling, threatening or promising. Even now, having been warned by what was a very near thing, I cannot keep my attention fixed for long on the matter of morale. Nor on the condition of my two patients. At the start of their illness I carried concern for them in the forefront of my mind and found, as a result, solutions to many different aspects of the problem of caring for them in these wretched circumstances. But now I come to their sickbeds with a blank mind, almost resentful at the interruption of other trains of thought.

Is this why nursing is considered woman's work? Because it takes complete dedication as well as compassion? Men are not lacking in compassion. (Flagg, for example, is a paragon of that virtue.) But men think of themselves firstly as captains or mates or sailmakers or carpenters and only incidentally as keepers of their brothers.

This is nothing but idle scribbling, done to avoid looking squarely at the problem, which is that there are more calls on my time than I can properly answer. I shall have to learn to divide it so as not to neglect any important duty, however distasteful. The care of our sick is every bit as important as knowing the ship's position.

·✧·

That resolution firmly taken, she went to look in on Jonathan. Willy was dozing on the sea chest, his chin in his hand. He put his finger to his lips to warn her to be quiet. But she woke the sleeper and began briskly.

"I don't want to tire you, Jonathan, but I must have your counsel. By the look of the sky, I shall be able to get a noon observation. Once I know the latitude, I will be ready to correct our course. How much northing ought we to have for the run east?"

He answered, in a whisper, that a whole degree would be desirable but that it could be managed with less so long as the compass error was known and compensated for.

"I'll see to the compass night and morning, so long as the horizon is clear," Amanda said. "Now, what about longitude?" And seeing his lips begin to form the word "chronometer," she hurried to get the

144

worst behind her.

"The chronometer won't help. No one thought to wind it when you were taken sick."

Jonathan's head came off the pillow with a jerk. His forehead furrowed. His voice returned, powered by outrage, and he railed against Horace:...little as he had to do...much as he had pushed off on Amanda, who had two sick men to nurse...couldn't remember to wind the instrument on which—as any fool could tell you—the life of the ship might depend!

Jonathan's tone was as shocking as his ignorance of Horace's death—an old man's treble, quarrelsome and querulous. Amanda was too shaken to deliver the coup de grace that would bring the tirade to an end. But Jonathan was already faltering, running out of breath, falling back on his pillow, panting.

"You'll have to...try a lunar...must have your...longitude...coming up on that coast...all in Bowditch...Smith can help."

He could not continue. Amanda felt his forehead. The fever had risen again.

Smith was better. The disfiguring blotches were fading. His eyes were no longer red where they should be white, as they had been at the height of his fever, nor dull and cloudy as they had been later on. Amanda could tell him with conviction that he was on the mend.

"Thanks to you, ma'am. Oh, Chips and the lad, too. But mostly yourself I been thinking...laying here...I don't rightly know...." Tears were invading his throat and eyes.

"I need your help," Amanda said. "The chronometer has run down."

"Aye. So Chips was telling me."

"Did he also tell you about...?"

"Young Mr. Martin? Aye." Locked in a struggle with tears that rose and words that wouldn't, Smith gulped. His Adam's apple pumped wildly for a moment, then sank out of sight.

She wondered that Flagg should have carried such intelligence to the mate and not to the master. But perhaps he thought it her office to give or to withhold information from her husband, to choose at what moment he could best sustain the blows.

"The help I need is with lunar distances. The captain says that is the only way left to us for finding our longitude."

Smith was sorry to say he knew nothing of lunars beyond having taken altitudes for them. "It's the distance is the trick of it—that and the figuring." He had sailed with captains who could do lunars and come out—though more often than not they would fill up sheaves of paper and not come out. "But for myself, I rely on the reckoning. Use a traverse board if I have to. Better than having all that," he waved a weak hand, "to do with."

"What do you mean about the distance being the trick of it?"

"Well, ma'am, what it is, is: You have to hold your sextant so, to measure how far apart they are, the moon and whatever else. And that's awkward, you see. While you're about it, there's others taking the altitude of the bodies, and a man on the watch. Three sextants and four men." Parenthetically, he would be more than glad to offer his sextant if Amanda could find a man who knew the use of one.

"Rory claims to." She related the incident in which she had tested that claim, hoping Smith might interpret it, but he found it as baffling as she did.

"Funny thing is he didn't ask you for the declination afore he worked the shot."

"That's right. I never thought of that."

"Whatever he was up to, it's well you were able to scotch it, ma'am," Smith said with conviction. "I marked him down for a troublemaker, time he come aboard." But if she didn't mind him changing the subject, was it true, as Chips said, that nothing was being done to replace the lost top gallant mast or the jibboom?

Amanda thought it was true. She had paid almost no attention to the problems of masts, yards, rigging, or sails, feeling that there were others fitter than she to deal with them. But she had heard it said they were making good time, "considering the loss of the t'gallants and royals."

"That's just it, ma'am. Your t'gallants are your passage makers." Smith was distressed at the slowing of the ship's speed and even more by the loss of steering control. "You ought to have a jib set to keep her from broaching to again when she's running off the wind."

"Is it possible to make that sort of repair while we're under way?"

Smith said it was, so long as the fine weather held. If it hadn't been washed over in the broaching, there was timber aboard for this purpose. A good crew should be able to sway up a top gallant mast one day and get a jibboom in place on the day following.

"Very well," Amanda said. "If you'll tell me what orders to give and to whom…or," remembering her gaffe with the bosun, "perhaps you could talk to the men yourself?"

Smith said he would talk to Davy, who could then report to Amanda, who could give the orders to Crank to release the necessary supplies.

It lacked less than an hour of noon. Amanda had prefigured the angle at which the sun should stand if the ship was at 50°; where, if they had half a degree of northing; where, if they had a whole one. She was not ready to face the lunar; one bite at a time was enough. While she waited for the sun, she began a new letter—began without thinking what she would write, letting her pen and her hand take command.

September 14, 1851
My dear ones:

> *Yesterday evening while I was sitting at table, trying to satisfy my hunger with what I take to be the nadir of seagoing gastronomy (cracker hash garnished with some very sour pickles), there was all at once a great commotion on deck. I hurried up, hoping against all reasonable hope that we were about to speak a ship from which I might obtain some estimate of our position. What I saw instead was a large, handsome, blue-and-silver fish, gasping its last on the deck while another of the same sort was being hauled in over the rail.*

The hook was rebaited and thrown back, and in the interval before a third fish was landed, I was regaled with an account of the preceding events, part in pidgin, which I shall not attempt to reproduce, and part in English, spoken with various accents, from cockney to Finnish, and all at the same time. It appears that someone had noticed a gaggle of seabirds a point or less off the bow and surmised that a school of herring or other fry was troubling the water in an effort to escape a school of large fish preying on them. The helm was persuaded to alter course enough to pass close.

By the time the ship had reached the birds, lines had been baited and thrown over, but there were no strikes. Having gone to such trouble, the men were loath to be robbed of all sport, so they began fishing for birds—a trick played for the most part on the greedy gulls, less frequently on the albatross. (Bearing in mind the warning of the Ancient Mariner, I should have forbidden it, had I been on deck.)

As it happened, there was an albatross following the ship. But even when the lines were baited with bright pieces of metal (cut from the tins in which our salt beef is kept), the bird ignored them. At one point, so I was told, he settled on the water near one of the lures and turned his head away as if revolted by it, permitting the ship to pull some distance ahead before again taking to his wings.

Just as he caught up with us, the line was struck, not by him, thank heavens, but by the first of the fish, which are called bonito. Three were caught within a quarter of an hour. The flesh is dark, firm, and free of small bones. I look forward to a day or more of feasting!

The weather has cooled by several degrees, and the change is very hard on our Hawaiians, who go about with bare feet and thin shirts, pinch cheeked, goose bumped, and sorrowful.

Flagg says these men were lured aboard by a promise (made them by the crimps) that we were bound for California, where they intended to jump ship and join the gold hunters. In any case, they brought along none of the clothes one would need for a voyage in high latitudes. Today I tried to alleviate their discomfort by distributing

Heyerman's clothing! She had backed—or sidled—to the brink of the telling. Perhaps if she began now with no preface.

September 14, 1851
My dear ones:
 Forgive me that I have taken so many days to bring myself to tell you of our loss

But the words lay like dead things, crushed by the effort that had brought them forth. She could not find others to bring them to life.

The noon shot went well.

She had preset the sextant for the angle she was expecting. When she found the sun in the silvered pane, it was well below the line of the horizon. But it would rise. She need not change her setting. The sun would come to meet it.

When she looked again, it had come half the distance. Then, with a quarter of its lower limb still below the line, it slowed. *("It will hang there for over a minute and then begin to descend.")* This was the meridian moment. Amanda turned the vernier screw to lift the image of the sun till it brushed the dark horizon line. When she looked the next time, the sun had dipped below it.

The altitude was 42°45′, which placed the ship nearly a full degree farther north than she had dared hope. That meant a margin of fifty to sixty miles of northing for the thousand-mile run to Nootka. *If* it was a thousand...*if* the longitude had indeed been 157° west when the course was changed.

Those "ifs" stood like a barrier reef between her and her objective. There might be passes through the reef, but she must depend on the moon to lead her through them—the uncertain moon, her own uncertain mind, and the abstruse oracle of the Bowditch.

"Lunar Observation." The section heading stood at the top of a page of solid print, impenetrable as granite. Amanda attacked it tim-

idly, running her eye down the lines till it caught on a sentence that had some promise.

"As the moon moves in her orbit about 1' in 2m of time, it follows that if the angular distance can be ascertained from the sun or star within 1', the time at Greenwich will be known within 2 minutes and the longitude within 30 miles."

In the *Nautical Almanac* there were tables giving the distance of the moon from the sun, and of the moon from certain bright planets and fixed stars, every third hour of every day of the year. At Greenwich. A navigator was instructed to measure the angular distance between the moon and whatever celestial body he had chosen, record the local time, search the tables for the nearest approximation to the angle observed, compare local time to Greenwich time, and translate the difference into longitude.

There were all sorts of caveats about corrections for parallax and refraction. Amanda skipped over them quickly lest her mind draw down shutters to protect itself from proportional logs and parts, sines and secants, and so forth.

Under the subheading *"General Remarks on the Taking of a Lunar Observation"* there were caveats about absolute accuracy, some hints about conditions conducive to such accuracy, and the requirement that there be *"observers enough to measure the altitude of both bodies when the distance between them was observed."* According to Smith, that was "three sextants and four men," which made it impossible. But she read on, looking for a different solution, half-dreading to find it. At the end of the section she came upon *"Method of Taking a Lunar Observation by One Observer."*

Here was her elephant! She attacked it bravely. It seemed to be a matter of finding the mean between a number of observations and times, a procedure for which there were meticulously precise directions, well garnished with footnotes.

> Add together the proportional logarithms (Table XXII) of the variation of altitude[†] of the object between the two times of observing the altitudes, and the prop. log. of the time elapsed between taking the first altitude and measuring the distance; from

the sum subtract the prop. log.[††] of the time elapsed between observing the two altitudes of the object; the remainder will be the prop. log. of the correction to be applied to the first altitude, additive or subtractive, according as the altitude was increasing or decreasing; to the altitude thus corrected, apply the correction for dip of horizon and semi-diameter as usual.

[†]*Table XXII is only calculated as far as 3°, and if the variation of altitude exceed that quantity, you must enter the table with minutes and seconds, instead of degrees and minutes; and the correction of altitude taken out in minutes and seconds must be called degrees and minutes respectively.*
[††]*Or add the arithmetical complement, neglecting 10 in the index.*

The shutters of her mind snapped tight, refusing to admit another particle of the stuff. She tried to coax them open by reading aloud, but her voice sounded alien, the words meaningless, laughable. It was like being outside herself and unable to gain entry—or inside, unable to call for help, locked in a darkness full of blind worms of words that crawled hopelessly in circles.

Davy came to make his report on the plan for swaying up the new topgallant mast. It was a pity, he said, that they had not been about it while the ship was becalmed, but good they had not waited longer, for the wind was freshening and the sea beginning to roughen. He was anxious to explain how it was to be done, what alternatives he had rejected and why, how the solution had come to him. First off, she would remember they had cut away the broken mast just above the doubling but left its stump in place....

He was testing his plan by telling it, reliving and relishing the struggle in which it had been born, preliving and savoring its achievement. Amanda knew these pleasures. She had tasted them in the days when she was taking her first steps on the path that had led her back to the blank wall of the prison of her mind. She would not be lured into ambush again.

"Do what you like with the mast," she said. "I have nothing to do with it."

Davy gaped. Then, diffidently, asked if there was something wrong. "The captain's not….?"

Nothing wrong with the captain, but much wrong with her. She had been asked once too often to do the impossible. No one could take a lunar distance without enough instruments or observers. At least, she couldn't. Perhaps she was stupid, but not so stupid as to believe she would ever make sense of the gibberish in the Bowditch. She sounded like Rory, intoxicated on self-abuse. But she didn't care.

Davy waited till she ran out of words, and then began to chide her. She should be ashamed to speak so when she had already accomplished what amounted to a miracle. "Brought us halfway out of hell—begging your pardon for the word, ma'am—and the rest, all plain sailing."

She tried to explain why it was not all plain sailing, why the longitude mattered, but he would not listen.

"Once you put us on the latitude line, there was nothing to it. We've only to run down our easting and we'll fetch Nootka."

He was not going to hear what he did not want to believe. Already he was hard at work repairing the damage she had done to his icon, a being half woman, half angel, endowed with powers beyond those of mere men.

"The three L's is all you need now: lead, line, and lookout." There were those who held with other omens, such as birds that flew back to their nesting grounds at sunset. But that was only if one knew which birds to watch for and how far they were apt to range during the day. It was the same with other portents, among which he seemed to be including lunar distances.

Listening, Amanda was almost converted to the folk wisdom that underlay his optimism. For it was true that men had sailed down their easting or westing for centuries before chronometers were invented or lunar distances calculated. Men like this man, who could not read a printed page, had made landfalls in every corner of the world and were still doing so. They had another sort of knowledge, competence of a different order from the navigator's. Who was to say which was higher? Davy's scheme for restepping a mast on a ship under sail or Bowditch's scheme for placing a ship on the curving surface of the sea by reading the heavens and a table in the *Almanac?* They were different sorts of mastery, that was all.

She had given up on the longitude, but the compass error was still critical. Davy had volunteered to help with the azimuth. He was handy with instruments, he said, but she would have to do the ciphering.

The sky was an enormous spectrum, shading from red-orange in the west to blue-violet in the east, luminous and unblemished. The sun was still several degrees above the horizon. While the two of them waited on the quarterdeck, Amanda strained to catch any windblown scraps of talk from the forecastlehead, where the evening concert was under way. It was several days now since she had done any eavesdropping—deliberate or inadvertent. Were the men being more careful because they now considered her a presence to be reckoned with, an officer instead of a mere appendage? Or was there some other reason, less flattering, more menacing?

Davy was going on about the ways in which the pull of the sails would be altered by the replacement of the fore-topgallants and the royals. Again Amanda had the impression of mastery in a man she had once put down as inferior because he could not read. Curiosity uncurled and stretched and spoke.

"Tell me, Davidson, are you married?" she asked.

Davy answered with a shrug but no words.

If he would not deny it, he was. But clearly he took no pleasure in the relationship. Probably it was not a legal marriage but one of those arrangements common among British seamen, so little of whose lives was spent ashore that no provident woman would have one for a husband. Sometimes a trull would take a succession of such companions into her care—or clutch.

"You'll be wanting to take the bearing now?" Davy put it as a question, but it was his way of serving notice that the sun was touching the horizon in the west.

Amanda nodded. Davy squinted through the vanes of the azimuth compass and pushed the stop. There was time for her to take a sight. Their observations agreed.

The variation was now 19° east, 3° more than she had been allowing. Davy suggested that she have the helm put up another quarter point. She gave the order and went below to sleep.

Sometime during the night she woke and, as she lay waiting for sleep to return, went over in her mind Davy's argument on the relative unimportance of longitude. She recalled now what Jonathan had said about sailing out one's easting—the dangers of coming unexpectedly upon a lee shore in storm or darkness. How would he reply to the claim that men sailed for centuries by nothing but lead, line, and lookout? She could almost hear him: that there were times when the lead could not be heaved, when a lookout could not see; that a captain who could not read the heavens would be forced to douse sail and heave to every night....

She would be willing to suffer such ignominy, but how was she to know when to begin? From the dark side of her memory came an answer—Jonathan's or Bowditch's? *"A full-day's sail from shore."* But how was one to know when that day had arrived?

THE FIFTEENTH DAY

S he was up before dawn and dressed to go on deck, but as she
passed Smith's stateroom, she heard a sound that brought her
back to look in. With the door open, it was ghastly—a moaning,
gasping, clacking of teeth, or dry tongue against teeth. The poor
man's body was jerking like a poorly manipulated puppet. She stood
beside him and called his name, but he did not hear. She tried to restrain him, but he was stronger than she. At last, knowing nothing
else to do, she turned up the lamp. If he was dying, let it not be in
the dark.

Slowly, while she watched, the seizure abated. The flailing limbs
grew weaker, or the agony easier to endure. Smith gave a shuddering
groan and lay still, open-mouthed and open-eyed. "Nothing but skin
and bones—" This was the meaning of that phrase: all flesh burned
away. But he was not dead. His eyes blinked at long intervals, and
his breath rasped in and out.

Amanda began the ritual procedure for reducing a fever: sponging his face and hands and wrists, cooling his pillow with a fresh
cover, offering him water—which he ignored—talking quietly, com-
fortingly.

Twice he stopped breathing, but began again.

Sometime later Flagg came. He had been in to see the captain and found him poorly. Mrs. Bright had better go to him. He would sit the deathwatch here. What could have happened that both men so improved one day had been taken like this the next?

Jonathan was in nothing near so desperate a condition. He was running a fever, but he was conscious and rational. Amanda gave him water with the juice of an orange in it and changed his pillow. His eyes were closing as she left.

AMANDA BRIGHT'S JOURNAL

September 15, 1851

Flagg says Smith is dying. Yesterday he said both men were past the crisis of their illnesses. I do not believe either of them can hold out against another. What we can do for them is so little, so point-less in the face of their suffering, that I play the coward and re-treat, using the excuse of other duties.

·◇·

The trouble was she no longer had much to excuse her. Since she had given up the battle of the longitude, there was only the taking and working out of a noon observation, an occasional azimuth, and the keeping of the log—enough to occupy at the most an hour of her day. She was retreating from the sick men, not because her ef-forts were futile nor because the labor was distasteful (though it was), but because her indifference frightened her. She was hardening into a woman of wood, like a figurehead, cleaving the water, breasting the oncoming seas.

There was a noise from Smith's stateroom, and she was in the doorway, braced. But it was only Flagg, moving the sea chest so he could lean against the bulkhead and rest his back.

"He hasn't…?"

"No'm, just the same.

Amanda sighed the terror out of her lungs. "I think I'll go above."

Flagg thought that a good idea, but he ventured to suggest that it would be best not to let the bad news spread. "You always do keep a cheerful face, I'll say that. And it'll never be needed more than now."

The bright air made her breathe fast and deep, and calm fell on her with the sunlight. There was a four-legged stool made fast to the quarter rail, and she settled herself on it, tired enough to sleep sitting up.

A throat was cleared.

She opened her eyes and saw No-Name and the tall African waiting to be noticed. No-Name (who had lately acquired a habit of staring at her with what seemed to be adoration) stepped forward and thrust out his hand. In it was an offering—a piece of carved wood.

The work had been done with much patience but little skill, and it was hard to grasp the carver's intention.

"Kee-way…" No-Name spoke so tentatively that she was not sure whether it was a statement or a question.

"Make for missis," King John explained. "Don' good, but all same good luck. Make kittiwake."

She saw now that it was a bird with wings lifted to rise from—or perhaps to settle on—the water. Moved, she thanked the giver in pantomime, as if his inability to use words implied that he did not accept them as legal tender.

They were still beaming at each other dumbly when the bosun came up. He had urgent business with the skipper, he said, and would like the lady's leave to go below.

Amanda led the way, saving her explanation—that Jonathan was asleep and not to be disturbed—until there was no one else to hear it. "You can tell me what you want him to know. I'll carry word to him when he wakes and bring you back his answer."

Crank was agreeable to that. He had the air of a man who considers obligations met once he observes the forms. His business concerned Rory. The man was up to new tricks. To let him continue unpunished made nothing the discipline and not safe the ship. That was Jonathan's dogma translated into Finnish and halfway back to English.

"What do you suggest be done to punish him?"

That was not the bosun's concern. He had made his complaint. The remedy was for others to find.

157

It seems Rory is become an apostle to the Polynesians. As high priest of Tangaroa, he is spreading the alarm that the cold from which the Kanakas suffer is a punishment visited on the ship by the sea-god whose taboo has been violated by my presence.

Islands of ice are to be floated across our path, and if that warning is not heeded, they will crush and sink us. Just how the omen is to be averted is not specified—at least not in the report to me. I doubt the Hawaiians would have me offered in sacrifice, but the Marquesan seems made of sterner stuff. In any case, our bosun believes that the appearance of even a small berg would be regarded as fulfillment of the prophecy and might put me in jeopardy.

I think we are not likely to encounter floating ice in these latitudes at this season, and it may be that the failure of his prophecy will erode Rory's standing as mouthpiece of a deity he does not pretend to honor. But there ought to be some more forthright way of dealing with this threat.

I cannot bring myself to order physical punishment of a man with a broken leg, and there is no practicable way to confine his tongue, which is the real offender.

·◇·

Except to put him in irons. As Horace had threatened to do. As Jonathan most assuredly would. To whom would she give such an order? Kankkonen was incapable of carrying it out. King John? Tono? Either of them would obey an order from Jonathan, but she did not believe they would obey her. Davy would obey, but was he strong enough to handle the Bull of Bashan without help? And who could be counted on to help him? Better to cast about for some stratagem, something on the order of the trick she had played with the sextant.

The sextant. Rory had a sextant, or so he had told Horace. So there were three instruments on board after all. With three instruments, the lunar distance was not beyond her reach. If the sky stayed clear, they might make a trial this afternoon before the moon went down.

Eight bells struck—and she was not on deck. But her sextant was preset for the expected altitude, and that gave her a full minute of grace.

The sun reached and passed the present altitude, which meant that the ship had lost some northing. Either the compass variation was increasing, or some current was pushing them south. Amanda ordered the helm put another half point higher and looked about for Davy. He was just emerging from the forecastle companion, starting aft.

All was in readiness, he reported: the new mast had been worked by Chips and the stays attached; the old mast's stump had been cleared from the cap; the block was rigged at the crosstrees. Most of the sails would have to be doused for as long as it took to complete the swaying up. And the sooner it was done, the better. Should he go down for any last orders from Mr. Smith?

Amanda hesitated. Flagg had said not to let the bad news spread, but surely he had not meant to exclude Davy from the circle of trust. "Mr. Smith won't be able to give you orders. He's worse. A good deal worse."

Davy absorbed this gravely. "And the skipper?" he asked.

"Neither worse nor better." And she signed that there was nothing to be gained by consulting him. (It struck her that she and Davy had begun to communicate more by silence or impassivity than by words or even gestures.)

"Well, then," he said slowly, "I'm to see it done?"

"Please. Give whatever orders are needed."

Davy shook his head.

"You want me to give them?" she asked.

He nodded. "To the bosun, if you please, ma'am." That reminded her that she had been wanting to discuss with him Crank's report. Setting her back against the jeer capstan so that she had an unobstructed view of the deck, she repeated as accurately as possible what the bosun had said. Davy was scowling when she was done.

"You probably knew all this anyway."

"I wouldn't say that, ma'am." He shifted his weight and stared at his feet.

"You didn't know? Or you don't put any stock in Crank's opinion?"

Davy looked aft, then forward. His expression changed. She turned to see why. Rory had come on deck and was looking in their direction. But there was no possibility of his overhearing them.

"Which?" she asked.

Davy had a hard time framing his answer. His vocabulary did not lend itself to gradations of feeling or judgment as delicate—or as vague—as these. He had told the Scot more than once to belay it. He would tell him again if need be. But he had not thought it necessary to carry tales. "We can take care of him amongst us, ma'am."

"I have something in mind that might distract him from his plotting." Amanda explained her notion of using Rory as third man on a lunar-distance observation.

"Does he have a sextant?"

"He told Mr. Martin he did. What do you think? Will it do any harm to ask him?"

Davy considered carefully. He couldn't see that it would. "If you've come to think you do want to have a try at figuring the longitude after all."

Only then did she realize that she had come full circle—was looking forward to the trial.

The Sixteenth Day

The swaying up of the new topgallant mast took most of the afternoon and evening of the fifteenth. Amanda missed the excitement, being confined belowdecks on nursing duty because Willy was needed in the upper rigging and Flagg had to attach the fittings of the new mast. She used the time, while her patients slept, to go slowly and carefully over Bowditch's chapter on lunar observations until she was sure she understood the anatomy of the elephant she was required to eat.

The heart of the matter was the concept that longitude was time. To know how far east or west of Greenwich the ship stood, one needed to know the time at Greenwich and the time at ship. The *Maria M.* had lost track of both. Greenwich time could be recaptured by measuring the distance between the moon and some other celestial body—by one observer at three different times, or by three at the same time. For the time at ship she would have to work a time sight.

Bowditch's directions for that operation were horrendously complicated but not impossible to follow if one took them in the proper order. To get the end result she wanted, she must have the latitude, which could be got from a sun shot at noon. Then she must make sure the ship held to the same parallel until the sun bore directly west. That required a reliable helmsman and a compass of known variation. The first step, therefore, was to measure the compass variation, and that could be done only at sunset or at dawn.

AMANDA BRIGHT'S JOURNAL

September 16, 1851
    Up before dawn to take a bearing of the sun at rising. variation is now 22° easterly. I should be more easy if I knew the reason for this rapid and constant change.
    Mr. Smith seems to have survived what is called a coma vigil. Flagg, whose optimism is again in the ascendant, says Jonathan need not pass through such an ordeal and is already on the mend.

·⟡·

Flagg was no longer distant or evasive. As they worked together, changing the sick beds, he made obvious attempts to melt her reserve, firing great salvos of flattery: how well she was looking—"Say what you will, there's no tonic like sea air, even for a woman!"; how proud her folks would be to see the way she was shouldering the burdens that had fallen on her; how deeply all hands appreciate what she was doing— "An angel, they say you are, sent on purpose to bring the ship safe."

Amanda recognized the words as Davy's and was provoked to ask, "Are you sure all the men feel like that?"

"Well, now…" To speak the truth, he would have to admit there were exceptions. But *most* of the *men—almost all* of them—had the highest regard for her.

"All except Rory?"

Rory was no friend to her, that was a fact. Still, one could see how it was with him.

"I'm not sure that I can," Amanda said. "Perhaps you will help me."

Flagg stopped what he was doing to give his full attention to the effort. "The thing of it is, you see…you see, it's not so much forecastle against quarterdeck, as it is…I mean to say, if you stop to consider…" Which he did. And having considered, saw that he was running into danger, fell off a point or two, and came on the other tack. "You know yourself, ma'am, it's not often there's a woman—a lady—aboard ship; it hits different men different. Bound to."

"I know the Sandwich Islanders have a taboo."

"There you are!" As if this made further explanation unnecessary.

"But you were saying how it is with Rory, why he is stirring up mutiny."

"I wouldn't go so far as to say—" Flagg swallowed on the dreadful word.

"The bosun does. He wants the man punished before matters grow worse. I don't know how that can be done. The mate knocked him about at the start, but it seems to have done no good."

"Takes a while with a customer like that."

"In any case, I'm looking for some other way to handle him. That's why I hoped you might help me."

Flagg folded his mouth in on itself and considered again. "What I say is…a man who respects himself gives others their due."

"I don't follow."

Purpling with embarrassment, he floundered into a confused analysis of the significance of a man's boasting of his prowess with the opposite sex, "as if to make himself more of a man, don't you see?"

She didn't see what this had to do with the question she had asked. Unless Flagg was implying that Rory had boasted in the forecastle that he could wield the power of his masculinity over her. She recalled the flirtatious tone, the cocky approach to his request for advancement. When she humiliated him publicly, had he felt his manhood, as well as his navigation, challenged?

"Let me ask you something, Mr. Flagg." She had decided to speak plainly, to force the old man to do the same. But at the last moment, she funked it and asked, "Is it true, do you know, that he has a sextant in his gear?"

Flagg didn't know, but it would be easy to find out. Rory had left his seabag behind when he moved to the deckhouse. "You'll be wanting another sextant then?"

"A sextant and a man who knows the use of it.

Surely she was not thinking of restoring Rory to the status from which she had just succeeded in toppling him. "That's where he lost out, don't you see? By you showing him up as a faker."

"He's not a complete faker. He can measure in altitude, which is all I want. It doesn't prove he's able to navigate."

Flagg said he understood that, but the impressionable Kanakas would not. With them it was a choice between masters: the lady or the Scot. One was Deliverer, the other Devil. Collaboration between them was inconceivable.

"What I been telling them is it's the book that counts. 'It's her has got the book and knows how to use it,' I say."

"And does that outweigh their taboo against women on shipboard?"

Flagg assured her that it did. The Kanakas were not bad hearted— only heathen. "They'll come round once they understand that you're carrying on for the captain. In his place, so to speak."

Amanda was puzzled by "once they understand." Was there criticism hidden under the layers of ambiguity and adulation? Was she at fault if the foremasthands did not understand her position? What should she do to make it clear? It was also puzzling that Flagg had not even commented on Crank's suggestion that Rory be punished. Was he, too, afraid to try?

September 16, 1851
> *Latitude by observation: 50°17' N.*
> *Longitude by reckoning: 148° W.*

Remarks aboard:
> *4 minutes of northing lost since noon yesterday. For the purpose of a time sight, I shall assume that the correction made this morning has prevented any further southward drift.*
>
> *The longitude is assumed and must be corrected by a lunar distance as soon as possible. But if this is accurate, we are now 21° west of the entrance to Nootka Sound.*

Well before the end of the afternoon watch, Amanda prepared herself to check the compass variation. She carried up both sextants, the azimuth compass, and the deck watch, and took her station on the forward lee corner of the quarterdeck. Every hand on deck slowed his work to watch her. A witch preparing a potion to induce love—or death—could not have been observed with more interest or awe.

The sun did not yet bear directly west, so she passed the waiting time trying the sextants, first one, then the other, with as short an interval as possible between. They agreed within seconds, but it would be better to test them at the same instant. That took two observers. She looked to see if Davy was within call, but he was not. Rory was perched on a keg beside the galley door, watching her. She wavered on the edge of the decision Flagg had opposed, and pulled back.

By four o'clock the sun's rate of descent was increasing. The bearing was not yet due west, but it was now or not this day. She took the deck watch from her pocket and held it in her left hand, lifted the sextant with both hands, and tried to operate the index arm with her right. It was impossibly awkward. Holding the watch in her right hand was worse. Jonathan always had Smith standing by to hold the watch and record the time. Surely, she too had a right to a first mate.

"Is there someone who can take the time for me?"

A little circle of onlookers had formed around her. They were keeping a respectful distance but close enough so that any one of them could have stepped forward to comply with her request. No one did. They were all dark men, as it happened: the Kanakas, Tono, Cook, and King John.

Crank was too far aft to have heard her. Flagg was not on deck. Nor was Willy. If Rory had heard, he did not choose to move from his keg. No-Name was at the helm. Every hand in the crew was on deck except Davy.

As she spoke the complaint in her mind, he was beside her, taking the watch from her hand, apologetic as if there had been some prior appointment for which he was late.

Amanda raised the sextant, taking the time she needed to make sure of the horizon, brought the filtered image of the red globe to meet it, rocked the instrument once, twice, and then called, "Mark!"

"Four fifty-one and twenty seconds."

Both of them were imitating the performance of the officers they were replacing, even to the tone of voice. Amanda read the sextant angle. She had forgotten the copybook in which she made notations and would have to carry the figure in her head. But she lingered long enough to test the sextants against each other while she had Davy there.

He held one instrument, she the other. They followed the rapidly dropping sun.

"Mark!" Amanda called.

Davy read off his angle.

"They're within three—no, *two* seconds of each other." The watchers seemed to understand or at least to interpret the triumph in Amanda's voice as a favorable omen. They were all smiling as she gathered her paraphernalia to go below. All except the tattooed Marquesan, who did not know how to smile but who looked less dour than usual.

She opened the book to the procedure for calculating the time at ship. Like an apprentice alchemist, she was manipulating mysteries whose true nature was unknown to her, searching columns for cabalistic symbols, trusting that when she had followed the last arbitrary, arcane instruction, a truth would emerge—hours, minutes, and seconds—with which she would be armed against the deceptions of the watch that lay ticking malignly on the green baize of the table.

Patiently, methodically, humbly, she worked, stumbling now and then, falling into error, having to go back. Once it was the difference between adding seconds to make minutes and adding fractions to make integers. Another time it was finding the logarithms required. None of the angles for which she needed log. sines or secants appeared at the upper corner of the pages of the tables. Only after much leafing back and forth did she notice that there were angles in the lower, as well as the upper, corners of each page. All her angles (for some reason she dared not stop to ponder) appeared in lower corners. She found their logs and went on.

The final step was the addition of a sum of four lines, each of which was a number of six digits: *"Half the sum of these four logarithms, being sought for in the column of log. sines, will correspond to the apparent time of day in one of the hour columns."* She added and divided and achieved—a number that did not appear anywhere in the columns!

She had made an error, probably a simple one, of addition or subtraction, or perhaps she had copied a wrong figure. Her eyes were gritty with weariness, but she must go back and look for the mistake. If she took time to rest them, she would lose what little foothold she had gained.

She was halfway through her review when Willy came with a question. Even ordering him not to interrupt broke her train of thought. She began from the beginning, but she came out with the same wrong—impossibly wrong answer. She would have to try yet again. But first she had better find out what Willy wanted.

He was in the pantry, squeezing the juice of an orange into a cup of water, and did not look up when she entered.

"What is it?" she asked crisply.

"He said to call you." And he offered her the cup.

"Call *me* to bring him something to drink?" Jonathan had not asked such small services from her since he had begun to make requests. He expected Flagg or Willy to serve him, or at least that is what she had assumed.

Willy answered her question with a sulky shrug. She sensed that he was trying to trap her. If she carried refreshment when she answered Jonathan's summons, she would be feigning a solicitude she did not feel, one that Willy was implying she ought to feel.

"You take it to him," she said. "Tell him I'll come when I've finished."

But when she came, Jonathan was asleep; the cup, almost full, stood in the rack that served as a night table. She considered whether she should wake him, decided against it, tiptoed out of the state-room, and went on deck.

Stays from the new topgallant mast were being made fast to the tip of the new jibboom. She watched the men moving about on their swinging perches, or balancing on the end of a slender spar that jutted from the bowsprit, or moving without hesitation to obey a shouted order by reaching for one particular pin on the crowded rail, one rope among a hundred others: marvelous manipulations, performed by men over whom she presumed to exercise authority. She, who could not perform the task that was hers.

"Be squall from no'east," said King John. "Catch plenty water you like."

That was good news. The supply of water for bathing the sick men was low. She must make sure the catch basin was set under the spanker. But as she started forward to give the order, she saw that the basin was already being lashed in place. Everyone was about his proper business. Except her.

She sat again at her workplace, but with a new plan of attack. She would set aside her own observation and use one of the examples in the Bowditch: the working of a morning time sight at latitude 50°30' N. It was close enough to her position so that the figures should be roughly equivalent.

She copied out the givens, made the correction, performed the additions, achieved the right sums, half sums, and remainders. But when she consulted the logarithm tables, she ran into the same wall of error. Not one of Bowditch's log. sines or secants was where it ought to be. Her eyes would not stay in focus. She closed them, rested her head on the sheet of foolscap, and drifted into nightmare.

She dreamed (and knew she was dreaming) that the ship was running large before a wind as wild as the one that had broached her. Great waves curled over the stem. She stood at the taffrail, staring up at their crests, unable to move away though she recognized her jeopardy. Someone shouted a warning, and she saw that the wave was forming into a face—a huge snarling visage like one of the idols in the Polynesian pantheon. It was Tangaroa—not his image but the god himself, forming out of his element, making good his threat to avenge the breaking of his commandment. The wave hung over her. She waited for it to engulf her....

The fall of water knocked a book from her hand. She came awake.

Flagg said the one who had the book was master—had the book and knew how to use it. Rory knew. What if he were to steal it? With a sextant and the Bowditch he would indeed be master. She must never let it out of her hands again.

Amanda got to her feet. It was too late to work anymore, too early to retire for the night. She decided to lie on the sofa with the book under her pillow, doze if she could, and be ready to go straight to work when she woke, refreshed.

THE SEVENTEENTH DAY

The squall that struck soon after midnight rolled Amanda off the sofa in the cabin. By the time she had found the fiddle board and wedged it in place, she was wide awake, ready to tackle the tables again. Her papers had slid off the desk, and as she reassembled them, she was impressed with the stubborn persistence they evidenced. Sheet after sheet was filled with identical columns of figures, as if she had hoped that repetition, sustained long enough, must batter a breach in the wall.

She began again to work her example, covering Bowditch's figures so as not to be tempted to copy them. This time she must do it on her own, learning in the doing what it was that was being done.

First, to find the log. secant for 51°30' in the table of log. sines, secants, and tangents. As she flipped through the pages of labeled columns, looking for the one on which 51° was printed (in the lower right-hand corner), she noticed for the first time that each page bore not one, but four, angles—a different one in each of its corners. The page that carried 51° also carried 128°, 39°, and 140°. The top two, added together, came to 179°, one less than 180°. The bottom two did the same. All four added together came to 358°, two less than a perfect circle. Every one of the forty-four pages of tables had four angles that added up to the same sum.

She waited for an insight to arise and illumine these relationships, but none came, and she went back to her example. On the outside margin of the page was a column of figures representing minutes of arc from 1' to 59'. She ran her finger up to 30' and across the columns to the one marked Secant. Her eye kept sliding off the line, so she laid a folded sheet of paper across it.

There, on the fold, was the figure Bowditch used: 0.20585. It most certainly had not been there before. Her skin gathered tight across her ribs and tingled along her spine. She looked over her discarded work sheets for the figure she had found on her other attempts: 0.10646. It was also on the line of folded paper, but three columns over, in the column marked Secant. The correct figure was in the column marked Cosecant. Just reversed.

For an instant she believed it was Bowditch who had made the mistake. But that seemed improbable. She looked up each of the logs. used in his example. They were all on the page, but all in the wrong column. In every case, the log. she needed appeared in the column of a complementary function. Also, the angle whose log. she wanted always appeared in a lower corner.

Her eyes moved along the lower margin of the page, and the mystery unraveled. Each of the columns bore different labels, top and bottom. The one labeled Secant at the top was labeled Cosecant at the bottom. If she had worked from bottom up instead of from top down, she would have found what she was looking for at once. But how was she to have known? Bowditch presented his tables as if anyone who used them must already know how.

Perhaps if she understood how they were formed, what reality they embodied, how the numbers changed into forms and back into numbers...For a moment, closing her eyes, she could almost make out that movement—a dream she could dream if she tried—in which the inner life of numbers revealed itself. But the effort required was too great, and she had pressing business, business that was now within her competence. Her own time sight figured out to 4 hours, 32 minutes, 8 seconds. The watch time was 4 hours, 51 minutes, 20 seconds. So the watch was fast by 19 minutes, 12 seconds, or had been at the time of the observation.

It might have gained or lost in the 12 hours that had passed since then. She ought to have wound and set the chronometer, it would at least have preserved the local time, once she established it. Now the whole procedure would have to be done over: amplitude at dawn, latitude at noon, time sight in the afternoon, and finally the setting of the chronometer to time at ship.

But she had mastered the problem of time, and she could master the lunar distance. With no one's help.

The squall that wakened her had blown itself out without her noticing. The ship was moving so smoothly that she could not guess its speed. The wind must have hauled west or northwest again.

She was on deck for the sunrise. The amplitude observation showed the compass variation still 22° east. The ship was so nearly becalmed that there was no visible wake. A covey of small birds rocked on the quiet surface, pretty birds with reddish sides and dark gray backs. They floated higher in the water than gulls and carried their necks proudly. When the ship drifted too close, they rose and flew off to the west, using their wings in a way that made her think of sandpipers on a beach where she had once walked with Jonathan.

The wind picked up just at the time she was ready for the morning time sight, a rehearsal for the critical one that would come in the afternoon. Davy had offered to take the time for her, but he was busy with a sail change. She watched him from the quarterdeck.

The man had changed. Already he had more of Heyerman's authority than Kankkonen would ever have. And he was still changing—as Horace had and for the same reason: in this situation one changed or went under. What Davy lacked—*all* he lacked—was self-confidence. He was resourceful, intrepid in emergency, steady as bedrock. If he were not handicapped by ignorance...

Not ignorance, she corrected herself. Illiteracy was not the same as ignorance. Davy had many kinds of knowledge. But it was learned from experience. He was impotent to acquire other kinds of knowledge because he could not read. If it was not too late for him to learn—if he was willing—he could be freed like the great canvases he was unfurling now.

Squinting her eyes to slits, Amanda imposed on the image of the real man a vision of her own making: Captain Davidson, a man of substance, heavier in body, bearded perhaps, in the brass-buttoned coat of a shipmaster, his braided cap set at an angle over his eyes. It was not impossible. There were captains sailing out of New England ports with little, if any, formal schooling—"come up through the hawsepipe."

Davy looked her way, signaled that he would be at her disposal in a few more minutes, shouted an order to someone aloft. He was already charged with many of the responsibilities of command—the maintenance of discipline, the setting and furling of the ship's wings. And he carried the burden without even as much recognition as Kankkonen had been given.

What if she were to appoint him captain *pro tempore?* To serve until Jonathan was enough recovered to give orders again? Or better yet, have Jonathan appoint him. Before witnesses. So that Davy would be vested with all possible authority for the confrontation— if it came—with Rory & Co.

She began to word the arguments she would make when Jonathan was enough improved to listen.

The latitude at noon was 50°10'. They were still slipping south. The possibility of treachery by the helmsman flickered in her mind—the possibility that when neither she nor Davy nor the bosun was on deck, the wheel was being put over on orders from Rory. Or perhaps in response to some tropism on the part of the islanders, yearning to escape from the prison of cold.

"The blotches are changing color," Willy said as he set down her plate. "They look like bruises all over him."

Amanda was as surprised by his speaking without having been spoken to as she was by his rude tone. She decided against a reprimand, expecting silence to do the office for her that it used to for Jonathan. But Willy was not abashed.

"You better begin pretty soon to worry how he's getting on. And the mate, too. I'm no nurse and neither is Chips. We can't do for them when they're bad off like this."

"What is it you think I could do that I'm not doing?" She regretted the question the moment it was uttered. It put her on the defensive. But perhaps that was why she had asked it—because he had touched the weakest spot in her armor of authority.

Willy was saying that it was her business to know what ought to be done. She had all the books. "If you'd read in them sometimes instead of always doing sums, maybe you'd find out."

She wanted to slap him. Or spank him—to reduce him to a manageable size and age. She could see him as a stringy nine-year-old, laid over a wide maternal knee, his trousers pulled down, his buttocks and his pride raw.

In the silence that lasted till she had forced down the last bite of food and drop of liquid, Amanda caught herself framing stinging rebuttals and rebukes in which the word "ungrateful" was used. But it was no longer appropriate. The ties of loyalty and affection that were the context of gratitude had been severed by Willy's defection. She must school herself to think of him as one who owed her nothing but obedience.

She looked in on Jonathan after lunch. The blotches had indeed turned an ugly blue, but they had also faded and flattened, and he was resting more comfortably. When he woke, she would speak to him about Davy.

To be on hand for that moment, she got out her embroidery—something to keep her relaxed, without sleeping—and sat at the round table close to the stateroom door. But the ship was swinging with its most seductive and soporific motion, and before she had taken half a dozen stitches, she slept.

When she woke, it was time for the afternoon time sight. The wind had freshened and the ship was rolling more heavily, but she got a good shot. Davy marked her time. Then he took the sextant, and she marked the time for him.

Working the two shots, she established the fact that the watch had lost two minutes in twenty-four hours. The chronometer was wound and set to the new, correct time at ship. She was ready for the next step—the lunar distance. And the step after that—calculation of longitude, which would finally fix the position of the ship.

The moon would rise at 9:30, by which time it would be dark and the horizon hard to find. An hour later the moon itself would give enough light so that sharp eyes (sharper than hers) would be able to make out the horizon line. She must choose a celestial body whose distance from the moon they would measure.

The *Ephemeris* offered her three choices: two stars of the second magnitude and the planet Saturn. She read in the section *""General Remarks"* a warning that *"it is rather difficult to observe the altitude of stars on account of their dimness, particularly Alpha Pegasi and Alpha Arietis "*—the two stars tabulated for this date. It would have to be Saturn, which was not at all a bright planet at this season.

The observation was made at a little past eleven, near the end of the evening watch. Even Davy had difficulty establishing the horizon line. Twice they had to go below to consult the Bowditch on the use of the reversing telescope. But in the end, with some help from Flagg, the altitudes were measured and recorded, and the angular distance and the times. Davy's readings agreed with hers. It was very promising.

But after an hour's work, Amanda had not finished her calculations and was too tired to go on. The men had long since given up. She was alone at the desk.

She left her papers carefully weighted, turned down the lamp, slept an hour, got up, and went to work again. She started from the beginning, reducing the several measurements and the time intervals to means, correcting for the *"second differences of the motions of the bodies,"* following with meticulous, uncomprehending care the rigmarole of directions, parentheses, and footnotes."

She came out with a "true distance that could be compared with the distance at Greenwich and a Greenwich time that could be compared with the ship's at 11:17 and 42 seconds—which placed the ship several miles inland!

She looked again at the chart to be sure.

There was no mistake about it, unless the latitude was farther south than she had reckoned. In that case, the ship might be south of the entrance to Nootka, in an area full of dangerous offshore rocks and shoals.

A week—even a day—ago, she would have been panicky. But she had since "taken hold." She knew better than to try to run down the error that had spoiled this effort. It might have been a few seconds of time, a few seconds of arc, a misreading of some table, or a mistake in arithmetic. The best way around the obstacle was to begin again tomorrow.

Begin again and cut the calculations in half by using three sextants. She was sure enough of herself to take advantage of Rory's offer, in spite of Flagg's fears. Meanwhile it would do no harm to post a lookout in the crosstrees, in addition to the regular bow watch.

She gave the order before she went to her bunk.

THE EIGHTEENTH DAY

AMANDA BRIGHT'S JOURNAL

September 18, 1851

Jonathan is distinctly improved. I shall speak to him later this morning and settle the question of a surrogate. Mr. Smith has less fever than yesterday but is barely conscious much of the time.

This morning I dressed the head wound of the Sandwich Islander they call Jerry. It has healed quite well despite the fact that he has been pulling his long hair over it (to protect it from the cold, I suppose) and holding that in place with a watch cap, the effect being decidedly piratical and not at all sanitary. Rory was among the group that gathered to watch me work, and I offered to examine his leg while I was about it. He declined. And in a manner I found offensive, implying that I was taking on myself more than I am able to manage.

It matters little to me whether or not his leg mends properly. If some shifting of the splint causes it to knit awry, it is he who will suffer. But I must admit to some curiosity as to the reason for his bad manners: whether it is that he cannot forgive me for his public humiliation in the matter of the latitude shot or that he is ashamed to incur heavier obligations to me while he is plotting rebellion. At any rate, his demeanor changed when I said I should be glad of his assistance and the use of his sextant if he had one. I had hardly time to explain what I meant to use it for, when he was his old garrulous and ebullient self, conveying without actually saying so that I had finally come to my senses and admitted that nothing in the realm of celestial navigation could be accomplished without him.

·⋄·

D avy and Flagg were waiting for her, one holding Smith's sextant, the other the watch and the copybook. Rory was stumping his way along the waist, Willy behind him carrying the instrument, which turned out to be not a sextant but an octant (adequate for taking an altitude but not for the angular distance, according to Bowditch).

He greeted his fellow navigators—all but Davy, as Amanda recalled afterwards—with hearty bonhomie and pronounced himself ready to begin. Amanda caught Flagg's eye and read a reproach for having ignored his warning, which was validated by the rascal's arrogant assumption of center stage and its effect on those who watched.

"We'll begin as soon as we have tested your instrument for index error," she said to Rory.

That would not be necessary. His instrument made no errors. It might not look much, but that was because it had been too long in his seabag. A little spit and polish would make it as good as new. Amanda tried to break in, but he was off on one of his windy flights, talking sentimental nonsense about how he and the sextant—he insisted on calling it that—were old shipmates who knew each other's quirks and crotchets and made due allowance.

He did not want the instrument examined and was talking to evade her order. Amanda understood, and it made her stubborn.

"I want all three instruments compared," she said firmly. "We know the difference between the sextants. And we must know how the octant differs—if it does. You will please give it to Davidson."

Davy made a move as if to take it from Willy, but Rory snatched it. "Belay that," he growled, lowering his head like an enraged bull. The air crackled with expectancy. She had ignited the old feud. Gael against Saxon.

"See here. No one is going to hurt your precious instrument. If you're so anxious about it, you can make the test yourself. Take a sight of the lee tip of the fore-t'gallant yard. I'll do the same."

Rory struggled with his temper. With one last baleful look at Davy, he raised the instrument and sighted toward the yard. Amanda did the same, read her angle, and waited for him to read his. He was fumbling with the index so ineptly that she might have thought he had never used an instrument before if she had not seen him use a sextant, which was, if anything, more difficult.

"You're missing a part there, ain't you, mate?" Davy asked.

There was no index mirror. None at all.

Amanda burst into laughter. It was rude and ill-advised. But the scene was irresistibly comic: after all the bragging and blowing, the growling and menacing, there he stood, the great booby, with the look of a child caught in mischief, ready to weep. Without warning, he lunged. Davy sidestepped deftly, as if he had been expecting the attack, and Rory fell heavily, stretching his full length on the deck.

"Your leg!" Amanda knelt to feel the splint. It was in place and firm. He had shifted his balance as he went down so that he took the impact on the other side, protecting both his injury and the octant, which he held in the crook of his arm. Too furious to feel pain or weakness, he pushed her away, cursing, not at her for having laughed at him but at the "Sassenach" who had tampered with his sextant and would pay for it.

"Him don' trouble you t'ing," said Tono, whom he permitted to help him to his feet. "No man trouble you t'ing. On'y boy come get 'um."

"That's it. It was him did it!" Rory turned on Willy. "It was you dug it out my bag. It must've been you smashed off the piece."

Willy blinked back tears as his new friend accused him of deliberate malice and then of criminal negligence. Rory was in one of his Bull of Bashan states and without the excuse of strong drink.

"Why don't you look in the case?" Amanda asked in one of the few pauses.

"It doesn't have a case," Willy said. "It was wrapped in an old

179

shirt, down at the bottom of the bag."

"Then empty the bag and look through everything. If the mirror came unscrewed, it can be put on again, and we can still try for a lunar this evening."

Rory would look for the mirror himself. No one was to come near his quarters. The shock and the fury were wearing off, and he was beginning to feel pain, but he did not give in to it. Grasping his crutch so that it supported him and menaced anyone who approached, he started away.

Willy looked to each of the men, then to Amanda, seeking answers. What had he done to call down this rain of fire? What should he do? Follow and try to appease the raging bull? Or transfer his allegiance? Amanda couldn't help feeling sorry for the boy, but this was the sty he had chosen to lie in. He would have to find his own way out.

Back in the cabin, she tried to recall the precise sequence of events, hoping to wring from them reasons, motives, meanings. It would be interesting to know what had happened to the octant. But more significant was why Rory had not noticed it. She tried to remember any earlier evidence of his hostility to Davy. He had turned on Willy because he needed a scapegoat to save what he could of face. But why had he lunged at Davy? As if he meant to kill.

There was a sound of movement from the stateroom, and she looked in. Jonathan was sitting up, propped against pillows, more alert than she had seen him since his illness began, but his face was troubled.

"Are you in pain?" she asked. "I've saved some laudanum."

"I'm all right, but I have been…well, there's no need to tell you how I have been. How long is it? What's the day?"

"Thursday, the eighteenth."

"And when was it I was taken sick?"

"It must have been the fourth—or maybe the evening of the third—when you first came down."

"Fourteen days?" He was appalled. "Two weeks!"

Now was the moment to tell him all that had happened in those weeks and lead from that into her proposal for a surrogate.

"And Smith?" Jonathan asked. "Has he been as bad off as I?"

"About as bad." She would have to start from the day of the catastrophe, the double drowning. She had not prepared herself. The words were sticking in her throat and needed to be gentled out.

"Excuse me, ma'am." It was Flagg, discreetly urgent. "You wanted to be let know when the sun was bearing due west and falling."

"Thank you." She told Jonathan she would be back directly, knowing that he would almost surely have fallen asleep.

Amanda and Davy were waiting for Flagg and the moon. She had decided to try another lunar distance, using Saturn and Aldebaran. There would be only one sextant, but with the chronometer rated and running, she hoped she could manage.

Flagg was finishing some work in the carpenter shop, and the moon was pulling itself free of horizon clouds. Amanda asked if Rory's missing index mirror had been found.

Davy shook his head. It was most likely broke off long since, when the seabag was tossed on the deck of some other ship and its owner on top of it.

"If it happened a long time ago, shouldn't he have known it was missing?" Amanda asked.

Yes, if he had used the instrument; otherwise, no.

"Even before he knew it was damaged, he was dead set against letting you touch it. Why was that?"

That was the way of your Scotsman. If he could find an Englishman to blame for his misfortune, it relieved his pain.

Hardly an answer to her question, but Amanda had learned to accept the reluctance of any member of the foremast fraternity to discuss his mates with one of the quarterdeck elite. Would it be different if Davy was made captain? Even *pro tempore?* If he crossed that invisible dividing line, would they meet as equals, speak their minds freely, have each other's confidence?

Flagg came up and the work began.

They took two complete sets of observations: the moon against the star, with three altitudes of each; the moon against the planet, with four altitudes. The shots took time and patience. The calculations took even more.

Amanda spent two hours bent over the volume of tables, the alembic in which the alchemy was to be achieved, dross transmuted into gold—the golden time of Greenwich, mated with the silver time of the ship, and transmuted into distance, the treasure of longitude west.

The Saturn–Moon distance worked out to 135° and some minutes. Aldebaran–Moon to a little more than 134°. Her estimated longitude had been 142°. They were three hundred miles nearer land than she had supposed. Two days' sailing if the wind held fair. Even less if the ship moved faster than the chip log showed, and she believed that it did.

Davy came to see how she was faring, and she showed him the little crosses plotted on the chart.

"That means we could be dropping a hook in Nootka before the end of day after next?" he asked. "There'll be cheer in the forecastle when I tell them the news."

"Before you do that," Amanda said, "there's something I want to ask you. We're going to need a captain—a substitute captain. My husband will not be well enough to manage the landing and all."

He waited, head a little to one side, puzzled, but not apprehensive about what was to come.

"How would you feel about taking it on?"

A tremor started along one of his nostrils and ran down to his lip. For a moment or two the whole layer of muscle seemed to be heaving under the skin, but all that emerged in the way of sound was a dry, embarrassed laugh.

She should not have spoken. It ought to have been done only after consulting with Jonathan; by him, if possible, rather than by her. And she had done it all wrong. The offer should have been put in some plausible context—a specific solution to a specific problem, such as letting go the anchor or the posting of a watch against boarding parties of Indians. She had diminished him in his own eyes by asking too much.

THE NINETEENTH DAY

September 19, 1851   Compass variation, 230E.

Course	Dist.	Diff. Lat.	Dep.	Lat. D.R.	Lat. Obs.	Diff. Long.	Longitude by		
							D.R.	Lunar	Chr.
NE by E	120				50°10' N		133°	133°23'	

She had taken her third lunar distance, this time with the sun, which was easier. It rose long before moonset, and by 10 A.M. both bodies were in the best possible position. The result, achieved in half the time of her first attempt, tallied with her dead reckoning estimate so closely that it gave her courage to set the chronometer to what she took to be Greenwich time. She had restored the Promethean fire.

Her pride was diminished only slightly by a warning in the *Ephemeris: "Since so much depends upon skill in measuring the distance, the observer can only form a correct judgment of the degree of dependence to be placed upon his own observation by repeated trials and a careful comparison of his several results."*

She would make as many trials as there were opportunities before landfall, which would constitute final, definitive proof—or disproof.

Landfall—real and imminent. She was glad now that she had said nothing to Jonathan about Davy. She would manage without a surrogate. The bosun and Davy could see to the anchoring, consulting with Jonathan or Smith if there was a need to. Both men were stronger today than yesterday and would be still stronger tomorrow. For the rest there was no one as fit as she to make the decisions that would have to be made. Even in the matter of barter: the trade goods they had brought, the furs they wanted to buy, the precautions against any outbreak of hostilities with the Indian inhabitants—she could act for Jonathan in all of this as she had acted on the open sea—

The sea, the sea, the open sea,
The blue, the fresh, the ever-free.

The verse came back to her, strong and exultant. If it had been set to music, she would have sung it aloud.

Jonathan was ready to be filled in on the events of his lost days. Amanda offered him the logbook to read, but his eyes were weak from the fever.

"If you'd read the entries to me—beginning with the last."

This was the moment she had looked forward to since the night she had made Deneb her witness, the moment when Jonathan's praise would confirm and crown her achievement. Like a painter unveiling his masterwork for its first and finest audience, she began: the variation of the compass, with a comment on the strange increase, which had finally slowed; the course steered, with a comment on the persistent loss of northing despite the compensation; and finally the longitude.

"I established it by a lunar distance this morning. I've set the chronometer to Greenwich time, so from now on it will be possible to get our longitude from a time sight when a lunar is not to be had."

She paused and waited for the accolade.

"When is Mr. Martin going to do me the honor of reporting for orders?" Jonathan asked.

She had fallen into icy water that took her breath. She had been so taken up with herself and her achievement that she had forgotten—had ignored the opportunity for which she had waited so long. Jonathan had asked for the last entries first because he had no inkling of the catastrophes of the early days of his illness. While she tried to think how to begin the telling, he was berating Horace, not only for the high crime of letting the chronometer run down but also for hiding behind a woman's petticoats, letting her bear the burdens created by his negligence and ineptitude.

"Horace is dead, Jonathan! Drowned. And Heyerman with him."

Clumsily, cruelly, she blurted it out: the injuries to the hands, the damage to the ship, the threat of mutiny—everything but Willy's defection. She left that out and wondered who it was she was trying to spare.

Jonathan stared at her as if she were an apparition.

"You've had to bear this alone? For fourteen days? Looking after the two of us…alone?"

"I wasn't alone." She explained how Willy and Flagg had relieved her in the sickrooms, how others had risen to meet other aspects of the emergency. Jonathan's lips were moving all the while she was speaking. When she stopped, his words became audible, hissing out between teeth so tightly clenched that they had to make their way through cracks that distorted them. He was abusing himself as he had abused Horace. Out of all proportion. Begging her for forgiveness.

"What is there to forgive? It's not a sin for you to have fallen ill."

Bringing her on this voyage, that was his sin. Indulging his own selfish desires, forgetting that he had promised to cherish and protect her. Exposing the woman he loved to a thousand perils and degrading drudgery. If God forgave him, if with His help he got her safely home, he would never again succumb to this temptation. He swore it.

By the time he had run out of breath, Amanda was too angry to spare much of hers. She reminded him that it was by her own choice that she had been exposed to danger. "And if I'm to be got safely home, I had better be about the noon shot. Noon comes two minutes early today."

The noon shot was the last she was able to get. Clouds blew up from the southeast, and by midafternoon there was no blue sky showing. The barometer was falling, and Flagg was predicting a line storm. It was close to the time of the equinox, when southwesters were to be expected hereabouts.

There was one consoling prospect—if they were blown off course, it would be to the north. More northing would be an advantage in the final approach to Nootka Sound. But lookouts would be needed at all hours from this day on. It might be wise to lay to, if not this night, then surely the next—if there was another night before landfall.

Amanda lay in her bunk that night and thought about her quarrel with Jonathan. Her anger had not melted and thinned but grown heavier and colder. He, who had asked the all-but-impossible of her, had not even noticed her achievement. Her victory meant nothing to him; that made it meaningless to her.

He blamed himself for failing her, failing to protect and cherish. To love, honor, and cherish—that was what he had promised. But to cherish could mean something other than to protect. It could mean to nurture. Nurture what needed to be nurtured in the woman she had become.

Jonathan did not see that woman. Perhaps he would not have chosen her to love. Did men ever see the women they loved as they were? Or always only as extensions of themselves?

What about the other men—the ship's company, those that ranged themselves for or against her? How did they see her? "An angel sent on purpose..." Davy had called her that once, but she did not think he would use such a word now. They were friends now, comrades, linked by a bond that had nothing to do with love between male and female.

She thought her way back to the noon hour.

She was standing on the quarterdeck, Davy and Flagg on either side of her, the lookers-on, below, amidships. The wind sharp enough to keep blood coursing and energy high. The sun hot on her skin under the coolness of the air. The moon frosty in the blue of the west, submitting to her will, permitting her to bring it into conjunction with the white gold glory of the sun, greened by the sextant's filter.

"Stand by."

Flagg's pencil pointed like a hunting dog's tail. Davy's eyes followed the second hand of the watch.

"Mark!"

Davy read off the time; Flagg wrote it in the copybook. Amanda read off the angle; Flagg wrote that down. They were parts of a single machine, but she was the moving part that drove the others.

The men paid her deference and obeyed her because they depended on her for their survival. She had power over them because she had power over nature, whose forces obeyed and served her. This was the heady wine Horace had tasted and Jonathan had grown addicted to.

But there was a difference. The men obeyed her as they would have obeyed any competent captain. But because she was a woman, they perceived her as an anomaly, a being of another order who had inexplicably—miraculously!—assumed this function. They all did but the Polynesians…and Rory.

She was nearly asleep when the thought of Rory brought her awake. Where had he been in that scene? Not present, she was certain, although she had not been conscious of his absence at the time. Perhaps he had kept to his bunk because his leg had been injured in his fall. She must have a look at it, redo the wrapping and replace it with a clean one…tomorrow.

THE TWENTIETH DAY

September 20, 1851
  Sky overcast, wind variable, mostly NW.
At 10 A.M.
    Lat. by D.R. 50°10' N.
    Long. by D.R. 130° W.

AMANDA BRIGHT'S JOURNAL

September 20, 1851
  No observations have been possible since noon yesterday. The wind has hauled and veered, freshened and dropped. Also, there have been two fogs, one of which blew down from the north like a squall, lasted the whole of the first watch, lifted around dawn, and gave way to calm.

  I have a persistent sense of being in the grip of a strong current. It makes me apprehensive—while the overcast makes observation impossible—of being brought up with the coast much sooner than the reckoning predicts. Sufficiently apprehensive to ask the bosun to have the deep-sea lead lowered to see if they can strike soundings.

·⟡·

This was a procedure she had never witnessed, quite different from the heaving of a handline as the ship felt its way into the shallows of an anchoring ground. The reel, carrying nearly one hundred fathoms of line, was handled by a man stationed on the weather quarter, and the line was carried forward to the bowsprit. One man supported it amidships; another, perched on the cathead, swung the dipsey (which weighed nearly fifty pounds and was heavily coated with wax for bringing up a sample of the bottom), lofting it over the bow wave and into the sea. As the ship moved ahead—slowly, for it was nearly becalmed—the man amidships let go the line, and it ran free from the reel until—"No bottom at ninety fathoms," was called from the stern.

But Kankkonen was not satisfied with a single cast of the lead. He ordered the line reeled in for another. While Amanda waited, Willy came to say that Jonathan wanted her at once.

He was sitting up in his bunk, examining a revolver, which she had seen in the drawer where his valuables were kept but never till now in his hands.

"Would you trouble Mr. Smith for his pistols?" He addressed her in a tone that demanded unquestioning obedience. Without questioning, Amanda obeyed.

Smith was awake, weak but responsive to a request from the captain. The pistol case was in his sea chest, he said. If the missis would be kind enough to open the lid, he could tell her just where to look.

She carried the box back to Jonathan, who took it with no thanks but a nod and asked whether Horace had any small arms in his gear.

"I don't recall seeing any, but Willy should know."

"Willy has only what you gave him, and there was no weapon. So that accounts for all the handguns. Now for the arms locker." He handed her a key. "Open it and count the rifles. See that the ammunition for them is on the shelf above."

The arms locker was a small, separate compartment of the port locker. In it Amanda found eight rifles, neatly stacked, butt to muzzle, and a supply of powder and ball. She reported this to Jonathan, who nodded and took back the key.

"Are you going to tell me what's wrong?" she asked.

The feeling of being reprimanded for some unknown fault had weighed heavier than her resentment of his manner, but the balance was beginning to shift.

Jonathan said that Willy reported a conspiracy: a plan to seize whatever arms were issued at landfall, take over the ship, and sail it south.

"Arms issued? To whom?"

Under ordinary circumstances, he would issue arms to all members of the watch. The Nootkas were considered savage and treacherous—"though not as treacherous as some members of our ship's company, it would appear. And by the way, I must ask you to take care that the conspirators are not forewarned." It was important that Willy not be exposed to reprisals and that he continue in the confidence of the plotters. "We need to be kept abreast of what is being planned."

"And who is it that is planning all this?"

"The Scot is the ringleader."

"Willy says that?"

Jonathan nodded gravely.

"Willy is mistaken." It was too late to tell him of the boy's defection. She ought to have done it yesterday. The best she could do now was make her own report on the state of affairs before the mast. "I don't doubt that many of the hands would be glad to sail south. But they would not trust Rory to take them there. He is no navigator, and they have seen it proved."

Jonathan heard her out in the manner of a judge who has already reached his verdict but is preserving the forms by giving the accused his last plea. Then began the rebuttal. Once or twice she tried to argue a point. Each time Jonathan waited till she had done, then continued as if what she had said was immaterial.

She had the sense that they were conducting a debate—the one that really mattered—without words, that she was losing it because she did not defend herself against the real charge. What that might be she was as far as ever from suspecting until Jonathan said—almost as a parenthesis—that *this* was the inevitable result of the failure to maintain discipline.

"Are you talking about Horace? Does Willy say Horace didn't maintain discipline?"

"I am talking about you, Amanda." Jonathan's voice broke. He stopped and glared angrily at her. "I don't wish to be unjust. I mean to give credit where it is deserved. I am also at fault...my illness and..." His vocal cords betrayed him again, and again he stopped to master the weakness. "The fact is, discipline was not maintained while I was ill. The distance between the forecastle and the quarterdeck has been wiped out, and this is the result. All this talk—"

"Of mutiny? Is that what you mean? That I have opened the way to mutiny by being too familiar with the hands? Is that what Willy says?"

Jonathan refused to answer, but she went on anyway.

"I have asked for help from many of the men. I needed it. I was given it. I'm grateful."

"I understand—"

"I've had the loyal support of all the crew. Except Rory. And Willy!" Jonathan was ready to defend the informer, but she gave him no opening. "In particular, I've had the help of Flagg and Davidson."

"So I'm told."

"You're told that they have spent time on the quarterdeck."

"And in the cabin."

"That is true. Flagg, because he has done at least half the nursing." (Jonathan dismissed that point with a wave of his hand.) "Davidson, because he undertook the repairs to the foremast. At Mr. Smith's request and under his direction." Jonathan had evidently not heard that from Willy, and it had some impact. "And because both men have been helping me with the navigation."

"I can hardly believe you learned to take lunars from an ignorant cockney seaman," Jonathan said.

Jonathan was jealous! Of Davy! That was at the root of this. It was outrageous that he, a man who had lusted after the flesh of abandoned women, a frequenter of brothels, should accuse—or even suspect...He dishonored those to whom he owed a debt of gratitude by harboring, even for an instant…

"What I mean to say is this, Amanda. It can't help but undermine discipline when one—or two or three or however many—of the foremasthands assumes a familiarity—"

"If Willy says that—"

"I say it. It lowers the esteem of the men for those in authority."

"You are wrong. And you are a fool to listen to Willy. Listen for a change to me."

One part of her stood aside and wondered at the self-praise that poured from her mouth, but she believed passionately in the truth of what she was saying: that she had not lowered, but raised, the esteem in which she was held by the crew. She had done it not by relying on the taboos of distance, aloofness, mystery, silence but by accomplishing her object. By bringing the ship safely through perils and confusions. By putting down not one but two incipient mutinies by the quickness of her wit and the firmness of her action.

"If you have time and strength to spare on scuttlebutt stories, get someone to tell you the part Willy has played in the undermining of authority and conspiring to mutiny."

Willy was in the cabin. The stateroom door was half-open. She hoped he was listening.

"So, Jonathan, if you have no further unjust accusations to make against me, I'll get back to my place. On the quarterdeck."

Willy stepped aside as she came through the door—she would have slammed it into him if he had not been quick—and followed her to the companion ladder.

"Cousin Amanda, I want to tell you—"

"You stay below. Do you understand?"

"I know you think I —"

"Stay away from me."

She could have struck him. Could have struck Jonathan. She would if she were provoked any further.

She did not go below for the noon meal but asked for and was given a cup of soup and a ship's biscuit, which she ate on deck. There were anxious looks from several of the watch, and at last Flagg approached her, diffident but concerned, to ask if she was feeling a bit offish.

She seized the opportunity to question him, beginning cautiously. Willy had been reporting certain things to the captain, she said, things that were alarming if they were true. She had relied on Flagg to keep her posted on any threat to the safety of the ship.

He reacted almost too quickly. There had been, he would have to admit, a good bit of gab. She would remember he warned her— "What the captain has been told is that Rory is plotting to get arms for a mutiny. If you warned me of that, I did not understand you."

Flagg looked over his shoulder for the eavesdroppers her tone invited, but she continued in the same deliberately audible voice.

"There is also gossip—so Willy says—that you and Davy have been permitted liberties, that this is part of the reason for the troubles."

Flagg's mouth sagged and then shut, nothing having come out of it. Sagged and shut again. She would learn nothing by increasing the pull of loyalties that had the old man on the rack.

AMANDA BRIGHT'S JOURNAL

September 20, continued.

If this overcast continues and I can get no observation, we shall have to lay to this night. I feel we are close to land. There is nothing to go on—no birds, no debris of vegetation in the water. But three times I have imagined that I heard the sound of breakers through the fog.

Perhaps the turmoil inside me is imposed on the natural world and my perception of it; perhaps it is because I am uneasy that I believe we are sailing into danger, rather than the other way round. It may even be that the danger of which I have so strong a premonition is not from wind or water or rocks or fog but from the men of the crew. But I am not convinced.

·-◇-·

All afternoon she worked on calculations that would stand her in good stead when and if the sky cleared. But it did not clear. At eight bells she gave the order to heave to for the night, with a double watch kept on the bow and aloft, and soundings taken every two hours. Her manner had changed since the quarrel with Jonathan. The men noticed and responded to it, but not with enthusiasm. He had succeeded in making her stiff and self-conscious; less, rather than better, able to discharge her duty of command.

She woke feeling that she had been called—summoned by some harbinger of catastrophe. Still and rigid, she waited for the call to be repeated. It did not come again, but she could not believe it was dreamed. She got up, grabbed her long cloak, and wrapped it around her as she went.

The doors of both sickrooms stood open. Dim lamps burned so that she could see each of the sleepers, see the rise and fall of bed linens as they breathed. Neither of them had called her or cried out.

It came again. Fainter this time. From the deck. Forward. Someone was hurt. Badly hurt. In need of help.

She groped her way to the companion ladder, pulled up it two steps at a time, and stepped out. The fog had come down so cold and thick it was hard to draw into one's lungs. The cry came again, raucous with anguish, hardly human.

She crossed the quarterdeck and started down the steps to the waist, but the ship rolled as her foot felt for the deck. She skidded on the slippery planking and fell, her ankle twisting under her so that it seemed to snap. Pain blinded and deafened her. She didn't know whether she cried out or heard again the cry that had waked her. Then someone was beside her, helping her up.

Davy. Did the man never go below to sleep?

"Better sit for a spell," he said. "Here's the hatch. It's damp, but your cloak'll likely keep you dry."

He was easing her down, talking to distract her, assuring her that the pain would pass, that no bones were broken. How could he know that? And yet she was comforted.

Breath by deep breath, she worked through the agony. Her teeth were chattering, but the pain was becoming manageable despite the chill.

Then the cry came again.

"What's that?" She caught at his arm and felt the muscles jump under her hand.

He laughed uneasily. "Brought me up, too. A bird. A bloody damn bird, that's what."

"What bird can make a sound like that?"

"Like a soul turning on a spit over the fires of hell, ain't it so? But it's only one of them little ducks. You seen 'em. The ones been swimming around us ever since we ran out of wind."

She did remember having seen the birds, always in pairs, barrel-chested, and so short of wing they could hardly lift off the water when frightened. Davy was explaining that the pairs were mother and chick. They got separated when one dived for a fish. The awesome shrieking was their way of finding each other in the dark.

"Then we must be near land. If there are birds…and such poor flyers…"

Davy agreed. "Crank was saying the same thing earlier. You can't see past the tip of the jibboom, but you'd ought to hear the surf if we're that close. He's there on the pulpit now, listening for it."

She listened too for a while, but the cold was penetrating, and her ankle was beginning to pain her acutely as the numbness wore off.

"I'd better put some sort of binding on my leg," she said. "Will you call me if the sky clears enough for any sort of shot?"

"Aye, but have a care you don't—"

He had not finished his warning when she fell. The instant she put weight on the ankle, it gave under her. Her foot slipped again. She cried out, was caught and held—caught and embraced.

The long, loose cloak came open as her hands grabbed for support. She clutched at his arms as they reached out to her. For a moment they held on to each other to brace against a swell that passed under the ship. There was a throbbing of blood in her throat, pain in her leg, and a heave of feeling like the heave of the sea.

"'Ere, now!" Davy's voice was cracked, weak, uncertain, utterly unlike the body against which she leaned: strong, male, firm as a mast. "You all right, ma'am?" She wanted to laugh.

"You all right there?" he asked again.

She tried to step away, to stand on her own feet, but another roll of the ship thwarted her. She staggered. His arms came back to sustain her. One hand clutched her right breast. She felt his fingers, hard and cold, through the thin fabric of her camisole. He must feel her flesh, warm, soft, all but bare.

It was a while before she came back into her body, but she knew what had happened in the interval. She had gasped. Davy had let her go. She had managed not to fall. They had stood, dumb, stunned by the bolt that had passed through them. Then she had lurched away, hopping like a cripple without a crutch, from the hatch to the ladder, pulling herself up, hopping to the capstan, from it to the companion, easing herself down that ladder, across the unlighted officers' mess to her bunk.

She did not bind her ankle. She had hardly the strength to pull blankets over her. Pain was lost in exhaustion. She let herself thankfully down into sleep....

Fire flowed from her like current from a river mouth. And the man was caught up in it, caught and drawn into the circular movement of this element in which they were both suspended, which moved like water and warmed like fire. The circle tightened into a vortex that drew him downwards, to where she waited, still and swollen with love.

They touched. Touched lips and then bodies.

His hands moved over her, seeking the places where the fire burned closest, stirred it so that it leapt up out of its confinement. And in the burning center there was an aching that gathered into a fist.

It struck. Her womb jerked as if it were forcing a child into life.

She was awake. The darkness arranged itself around her so that she knew where she was. The aching was undiminished. The mystery still promised.... She tried to move her body to meet it, but it slipped around and past her. Elusive as water.

Desperate lest she be cheated again, her hands moved as the man's moved in the dream. They touched her breasts; she felt the nipples twist; and her womb jerked once again. Her hands went to her belly, waited for it to knot, slid down, pressed on something hard in the soft flesh. The fist doubled and struck. Her hand pressed harder, and the fire in the crater spilled over.

Over and over. Jerk and thrust. As Jonathan's body jerked and thrust. She was feeling what he felt, what had been withheld from her till now.

Water lapped and sucked against the hull. She could feel it pass through her as wind passed through the rigging. This, then, was the mystery. Different from what she had believed, having nothing to do with the fusing of two beings or the making of a third. Union not with one other but with all others and most of all—first of all—with one's self. Nothing to do with the conceiving and bearing of a child.

She should have known that. For a child could be conceived without love—out of the very opposite of love. Force—of a man's brute strength or the brute strength of hunger or some other imperative— might impregnate a womb whose fruit would not bless but curse...a child who would punish not the sinner but the sinned against...shame its mother into abandonment....

"Shameless and abandoned..."

Ought she to be ashamed? And if she was not, was it because she was abandoned—*"abandoned to unspeakable, unnatural vice"*?

But it was her nature that had led her. Following it, she had found herself, freed herself, made herself whole and strong enough to cope with tomorrow, when there would be other mysteries—other imperatives—the sun and the sextant, the moon, which was changing, turning its face from her, hiding its secret in darkness, leaving her with no key to unlock the answer to where, on the surface of the sea, she floated and was rocked to sleep in the cradle of the ship.

5

Amanda Bright,
Master

THE TWENTY-FIRST DAY

Dawn was held back by the fog. When it did come, just before the change of watch, its light turned the sails a strange sick color like heaps of sea wrack bleaching on a beach. The calm was so absolute that pairs of guillemots—the fat little ducks that had shrieked so in the night—made ripples as they dived and rose and swam in circles close to the ship.

Amanda leaned on the railing near the break of the poop, listening to the men taking soundings. Her ankle pained despite the binding she had put on, but she could walk without a limp if she put her mind to it.

"Watch there, watch!" from the bowsprit. The plash of the lead. The man amidships let go the line as it came abreast of him. And from aft—"Seventy-five faddom."

They had struck soundings at last.

There was no audible comment, but the men's bodies spoke, slowing or halting whatever movement was in progress when the news reached them. Amanda felt her heart pound with fear or the prelude to fear. They were locked in this place of menacing silence, of savage dangers and dangerous savages, blindfolded, not knowing how they had been carried here so quickly—not, surely, by the familiar collaboration of wind and sail—not knowing what lay behind the wall of whiteness....

She went below to look again at the chart.

The course she had been steering should have brought them into sounding depths forty miles north of Nootka Sound, off an evil-looking, unnamed cape, footed by many islets and rocks. South of the westernmost point of this headland, the shore ran northeast for several miles through a rubble of reef. If they should fall in with the coast in this region, any wind at all would be likely to blow them onto some submerged death trap.

But the current that had hurried them east might also have carried them south. The ship might stand anywhere along the western face of Vancouver Island. Off the entrance to Esperanza Inlet, for instance, where the chart showed safe anchorage behind a screen of dangerous Islands. Or near Bajo Reef, which was marked "Covered at High Water." Or close to Friendly Cove at the north jaw of Nootka.

There was no way to tell which, so long as the fog hid the shoreline and the sky overhead.

Four bells, ten o'clock, two hours till noon. Amanda asked the bosun whether he noticed any thinning of the cloud cover. He did not. Fog sometimes held for weeks on this coast, he said.

"Ought we to drop anchor and wait?"

From his expression she suspected she had exposed her ignorance by the question, but all the man said was something about getting the anchor cable ranged and bent on. Anchoring, she remembered, was the mate's province, so she went down to see if Smith was awake.

He was, and curious about what was afoot, glad to advise her that it was impossible to anchor in any depth over twenty fathoms, unwise to edge closer in search of such a depth. Vancouver Island had a bad name for sudden, violent blows from the south.

"You might could find yourself clawing off a lee shore with no room to wear ship."

Amanda went back to her desk and worked a series of possible meridian altitudes. Not that there was any use in presetting the sextant, but simply because it was soothing to work with numbers—clear, immutable, manageably real.

When that palled, she opened the Bowditch, hoping for an oracle, but she was mocked. The book fell open at a passage on finding longitude by an eclipse of Jupiter's satellites, as if the old man of Salem were saying that she was as likely to find one as the other.

On the next cast she did better: *"To Find the Latitude by the Moon's Meridian Angle."*

There was a way to get latitude without the sun!

The moon had crossed its meridian an hour ago, but Amanda learned by reading on that there were other possibilities of which she had been unaware: ways to find latitude by double altitudes of sun, moon, or star; by *"altitudes of two different objects taken within a few minutes of each other, or by observing the altitudes of two different bodies at the same instant."*

That was—or could be—part of the taking of a lunar distance. She could get longitude as well as latitude and fix the ship's position by one more lunar distance. She would need two sextants for simultaneous observations. Davy could use Smith's instrument. Flagg could hold the deck watch as well as his notepad. It was an elephant they could eat.

At noon the fog still covered the sky, although there were smears of brightness in the west. The calm still held.

The guillemots still swam in pairs, mother and chick, close to the ship. Amanda sent for Davy and explained what she would require of him and what of Flagg. Once, while they were talking, the quiet was splintered by the cry of a guillemot. Their eyes caught and held like burrs. It was hard to pull loose. Amanda was careful not to look at him again.

Just before three bells, the sun burned through in the west. As soon as the area of blue widened to include the moon, they could begin. She went down for the sextants and the deck watch.

Jonathan was standing in the door of his stateroom, holding to the jamb, gray-faced, and so thin that his trousers and shirt hung on him like another man's garments. She asked how he was feeling. She was surprised at how her own feelings had changed, from a dilute pity, strained through the mesh of other, more pressing concerns, to a grudging admiration of his fortitude. How he fought to master weakness, to pump the strength of his will into his emaciated frame.

Jonathan answered her question with a curt "Better," and asked one of his own: "Is the sky clear?"

"It is in the west."

He watched her as she moved about the cabin, then asked if she intended to try for a time sight.

"For a lunar distance and a latitude."

"Who will be taking the times?"

"Flagg." She turned and met the thrust of his question. "And Davidson will be using the other sextant."

"You're making trouble for yourself, Amanda."

"I don't think so."

"Because you don't know what it is you're dealing with." And she had better listen to someone who did. If not to her husband, then to the testimony of tradition. Eternal verities. "A woman can't…a woman doesn't…a woman has only herself to blame if…"

Amanda's fingers fiddled with the vernier screw of the sextant while the sermon poured over her, delivered from the height of his superior knowledge of the ordinary seaman, a creature so simple he could be summed up in a few pejorative phrases. Especially in regard to his view of the female sex.

"You could hardly expect your average foremasthand to understand a lady. If you had the least notion of the lives these men lead…"

"I have some notion that brothels are frequented by masters as well as by foremasthands," she said.

"What are you talking about?"

She would not be in a hurry to answer. She would speak impersonally, judicially; say something about knowing oneself—one's worst self—before presuming to prescribe and proscribe. But she had not honed the edge of the phrase when Willy came to call her for the observation.

"You must excuse me, Jonathan," she said. "We'll talk of this some other time."

She saw the blaze of anger in his face and remembered when her own concerns, no matter how compelling, were expected to wait upon the master's convenience.

There was still an unbreached wall of white to the east, but elsewhere the sky was blue, the sea bluer, the horizon sharp. They began with the simultaneous altitudes, Davy taking the sun's; Amanda, the moon's.

"Stand by."

"Mark!"

Flagg read off the time. Amanda and Davy read off the angles: degrees, minutes, and seconds. Flagg repeated and wrote. They changed around: Amanda measuring the sun's height—*da capo al fine*...for good measure, once again.

Then the angular distance—a new theme. They were working together like musicians in a trio: Davy playing the deck watch; Flagg, the tablet and pencil; while Amanda played the air, bringing the round limbs to touch, delicately as a kiss.

"Standby."

"Mark!"

As she started away, Davy followed to say something *sotto voce*: that she was not to worry...something about Rory. All she recalled later was the anxious crinkling of the skin around his eyes.

She sat at the desk as if at a keyboard, with the Bowditch, the *Ephemeris,* and Flagg's sheet of times and angles propped open before her like a musical score. Slowly, savoring the suspended harmonies, she began. First, there were the annotations to make: symbols for sun and moon, degrees, minutes, and seconds, and hours—each to be marked before the proper set of ciphers. Next, the columns to be set up. The tables to be entered, logs. taken out. Addition. Subtraction. Division by two, and the addition of the half sum to the remainder. Delighting in what she did, checking her mind's impulse to leap, teaching it to move in rhythm with the columns, toward the great diapason.

"To Find the Longitude from the True Distance." True distance. It had the sonority of ultimate consonance. Like the True Cross.

But the resolving chord was minor, dissonant.

127°04' west.

Almost a full degree east of her reckoned 128°! They must also have slipped south. How far, she would learn from the simultaneous altitudes.

Again the mode was minor, the chords resolving down, down—below the lowest of her several predictions—to 49°20' north. Nearly fifteen miles below the entrance to Friendly Cove.

She drew the coordinates on the chart, marked an X at their crossing, and measured the distance and bearing. It was twenty-two miles, northeast by north, to the spot where she had hoped to anchor. But it was still possible to make landfall at Nootka—if the wind came up and the coast cleared.

She tried to picture what would be revealed in that event, translating the lines and letters of the chart into a vision of shore and mountain, cliff and forest. For the first time she noticed how much this drowned coastline resembled that of New England: the same deep bays and coves, studded by a spattering of rocky outcrops, drained and flooded by powerful tides.

Tides! Something else to be reckoned before standing in to shore. The times of ebb and flood, the height and range. She would have to consult Jonathan.

Only then did she remember how they had parted. She had not looked in on him when she came down from the deck, and he had not made a sound. She tiptoed to the door and opened it quietly.

He was stretched across the bunk as if he had fainted.

Neither Davy nor Flagg was anywhere in sight when she emerged onto the quarterdeck. Kankkonen came clumping up to tell her something about the setting of sails below the bowsprit. It was the sort of thing in which she had no competence and little interest, but she kept him talking, trying to think of some way to have Davy summoned. She wanted to share both her triumph and her anxiety about the position, but she was self-conscious about her foremast friends. Jonathan had succeeded in locking her into the loneliness of a captain—his sort of captain—after all.

King John was at the wheel.

He answered her question about the heading by showing her that the spokes could be spun without changing the direction of the compass needle. The ship was making no way at all. The courses strained as if trying to fill their lungs and failing.

"Nootka?" He spoke the word with a rising inflection that made a question of it, his eyes roving up and down the wall of whiteness.

"Nootka." Amanda pointed on the compass card to North and then, approximately, in the direction of the bowsprit.

King John nodded and spun the wheel again. He would point up when he could, but for the present the ship was flotsam.

AMANDA BRIGHT'S JOURNAL

September 21, 1851

Both our patients have less fever today than yesterday. It rises in the afternoons, but not as sharply as before. Jonathan overtaxed himself this morning. Since then he has roused himself only to drink tea and then gone back to sleep. Mr. Smith makes less effort and may be the better for it.

All this afternoon the world has been split into opposites: bright on the one hand, dark on the other. To the west, the sea is lapis lazuli, flecked and streaked with reflections of the sun. The sky glows. To the east there is only the fog. While we were in it, it was gray, cold, oppressive. Outside, looking back, it appears invitingly soft. But blank. Utterly blank, so that it is hard to believe the lead is not lying, that we have really left the realm of the unbroken horizon at last.

Late this afternoon I saw a flock of birds—black birds with long necks and strong wings—passing like a flight of arrows into the white wall. They must have been returning to nests somewhere along the shore. If it is within their reach, it is within ours. We may yet make landfall before night.

THE TWENTY-SECOND DAY

S he went on deck not long after dawn.
It was an enchantment. The land was covered by a cloud
conjured up by a shaman charged to protect his people against in-
vaders, baffling them or luring them into traps set among the rocks.
Water black as obsidian covered the traps, flecked here and there
with ragged remnants of foam.

The port watch was turning to, and Davy reported on the four
hours just ended. The ship had been kept as much as possible on the
heading Amanda had ordered, but with no wind to steady her, she
had yawed about some. The lead had been heaved twice; once it had
brought up clay from seventy fathoms; once it had found no bottom.
It would soon be time to heave it again.

"Will there be wind before noon, do you think?"

Davy had no opinion on that. He was uneasy in her presence and
would have excused himself if he had known how.

"You were telling me something yesterday," Amanda said. "About
Rory. I'm afraid I was so taken up with my observation, I didn't truly
listen."

"No matter, ma'am."

"It mattered then." She watched his face for a sign that would tell her whether and how much it still mattered.

For a while there was none. Then all at once it moved like a shifting ice field, and his voice cracked under the same contrary strains. "He's daft, that one. But we'll look after you, ma'am. No matter."

"No matter what?"

Davy shrugged the same nonanswer he had given when she inquired if he was married. Was her ankle still hurting?

"Not badly. It pains a little, but I can put weight on it."

"I saw you was walking better," he said and got away.

At breakfast Willy informed her that he had moved out of the deckhouse and into the forecastle. If he expected her to ask why, he was disappointed. She could guess. But she wondered a little what Jonathan would do for an informer now.

She went to her desk to work on the tides.

Bowditch had a whole section with new tables, new procedures, new shibboleths such as "vulgar establishment" and "lunitidal intervals." Nootka Sound was among the points listed on the west coast of North America where the height and interval of the tides had been surveyed. Meridian passage of the moon—upper and lower transit—was tabulated in the *Ephemeris*. What she wanted was the hour of slack water, between ebb and flood, the best for an approach, all other things being equal. By combining ingredients as directed in the Bowditch, she arrived at the hour of four—morning or evening.

At eleven the fog was lifting to the west, and there was wind from the same quarter—an auspicious start. But the bosun reported that the lead had found no bottom on the last several casts. It looked to him as if they had "slipped off the shelf." Amanda discounted his pessimism. As soon as the sun cleared the overcast, she would take an observation, and they would see.

Meanwhile she leaned on the rail and watched the Sandwich Islanders trying to coax some birds to dive for bits of stale ship's biscuit: curious black birds with Mardi Gras masks—concentric circles of white, black, and yellow—and with orange-red beaks as big as parrots'. They bobbed jauntily on the wavelets, diving now and again, but never for the biscuit scraps.

A jellyfish drifted in the black water—a pale, milky transparency with the outline of a flower sketched in white. It moved slowly astern, which might mean that the ship was sailing slowly north or that the water was slipping south, carrying the ship with it but at a slower rate than it carried the gossamer flower.

The sun had been warming her forehead for some time before she recalled that she was waiting for it. Davy and Flagg were summoned; the sextants and watch brought on deck; and the ceremony of a lunar distance begun. It was so easy now—so brisk and businesslike—that Amanda had room in her mind for other impressions: Kankkonen, busy on the forecastlehead with the lashing of the bow anchors (they would have to be got over before the ship stood in for a landing); the men of the watch, some working with the bosun, some near the break of the poop, listening to the "Stand by" and "Mark." She could feel them, all of them, dark and light, Cook and Willy, as well as Davy and Flagg, connected in a system of attractions and repulsions like the solar system, a system of which she was at this moment the center and sun.

The result of the observation was a longitude of 126°30' west.

She knew before she drew the line on the chart that the bosun was right. They had drifted so far south that they were off the edge of the continental shelf. She worked all the altitudes again, using a different method for making the connections, but the result was the same within two seconds of arc. The angular distance was even more critical, but the figure she had used there was the mean of four careful measurements. Either she had made some enormous and consistent error of arithmetic, or the ship had fallen victim to a fierce southerly set. It had drifted twenty miles on a course that would lead into the Strait of Juan de Fuca, the boundary between Canadian and American territory. How long was it since she had been within sight and sound of her own, her native land?

When she came up with the sextant at noon, the hands made no effort to mask their interest. Alarm had spread from the center to the farthest orbit of the system. Even to Willy, who hung about the companion hatch, pretending to clean the brass bindings of the door.

The sun was too high for her presetting and still rising. The ship had drifted again. They had missed their landfall. The unfriendly cove, which she had never seen, was receding behind the enchantment of the fog, already out of reach.

The position of the ship was between the entrances of two great sounds: Clayoquot and Nitinat; thirty miles from one, forty from the other. The wind was brisk and northwest. It was possible to head up and beat into it, to regain some of the lost northing. But against such a current? And into such fog? Tomorrow the moon would be dark, and for five days thereafter. If the sun also failed them, if the fog did not lift, how long would the ship have to beat back and forth, reckoning by guess its gain or loss in the battle against the stealthy antagonism of the current?

The alternative, tempting as sleep, was to yield to wind and water; let them carry the ship into the strait, where the fog would not follow. She had heard there was a Hudson's Bay Company post at the southeastern corner of Vancouver Island, facing on a sunny, sheltered, inland sea....

Jonathan called.

Willy had helped him dress after breakfast, and he had been resting ever since. Now he wanted to be helped into the cabin, to sit for a while, perhaps come to table for the noon meal. It was Willy he had summoned, but he permitted Amanda to do the office, guiding him step by shaky step, like an old man, feebler than his own grandfather. The ship was bucking into the chop like a trapped man beating his fists against a door. Jonathan could not hold his balance against it. He had intended to sit at his desk, but the round table was closer. He let Amanda ease him into the chair beside it.

"Is there anything I can get for you?"

He said no and had nothing else to say.

She went back to the desk, to the logbook, filling in the squares that summed up the twenty-first sea day, leaving blank only the square marked Course. Strictly speaking, there had been no course, only a heading, which had no meaning as things had turned out. But the ship was moving now, and there would have to be a course laid out, an order given to the helm.

If Jonathan had not been so shaky, if he had not been so stubborn, if he had asked a single, civil question, she might have told him how matters stood and asked his counsel. Although if she asked, she would feel herself obliged to follow it, and she was not entirely sure that—at this moment—his counsel would be sound.

She made her own decision and filled in the Course box: SE by E.

"I'm going on deck," she said. "Willy will bring lunch in a while. I'll be down in time."

"If you see Chips, you might ask him for his engraving tools," Jonathan said unexpectedly. He had a piece of walrus tusk he had been saving for scrimshaw. It would do to pass the time while he got back his strength.

She felt the tightening ache of tears even before the image rose in her memory…another piece of scrimshaw.

Jonathan had showed it to her before slipping it into a drawer of his chiffonier. A polished piece of bone on which he had engraved the figure of a woman, seated in a chair—a small, delicate woman with a wire-waist bodice and billowing skirts. The chair and its high, carved back had seemed familiar.

"You don't recognize it?" Jonathan sounded a trifle hurt. "I thought I had it down pretty accurately."

Of course! Her father's favorite parlor chair, its black horse-hair up-holstery sculptured into deep puff and ridges…But the woman? "Is it meant to be…me?"

"It's not much of a likeness," Jonathan admitted. "I'm no artist." But he had spent long hours fashioning this talisman and carried it in his pocket on every voyage before this one. "I won't be needing it now that I have the original," he said with the odd little jerk of his neck muscles that did the office of a blush.

Amanda studied the image, wondering that he should ever have thought of her as dainty and doll-like, then—acting on the sort of im-

213

pulse she usually suppressed as indecorous put her arms up and lifted her
face to be kissed....

She relayed Jonathan's request to Flagg and ordered the helm
brought round to the new heading. The bark picked up speed,
heeled softly, and steadied. It was a perfect, joyous reach.

When she came down, Jonathan had gone back to his bunk. The
logbook lay open on the desk. He could have read her entry, in
which case he did not have to be told that she had decided to make
for the Strait.

September 22, 1851
Dear Aunt Aggie and Uncle Matthew:
  This dreadful voyage is coming to a close. We are coming into
waters where I expect we shall meet a vessel that can carry a let-
ter to you, and I must not postpone any longer

As she waited for the words to arrange themselves in her mind,
her eye went back over the lines she had written: *"dreadful voyage."*
And yet, thinking back, she did not find it dreadful. This was a voyage from one life to another, from one Amanda to another. What
stood out in her mind was a sense of fulfillment. The voyage had
taught her—or, striving with the sea and the stars, she had taught
herself—that the joys human beings experience had little to do with
the giving or taking of pleasure. Not the great joys. Those had to do
with the touching and transcending of limits, expanding, crossing
known frontiers, entering into terra incognita, exercising mastery.

Horace had learned the same lesson, had reached and surpassed
his limits and—however briefly—had known joy. Could she write
that to his parents? Would it assuage their grief if she could make
them understand? Perhaps, but she was too pressed for time to try,
and she dared not postpone again.

She went back to the letter, setting down the facts of the tragedy,
briefly, abruptly, and ending with:

  I cannot write more now—forgive me—except to say that
Jonathan and Mr. Smith are on the mend. If they suffer no re-

lapse, it is possible—though by no means certain—that we shall continue the voyage as originally planned. If not, it may be that we shall follow the ship that brings this letter, as soon as their health permits.

She felt a great relief, but there was still the letter to Louisa. That would be even harder. And there was no use beginning till she had a chance to go through Horrie's papers to find a name and an address.

Midway through the afternoon watch, Amanda decided to try for one last lunar. It was not a promising prospect: both sun and moon were in the west, too close to each other (and the moon too low) for easy or accurate measurement. But there was nothing to be lost by trying.

Waiting for her two assistants, she stared into the fog that had become the given, a musical note sustained till the ear went deaf to it. Suddenly there was a hole—a tunnel bored by some trick of wind—and at the far end of it, land!

White surf curling at the toes of black cliffs. A tumble of gray rock above like the ruins of a castle-fortress. A broad, horizontal brush-stroke of emerald, vivid in the sunlight. Behind that, the dark fringes of conifer forest. Behind that a gray black hump of mountain, shouldering its way between land's end and a range of high mountains, indigo streaked with snow, the highest of them struck off at the top by a cleaver of cloud.

Before she could call out for others to look, it was gone. The curtains had drawn. All was blank as before, except that she heard—or imagined—the roar of surf breaking on the black cliffs. Less than a minute later, there was a shout from the forecastlehead.

If there were orders given, she had not given them. Nor heard them given. But the men moved as she had seen them move in obedience to commands in moments of great stress. The helm was put down. The yards braced round.

Slowly the bow swung into and past the eye of the wind. The topsails flapped. The headsails hung shivering. The spanker slatted and tugged.

"Mainsail haul!"

The ship moved offshore into safe depths, heading to the south and west. Half an hour later they were clear of the fog.

Amanda bent over the chart. There had been no time to take a bearing, but she was sure that the land she had glimpsed was Cape Flattery on the American side of the Strait. There was nothing on the Canadian side high enough to keep its snow through the summer or collect it so early in the fall.

They had missed the entrance to the inland sea. The current had tricked her again—it must sweep down along the face of the great island like a river in freshet—had nearly driven her into the ambush prepared by its accomplice, the fog. One or the other of them she could oppose, but the combination was too strong. She would have to find anchorage somewhere, some cove in which they could wait for as many hours or days as need be. Fog could not last forever, even here.

The chart showed a sweep of shallow bay, twenty miles long, from Cape Flattery to Cape Alava, with rocks only in the vicinity of the two capes. Smith said the southerly arm would give more shelter from the storm winds. They would need to carry the least sail possible, creep in, heaving the lead continually, groping for a depth of something under twenty fathoms.

Soundings were struck first at twenty-three fathoms. Then at twenty-one. Then at seventeen.

"Can't we anchor here?" Amanda asked the bosun.

He looked uneasy. With a good sand bottom, maybe, but only if there was not much swell. And the swells here were awesome. Slow, but awesome.

A shout of warning from Willy on lookout at the crosstrees the main. Another from Jerry in the foremast chains. Amanda looked ahead and saw the great, green-white flower blooming up from the green depths. Swells breaking over a reef less than one point off the starboard bow.

Again there were sounds that took the place of orders: shouts, stamping feet, the creak and rattle of blocks and yards, the shudder of heavy timbers put under sudden strains. Someone said, "If she misses stays this time..."

But she did not miss.

The bark came up, passed the wind, caught it on the other side, and headed out to sea, into the setting sun, which warmed the wall behind them into a glory of seraph wings.

THE TWENTY-THIRD DAY

The quarrel flared before either was aware of its imminence. Jonathan asked what she was doing, and she answered.

"Working out the tides at the mouth of the Columbia."

"The Columbia?"

If he had upbraided her, she could have explained that she had not intended to disobey his orders. But that was what she had done. Without considering, without consulting, without even deciding, she had been carried by a current of events to do what she had defied Rory and his faction to do.

"You propose to cross the bar of the Columbia?" Jonathan spoke slowly, as if leaving open the possibility that he had misunderstood, that she had committed no such outrage.

"There's no other place to put in. Except two very shallow bays to the north, and then—"

"Why put in?"

Every seaman knew that the way to avoid the dangers that had daunted her was to run out to sea. Jonathan would most likely have begun a long northwesterly tack, back to the approximate latitude of Nootka. Amanda could give reasons for having rejected such a course, but the fact was it had not occurred to her until now. She had been attuned—was still attuned—to making port, making contact with the world of men and women where there was comfort, safety, and succor.

"The bar of the Columbia is said to be the worst in the western hemisphere, Amanda. Perhaps the worst in the world."

He elaborated, piling explanation on instance. The enormous bulk of water, gathered from the whole western face of the Rocky Mountains, moving through gorges that powered and sped it to meet the Pacific, the greatest of oceans, whose winds and currents moved inexorably east. The result was chaos: surf, riptides, shifting sands, fog, sudden storms, and fitful winds. Such a bar could never be properly charted. No prudent man would attempt to cross it if he could avoid it. Great ships had been pounded to kindling on its shoals. Boats overturned in the surf, drowning the sacrificial victims sent to seek out a channel.

She felt like such a boat, awash in a sea of guilt, fighting to stay afloat. "Why do you tell me all this now? You read the log. You've been talking to Willy and I don't know who else. You knew we were being carried south, knew about the currents and the fog and all. You could have warned me. But you wanted me to do something wrong. You've been waiting for the chance to look down your nose and tell me what a ninny I am."

She was arguing illogically, emotionally, "like a woman." But Jonathan was no better. He was dignifying her accusations by denying them. Suddenly, she was too weary to fight any longer. Let him take command if that was what he wanted. Let him wrestle with the sea and the wind and the men of the forecastle. She would gladly surrender—except that he was not yet fit to command.

Jonathan's outburst was proof that he had not yet recovered, in mind or in body. He knew it, or he would never have stooped to wrangle with her. He would simply have resumed his old role. He looked so thin, so tired…as tired as she. The pity of it was they could not help each other, face each other as colleagues instead of as adversaries. They would have to have started from a different premise, long ago.

219

It was past the midpoint of the forenoon watch. Amanda's rough reckoning put them less than five miles offshore, fifteen miles north of a cape called Disappointment, which marked the north entrance to the Columbia bar. But she could not rely on her reckoning. She had been too agitated to think of heaving the chip log for some time after the escape from the reef, and besides, the log was of little use for measuring current or drift.

And now there was another imponderable to be pondered.

Kankkonen had called her attention to a curious circumstance: although the wind was still northwesterly, the swells rolled up from the south, as if the sea were declaring its independence from the tyranny of the wind. The Finn had no explanation, except that it might be the influence of some great river, or perhaps a great storm, far to the south. In any case, there was the possibility of a northerly set, opposite to the one that had carried them away from Nootka and past the Strait of Juan de Fuca. Amanda's estimate that the ship could cover the 120 sea miles between Cape Flattery and Cape Disappointment by noon might be wrong by several hours if the current opposed.

She had figured the tides from the tables in the Bowditch. The flood would begin at three. That left three hours of daylight and one of twilight for the crossing. Enough, if the wind was fair, the coast clear, and the channels explored. If the ship fetched Cape Disappointment by noon, there would be three hours for such exploration. Enough, but not by a comfortable margin.

At a quarter to twelve, Amanda sent Willy for the sextant.

The sun was feeble through the overcast, but it could be seen. There was a horizon to the south and west. She could preset the sextant within minutes of arc to the angle she expected. It was, she had just realized, the day of the equinox. The sun would stand, at noon, directly over the earth's equator. At Cape Disappointment's latitude the sun should stand at 43°48'. Every minute of arc less than that would mean the ship stood a mile to the north of the cape.

Her highest reading was 43°08'. Thirty-six miles still to go—no chance of crossing the bar until the morrow.

Jonathan was sitting at the round table, his scrimshaw tools laid out in the compartment of the fiddle where once her embroidery basket stood. He was dozing, the walrus tusk and one of the incising knives half-falling from his limp fingers.

Willy came to announce dinner, but Amanda signed him to let Jonathan sleep out his nap. She was still working out a correlation between the hours of daylight and the tides.

The boy came to stand at her elbow and asked in a low, urgent whisper, "Cousin Amanda, will we see land today?"

She nodded.

"When?"

"By midafternoon, I should think. If the clouds lift."

"They're already lifting."

"Good."

"Some of the men say we'll be anchored inside the river tonight."

"Not likely."

He did not move away.

His proximity was a distraction. She looked up, ready to rebuke him but was stopped by the look on his face. In place of the sulky insolence she had grown to expect there was a look of supplication. He was asking—not for forgiveness, that she might have denied— for certainty. He was sounding her for certainty! As if she were Moses with tablets to hand down, or Bowditch, who was, in matters such as these, more reliable than any desert-dwelling prophet.

Part of her anger was melted under the sun of this flattery, but not all of it. "You warned Jonathan of a mutiny," she said. "But you did not warn me."

"You wouldn't talk to me. You wouldn't let me talk to you. I tried."

"That was the second time. The first time—the time it came into the open?"

"I didn't know. They didn't tell me for fear I'd tell you."

Amanda took this under consideration. The lad was trembling and sweating, as if the intensity of his effort to persuade her was like rolling a boulder uphill. But she had to be logically, as well as emotionally, persuaded.

"When you came to tell me it wouldn't do for me to take Jonathan's place, you would have proposed Rory. Isn't that so?"

Willy took in as much breath as he could hold and let it hiss out between his teeth. "Somebody had to...you see, the hands thought—most of them—that *he* was telling you what to do. With the sextant, I mean. Giving the orders. But I knew he was too sick. And *he* kept asking me did you know how to use the sextant, because if you got the wrong numbers or anything like that, we'd be lost." He was getting hopelessly tangled in his pronouns. But it was impossible to doubt his honesty. "I thought at first maybe he'd get better, but when he didn't..."

He looked as if he would soon be weeping. Amanda remembered letting him take her into his arms to comfort him. But she could no longer afford stratagems of sympathy. "You haven't answered my question. Would you have had him as captain?"

"Well, somebody had to do the navigating, didn't they? And he said he could."

"And you believed him?"

Willy hung his head.

"Even after you heard him read the wrong angle—" She corrected herself, "heard him give the wrong latitude from the angle he read?"

Willy reminded her that he had not been present on that occasion. "He said he did it to get you to head for California, and that was what they all said we ought to do. ...I tried to talk to you. Why wouldn't you talk to me, Cousin Amanda?"

If she knew the answer to that, she was ashamed of it.

Willy swallowed, heaved another long, hissing sigh, and went on. "I didn't *want* him, but there wasn't anyone else. And if he *did* know...but when he *didn't*...when he looked such a fool and got so angry...then I knew for sure he didn't."

"When Rory asked you if I knew how to use a sextant, what did you say?"

"I said I didn't know. But I didn't think you could. Well, nobody else did either. No one ever heard of a lady...you can ask anyone, Cousin Amanda. It's a marvel how you came to learn it."

Amanda had to smile. And having smiled, she could no longer harbor doubt or anger.

They sighted land at two o'clock.

The cry came from aloft and was repeated, echoed, from places in the rigging and on the forecastlehead. By the time Amanda had found a place from which she could see, Willy was yelling exultantly in her ear.

"You were right. See there—just where you drew the line on your chart."

The lubber line of the ship pointed straight to a dark hump of coast. Her noon position had been accurate. Her estimates of compass error, current, wind, and all the rest, lucky. She must remember that. Luck had played a larger part than skill.

A captain was not expected to show anything more than silent satisfaction in the maintaining of his (her!) record of omniscience. But she could hardly contain herself. She was ready to laugh, to cry, to scramble into the ratlines for a better view, to shout back at Willy, pound his shoulders, fling off his cap, throw back her head, and howl for triumph like a wolf. And it might have all gone unnoticed if she had. The men were in a state of euphoric intoxication. She had never seen a landfall elicit such a response. It was a measure of the depth of anxiety that had preceded it. Ashamed of their skepticism, they pressed forward to thank her. One of the Kanakas touched a fold of her cloak, as if to borrow *mana.*

Only Davy kept his distance, he who more than anyone had a right to share in the victory. That was Jonathan's fault. And hers, for repeating his accusations to Flagg, knowing that Flagg would relay them. It had dissolved the comradeship, dimmed and tarnished even the memory of it.

Rory had crawled out of whatever hole he had been keeping to and was hobbling about the deck, agile as an ape, full of babble and brag. Bent on establishing himself as an authority on this bar and the lands and inhabitants on both sides of it, he was telling Cook and King John a tale about one of the survivors of the *USS Peacock,* a Negro called Saul, who had settled at the cape and made a living acting as pilot to incoming ships.

"You'll see his skiff put out for us once he sees that we're bound in."

Amanda went below resolved to make peace, to ask counsel, to accept it, even to apologize if necessary. If Jonathan still opposed putting into port here, she would offer the arguments of the almost-perfect weather conditions, the possibility of reprovisioning and making repairs, Smith's need of special care and rest.

Flagg was at the bunkside. "I was telling the skipper here how you fetched the cape. Neat as if you was following a line of buoys."

Jonathan looked pale and tired still, but no longer hostile. There was an overtone of genuine respect in his manner as he congratulated her. It was easier than she had foreseen for them to speak as if there had been no ugliness.

"I found a chart of the mouth of the Columbia," she said and got it for him to look at. But the print was fine and Jonathan's eyes still weak.

"Is there some way of making sure the cape you've fetched is the right one?" he asked.

She read from the notes at the bottom of the chart: *"Cape Hancock (also called Disappointment) has several trees trimmed up showing a 'broomtop' and may thus be known from the cape to the northward of Shoalwater Bay."*

Jonathan was satisfied with that.

"There are two entrance channels," Amanda went on. "The north one is difficult for sailing vessels. It's shorter, and there is good anchorage inside the hook of Cape Bluff, but there is a baffling wind and *'in the narrowest part of the channel vessels must generally beat in a cross tide.'* They recommend taking a pilot for the crossing."

"By all means, if you can find one."

"Rory has been saying there's a man who will come out in his skiff."

"And what does Rory know of the matter?"

Flagg answered that Rory claimed to have touched at Astoria on coastwise schooners that brought supplies to the North West Company fur post and the settlement that had grown up around it. "It could be just talk, what he picked up from shipmates. But he makes out to have local knowledge of sorts."

Jonathan did not appear impressed.

"I thought of sending a boat to sound the south channel," Amanda said. "You mentioned that the charts are not to be relied on because the sands shift."

Jonathan agreed that a boat must be put out. "It's hard to make out the gap in the breakers from the deck of the ship. You see only their backs."

"Four men to a boat?" Amanda asked, having already decided: two for the oars, one to steer, and one to heave the lead.

"If you can spare them. Bearing in mind that you may lose them all."

"Is it really as risky as that?"

Jonathan began to tell the familiar tale of the *Tonquin's* ruthless captain, who had lost two boats with all hands in the terrible surf of this bar.

"But it's not blowing today. And the men have volunteered to go. Even Rory. He says he can slide down a rope as well as the next man and steer better than most."

"I forbid you to let him!"

She had not seriously considered Rory's offer, had mentioned it only to make small talk, perhaps to provoke a smile. But Jonathan was seizing on it as a pretext for another of his tirades on discipline and her ineptness at dealing with "men of this sort," who were only looking for the chance to desert. No doubt Rory could steer a skiff. Through the gap in the breakers and on to the beach. "We'd see no more of boat or men." The fellow should have been clapped into irons long since—would have to be when the ship made port, here or elsewhere, sooner or later.

Flagg had turtled his head deep into his shoulders and shut his eyes. Amanda judged from his reaction how outrageous the outburst was. But it did not touch her as this morning's quarrel had. Then there had been substance in the charges brought against her. Now she read them as signs of Jonathan's state of mind and health, as proof that he was less in command of himself than he believed.

She stood at the rail, watching the longboat creep toward the thin line of white, oars flashing now and then as they caught the sun. Already the face of Cape Bluff was turning red. Far to the south stood another cape, higher and darker, marked on the chart as Killamook Head. Inland and north of it was a great saddle-shaped mountain, behind which range after range of timbered hills were limned in indigo at their crests, fading to mist gray below.

Flagg leaned on the same rail but at some distance. She was grateful for his presence and his silence. He did mumble a word or two now and again, but she did not listen. She was busy with her own thoughts—mournful musings she could share only with Louisa.

Landfall, toward which she had yearned from the instant of departure (as recently as this time yesterday it had been the goal that blinded and deafened her to everything else), now hung over her like a verdict. She had thought of the end of the voyage as release from constraint, as the breaking of bonds, as freedom. How had she been so misguided as to take things for their opposites? The return to the world of men and women would cost something more precious than it could bestow: the power to control fate or at least to manipulate alternative fates, to make decisions that would affect the outcome of the struggle—a struggle in which her will was one element, only one among many, in which her life found its meaning, without which it was drift stuff.

The struggle was coming to an end. Words to console the dying. Life was struggles, one after another, overlapping and receding into the future like the blue-limned hills beyond the mountain there. Once such a vision of life would have dismayed her. What dismayed her now was the verdict that cut her off, required her to submit, resigned her to a long, gradual descent into limbo.

Flagg had edged closer, had just asked a question of her, was waiting for her answer. She nodded—it was easier than to ask him to repeat. He went on.

This time she listened with half her mind, caught a phrase here and there, lost others to the gulls that screamed indignation overhead, but she was able to fill in the gaps. It was as familiar as Mother Goose: words of counsel and comfort, the wisdom of old wives—and old husbands too, it seemed.

Men and women, being opposites by nature...and it stood to reason He had created them opposite, or why would He have fated them to be paired off? The good Lord knew what He was about. Male and female created He them, proving that disagreements were to be expected. Especially between such high-spirited folk as Jonathan and Amanda, who would strike sparks quicker than most. A marriage was a sort of voyage, when you came to think, bound to run into some bad weather along with the fine.

"Voyages come to an end," Amanda said.

Flagg sensed that his wisdom was being assailed, but he could not find a maxim with which defend it.

"And marriages too," she added.

Flagg looked at her as if he could not believe he had heard aright, but he dared not ask her to repeat. He licked his lips as if they had gone suddenly dry.

"I hope you'll do nothing in haste or in anger. For your sake as well as the skipper's," he said after a time. "Alone is hard. Very hard. Even for a man."

They sighted each other across the abyss of generation and gender, like ships that pass close in a storm, shout their names and home ports, but are forced apart without knowing for certain whether they were heard and understood.

September 23, 1851
2 P.M.   Cape Disappointment, hearing ESE, distant 6 miles.
  Latitude 46°16' N.
  Longitude 125°05' W.
Middle part of this day, weather clearing, wind NNW, fresh.

AMANDA BRIGHT'S JOURNAL

September 23, 1851

The longboat crew found an ample, though somewhat circuitous, passage through the sands at the river's mouth, and I intend to stand in for the bar soon after sunrise tomorrow. The flood begins then, high water just before 12:30. No pilot has appeared. On the chart I find assurance that a pilot schooner "with a fly at the main" is to be looked for near the entrance to the south channel or will respond to a signal gun. We shot off Mr. Smith's pistols at sundown. Perhaps by morning there will be some response.

-◇-

THE TWENTY-FOURTH DAY

I t was a sunrise of serenest peace. The air was fresh and cool but not chill. The land, blurred by the low, bright sun, was unreal as a mirage. The mouth of the river spread five miles from the northward cape of Point Adams, quiet as a pond, reflecting the sky, drawing the eye back into the apex of the perspective where it could make out the faint, perfect cone of a snow-covered mountain. Nothing moved anywhere in the scene.

Amanda was trying to keep track of the progress of the ship by the ranges it achieved and passed. They were moving south and east, parallel to the sands of Peacock Spit, passing the entrance to the north channel. *"Bring Point Adams in range with Coxcomb Hill...."* If she decided to enter by that channel, this was the moment to have the helm put down and the bow pointed east. *"Proceed till the beacon on Sand Island is in range with the second or inner peak of Point Ellice...crossing the south end of the north breakers."*

There was hardly enough wave movement to qualify as breakers, hardly enough breeze to keep the ship on course. They passed the first range and moved toward the second, where she would *"bring Point Adams in range with Flat or Table Hill, which will be seen a little to the nrd of Pillar Hill tree, remarkable as appearing like a tower on a high hill..."*

When ship and point and tree-topped hill were joined by an

imaginary line, the *Maria M.* would enter the "safe-beating channel," pull herself through the gauntlet, begin the final stanza of her saga....

The ship was hanging back. If she had been alone on the quarterdeck, Amanda would have spoken words of encouragement, as woman to the woman spirit indwelling in the bark: not to be daunted now, after all the dangers they had passed. But the quiet was such that even a whisper under her breath would be heard. Someone amidships called a question to the lookout, who answered that there was neither skiff nor schooner in sight. Someone else grumbled that a crew of good oarsmen could tow the ship faster than this. Someone else foresaw help from the tide that was coming on to flood.

The spanker boom swung and slatted. The configuration of hills and tongues of land was painted on a curtain of glass. Even in the near foreground nothing shifted position. The men stared at the drooping topsails, the limp jibs.

Amanda turned to ask a question, and her feet caught as if on the threshold of a doorway. She saw the men forward take the same staggering step. It was so gentle a shock that she did not know it for what it was. Movement that had been imperceptible was perceptibly halted.

"She's taken ground!"

The men turned to her for orders.

Jonathan was trying to get out of his bunk, but he was too weak. It was clear he could not manage the journey to the deck. He gave her commands to be relayed, the last being that Flagg and Willy were to come for him, to carry him up, as soon as they could be spared.

Amanda issued the orders and was obeyed with alacrity. There was a tingling of emergency—as if this delicate nuzzling of the shoal were as calamitous as the broaching in the storm. Men flew about the deck and rigging, furling sails, frapping lines about gaffs and booms, rowing out to take soundings—in silence. Even such ordinarily noisy objects as blocks, oarlocks, timbers, canvas, and chains were mute.

By the time Jonathan was settled in a chair on the quarterdeck,

Davy was back from the exploration in the longboat. The vessel's bow was aground in ten feet of water; the stern was free; the bottom shelved sharply; there was four fathoms a few yards to seaward; and anchoring depths could be found less than fifty yards away.

"She might float herself off yet," Flagg told Willy within Amanda's hearing. "The flood's still coming, and there's no wind to drive her harder on.

Willy asked if it would help to throw weight overboard. No one answered. Jonathan must have heard, but he did not choose to respond, and no one else presumed to.

His orders, given in so low a voice that Amanda had to repeat them, were concerned with a kedge anchor. It was to be lowered into the longboat, rowed out to four fathoms, and let go. When they were sure it was holding, a cable was to be led through the freeing port of the quarterdeck to the jeer capstan. All hands were to man the bars.

"The stern is to be pulled off sideways. Mind that the angle is no more than forty-five degrees. And take care with the chafing gear where the cable goes over the plank-sheer."

The silence was overlaid by bustle and chatter, much ado about minutiae—like women outside a sickroom or in the kitchen of a house where death has come, keeping up their own cheer and making a brave noise to frighten off the devils of despair. But the men did their work well and quickly, coming back for new or more precise orders. Not from her, though it was she who answered them. She spoke for Jonathan. That was obvious to everyone. He was again in command.

The wind had revived, and there were breakers all along the flank of the Middle Sands, foaming around the hull and throwing spray almost to the deck. Despite the furled sails, the bark was pressed hard against the soft cheek of the shoal, so that little by little sand and silt gave way and began to re-form around the hull. For the first time, Amanda felt the passage of time as the twisting of a noose. There was nothing to do, no way to relieve the contorting tension, except to scan the horizon for the pilot schooner, as if its appearance even now would mean rescue.

The capstan bars were inserted in the pigeonholes. The men took their places, all hands except Rory, who hung about, looking as if he hoped to be called but feared to come without being called as long as Jonathan sat enthroned.

"Heave ho!"

Someone started a chantey, but there was no response. The line wound itself around the barrel of the capstan till the cable went taut and squeaked against the mat of sennit placed between it and the hull. Men strained and the ship strained. The sun shone hot and heartless. The wind died a second death.

Once there was a lurching movement. The men staggered forward and asked, "Did she move?" The consensus was that she had not; the cable had slipped a few inches to one side. The angle was not what Jonathan had hoped for, but it could not be corrected now.

Jonathan asked the time. It was a quarter after twelve. "And when is high water?"

"At 12:22. Seven minutes from now."

"We can have one more try at it."

But the ship did not budge.

Suddenly a distraction—voices hailing from the water level on the port bow. A canoe full of Indians had approached without being noticed. They were tying up to the longboat, which was tied at the foot of the Jacob's ladder.

The Indians were miserably clad in ragged remnants of white men's clothing and not prepossessing in other respects, but Amanda expected Jonathan to grant at least one of them permission to board. They had, after all, "local knowledge." Instead, he gave orders that they were to be driven off.

That was easier to order than to accomplish, and not until one of Smith's pistols had been reloaded and fired over their heads did they back their canoe off and head upstream in the direction of Point Adams. By this time the flood and the brief slack that followed it were past, and the ebb had begun.

Jonathan was exhausted, and the effort of concealing the fact was tiring him further. By a heroic—and, Amanda thought, unnecessary—effort, he made his way unassisted to the companion ladder and down it. But Flagg and Willy had to make a chair of their hands and forearms to get him back to the sofa, where he could rest.

As they carried him past Smith's stateroom, he said, "I'd like a word with the mate."

Amanda held the door open. Jonathan stood in it. Smith raised himself on one elbow to greet his visitor. Little was said, but something passed between the men. She could feel its substance but could not decipher its message. But she was sure it had nothing to do with the task that had united them in the past, nor the illness that had interrupted it, nor their chances of surviving. It was a recognition, not of each other as equals—they were still master and mate, superior and subordinate—but of something that took precedence over rank and difference and joined them in an exclusive fraternity of despair.

On deck the men were talking in low voices, silenced by her approach. Their manner toward her was altered, respectful but evasive, as if no one knew what to make of her now that she had been toppled from the eminence they had only just learned to accept. They were made uneasy, and she was made sad.

She relayed the captain's orders to the bosun: the chafing gear was to be reinforced in case the wind picked up, as it already had. If there was any sign that the kedge was not holding, Jonathan was to be called. The stream anchor could be lowered in deeper water if necessary. There would be another flood tide around midnight and another chance to pull her off—"If the wind hasn't whipped up a surf that beats us to death on the bar."

Amanda did not relay that last, but she could see in the faces of those who listened, that they knew.

September 24, 1851
Dear Mother and Father:
We are close to Astoria, an American port near the mouth of the Columbia. If all goes well, we shall be anchored here before long, and I hope to be able to dispatch this letter, along with one

to Aunt Aggie and Uncle Matthew. Together they will give an account of this unlucky voyage, which is coming to its end. At least so far as I am concerned.

Jonathan has been very ill and is not yet recovered, but I foresee he will insist upon continuing as planned. If he does, and does not require my assistance, I should like to come home.

She broke off to see who was moving about in the pantry. It was Cook, who had made some gruel and brought it himself, instead of sending it by Willy, because he wanted a word with her in confidence.

AMANDA BRIGHT'S JOURNAL

September 24, 1851

Cook is alarmed about a possibility that had not occurred to me nor—so far as I know—to Jonathan. He says there will almost surely be (from which I take it, there already is) a sentiment amongst the men to leave the ship while there is a chance of reaching shore in safety.

There are three boats: one already in the water, two others carried on the roof on the deckhouse. Room enough for all fourteen of us, including the invalids, and a distance of less than four miles to Baker's Bay, where there are said to be white settlers, as well as the Negro pilot and some Indians. The best chance would be at the bottom of the ebb, which will come after dark.

To leave the ship stranded would be to consign her and her cargo to destruction by the waves or pillage by the Indians who visited us this morning. To stay, on the other hand, risks the lives of everyone. (So Cook believes that the men believe.) I am incompetent to judge, but Jonathan has spoken several times of vessels larger and stouter than ours being reduced to splinters. Conditions are favorable, but they can change—and very quickly. This is a cape of storms.

·✧·

It was the old contradiction: the rights of the owners, of property, against the rights of propertyless men. The captain was the fulcrum on which the balance rested; sworn to protect and further the interests of one, his fate tied to the fate of the others; bound by something misnamed honor. To leave his ship would cost him that something; not to leave it might cost his life—his life and hers and all the rest.

Jonathan would not give the order to take to the boats. Not if the peril were twice as great or the chance of escaping it twice as clear. So long as he was in command, he would hold to the law by which he lived: the ship, the cargo, the course laid out, the quickest passage possible, the greatest profit.

And if Jonathan stayed, everyone must stay. Eight men had not been able to move the ship at noon; fewer than that number would not move it at midnight, even if the flood granted them a few extra inches of grace.

Amanda was not sure why Cook had brought his confidence to her. Was she expected to persuade Jonathan to make the impossible choice? Or warn him of the danger of rebellion? Or resume the mantle of authority and give the orders? She toyed for a moment with that notion: saw herself on the quarterdeck watching the boats being lowered from the deckhouse, waiting till all was ready, then sending someone below to bring the captain—sleeping? drugged to sleep? It was so utterly unacceptable that she pushed it away and with it the whole nexus of alternatives.

Low water came a little earlier than she had anticipated. The sands were not uncovered except at the foot of the beacon on Sand Island, which gleamed as if it held a lantern. The deck of the ship was listing perceptibly. Some loose object, forgotten in the general securing and battening, rolled from starboard to port, suggesting that the ship might also be tempted to roll over and rest on the bed of the shoal.

Amanda watched the sun sink and the light on the beacon go out. The men watched the cape or stared upriver.

There was something so unnerving in their silence that Amanda retreated from it and went below.

Jonathan was awake and drinking the soup Cook had left for him.

He had new orders for her to relay: the bilges were to be sounded; Kankkonen was to bring down the pistols for reloading; Cook was to brew some tea and lace it with rum to hand round at eleven, at which time, he, Jonathan, was to be helped on deck. He finished with a question. "How is the wind?"

"No stronger. And still northwest."

"It may change with the start of the flood. If not, we can count ourselves lucky. Unless the hull has worked more than I expect."

The report came back: not quite four inches of water in the hole. Jonathan was not alarmed, but he ordered the pumps manned. "It'll give them something to do while they wait."

Amanda went to her bunk and lay down, sustaining her position, despite the list, by a constant muscular effort that kept her from sleep, thinking back over those parts of the day that had given her no time to think—like that exchange of looks between Jonathan and Smith. She had felt excluded from some private anguish. Was it the vanquishing of *hubris* by which such men defined themselves? A recognition of their mutual defeat by an enemy whose victory was not yet apparent to the ignorant toilers before the mast...or to her?

She was drifting into doze when she remembered that the letter to her parents lay unfinished on her desk. She had forgotten to put it away. After her talk with Cook, she had made an entry in her journal and put that away when she was done, but the letter lay open, an arm's reach from the sofa on which Jonathan slept, if he slept. He could easily have glanced at it and learned that she intended to leave him.

She thought about rising to retrieve it and found she had neither the will nor the desire.

Some time after she fell asleep, there was a scuffle on deck. It did not wake her. She remembered it after the shots that did wake her.

Three men had escaped in the longboat: Rory, Tono, Kanaka Jim. The Polynesians had gone first over the side and down the ladder, then held it steady for Rory. He was clumsy getting his splinted leg over the bulwarks, made a noise, was discovered, and ordered to halt. Kankkonen fired both pistols and missed. If he had been trusted with a revolver, he said it would have turned out different.

Willy and Cook took the places of Tono and the Hawaiian in the midnight effort to kedge off the shoal, but the effort failed. There was talk of letting go the stream anchor in a more advantageous place, of lightening the ship by bringing up ballast from the hold. But all such measures were postponed till the morning.

If the ship lasted out the night—and it would if the wind did not rise—there was still hope. The morning flood might be a trifle higher. Even inches would make all the difference between victory and disaster.

THE TWENTY-FIFTH DAY

She slept poorly after the excitement. She wanted to go on deck, if only to reassure herself that nothing serious was amiss. But she had no place there now. The men would not welcome her.

At dawn she did go up to watch the light come, revealing an awesome stretch of bare sand that led almost from the trapped ship to the beacon, so that it seemed one might wade only a few yards and then walk ashore.

She looked in on Smith. They spoke of the wind, the time and height of tides. He thanked her again for her kindness to him, as if he felt obliged to speak before it was too late. His voice was toneless, flat, removed.

September 25, 1851

Cape Disappointment: 46°16' North, 124°01' W.

Ship took the ground on western flank of Middle Sands approx. 10:30 A.M., Sept. 24, in a dead calm.

Hull has worked some during the night. Four inches of water in the hole, but pumps keep it down.

Low water 6:45 this A.M., a minus tide. High water 12:50.

Wind moderate during middle part; dropped during midwatch.

Good prospects for kedging off if calm continues and flood is as high or higher than previous.

The log entry was Jonathan's, dictated to her, signed by him; it was the first he had made since his illness.

After she had helped him to the bath, where he wanted to trim his beard and wash up a bit, Amanda tidied the desk and found her letter. There was no way of telling whether it had been read.

Jonathan was dressed and ready to go up, when there was a hallooing from the stern. He emerged on the afterdeck, Amanda following to help him with the steps, in time to witness the skiff's approach. The man who rowed out from Cape Disappointment was not the black pilot Rory had talked of but a white man named John Pickernell. He lived near the "broom-top trees," he said, and had been a pilot till the "New York fellows" who owned the schooner *Mary Taylor* persuaded the territorial government to give them an exclusive franchise to guide vessels over the bar, in return for their promise to patrol the river mouth at all times.

"But you tried to raise them and couldn't, could you?"

Pickernell hoped the captain would report in Astoria on how Messrs. Hustler and White kept to their contract. "That is, if you get yourself off the shoal there. And you've them to blame if you don't." The delinquent pilots would most likely claim they had put in for supplies. But how long did that need to take? Unless, of course, one were putting in the sort of supplies that had to be slept off.

Jonathan questioned him about the tides and learned that the higher of the two floods came at midday this time of the year. Today's would be as high as yesterday's, give or take a few inches, depending on the wind. "The more wind you got, the more water. So long as it's from the nor'west, which is generally how she blows hereabouts."

"We haven't seen much wind from any quarter.

"Ah, but she'll fool you. Whistles up out of a dead calm and a clear sky. That's one thing makes the bar here bad."

Pickernell maneuvered his skiff close under the counter to ask if there was any way in which he might be of help. It had the sound of an offer of last rites. Jonathan seemed to hesitate, and Amanda thought he sighed.

"Could you put a couple of passengers ashore?" he asked. "We've had sickness aboard."

Pickernell could, and his wife, who was part Indian, had a hand for curing the sick.

"Will you ask Mr. Smith if he wants to be put ashore?" Jonathan spoke quietly to Amanda. "Explain to him that if we're not able to get her off this time, we may be in for trouble. There are places enough in the boats for all, if it comes to that, and if the weather is halfway decent…but if not…well, he will understand the position. He can decide."

She went on the errand and brought back the answer she could have given without troubling Smith. He was not up to the effort nor willing to risk being left in this wilderness. He preferred to take his chances with the rest of the company.

"I would like you to go, Amanda."

She refused.

Their eyes met and held as each tried to read what the other was thinking but not trusting to words. Amanda thought she saw anger. What if he were to order her to go? Could she defy the authority on which everyone's safety depended?

But all Jonathan said was, "Maybe you didn't understand what he said just now about the wind—I want to spare you, Amanda." He sounded close to tears, and that moved her. But while she groped for a way to explain her unwillingness to leave him, he offered the final, unassailable argument. "And there's no reason! You can do nothing by staying."

Nothing he could have said after that would have persuaded her to obey him. Perhaps he saw that in her face. Or perhaps Pickernell's next question drove everything else from his mind.

The man had pulled his skiff all the way round the ship—"like he was measuring us for coffins," someone growled—and now he was back at the stern.

"Meant to ask: did you lose a boat in the night? I see you got two on deck there but none in the water. Thought the one I seen might 'a been yours."

"You saw a longboat?"

"Floating belly-up in the cove just northward of the bluff there." He had searched the shore for bodies—as if this were one of his regular morning chores—and finding none had concluded, "She might 'a just worked herself loose."

Jonathan did not dispute the conclusion. The unlicensed pilot pulled away, leaving behind him a great emptiness of time and of hope.

The pumps had begun again. The monotonous ugliness of their racket scraped holes in the shell of fortitude, and doubt seeped in. The water creeping up over the sands was also creeping into the ship's strained hull, tying it down while the wind hurried from the north. The pumpers were shamans, menacing the devil with drum and rattle, but the devil was too strong for them.

Jonathan ordered the boats from the deckhouse lowered into the water and the bower anchors got over.

"Are you going to cut them loose to lighten the ship?" Amanda asked.

He seemed shocked by her question, but he answered it. Anchors were not the sort of thing one jettisoned; they would be needed to hold the ship once she was clear of the bar. "If the wind doesn't come up or comes up from the wrong quarter, we could be driven back onto the shoal."

They began with the kedging a little before noon. The channel had been sounded again. There was still plenty of water where the kedge had been dropped, and it was still holding. The possibility of using the stream anchor as well was discussed and discarded. Jonathan consulted with several of the A.B.'s—including Davy!— and there was consensus: neither a heavier anchor nor a better angle would materially alter their chances. It was simply a matter of strength, the tide's and the men's—one floating, the other pulling on the hull.

"All hands, then, heave!"

They strained against the capstan bars. Rested and breathed. Strained again.

It was hot with no wind to cool the sweat. Some of the men stripped to the waist. Others wore shirts as thin as a woman's scarf, which clung to them like wet drapery.

"Heave then, ho!"

They tried again and again to move her. Rested. Breathed. Tried again. Failed again. Ordered, cajoled, encouraged, berated, belabored, and begged by Jonathan. (What had become of his Jovian dignity?) Like the painted ponies of a merry-go-round, all shapes and sizes and colors: African, Hawaiian, Finnish, English, American, and the man from the country without a name, all moving to the music of the protest of their bodies: grunt, wheeze, fart, groan.

Everyone heard eight bells strike at the start of the ordeal. Amanda felt that only she heard the half hour strike. By the time another half hour had passed, it would be finished. The ship would be lost. There would be no way to save the lives of those she carried but by abandoning ship.

"Abandon ship...abandon hope..."

It was hard to believe in this silent, sunlit calm that the sea and the wind were still conspiring against man, the intruder—plotting how to destroy him, how to rise and smash his floating cradle with one blow of a watery fist, delivering his body to the icy water that would take his breath and never give it back. As it had done with Horace.

She had been watching Jonathan without seeing him. Suddenly she was aware that he was on his feet. His legs were trembling, threatening at any moment to give way under him, but he seemed not to notice. He had transcended his mortal weakness like a Greek actor who "became" for the moment the god he portrayed.

His hands clutched an imaginary capstan bar. His chest heaved—between shouts of encouragement to the men—as if he strained with them. He was making a magic to move the ship. Energy streamed from him and touched every man on the deck, binding them together, raising them to a power higher than the sum of their separate strengths. It was costing him more than she believed he could pay, but it was compelling. Amanda responded as if to a natural force like gravity.

The nearest man to where she stood was Cook. She motioned to him to slide his hands closer to the barrel and make room for her. Someone gasped a sort of cheer. There was a gabble of advice and encouragement, directions for getting a better grip on the bar, a better purchase for her feet. No-Name, whom she could see by turning her head a little, was making desperate sounds in his throat, trying to convey something. She smiled at him and shut her eyes so as not to be distracted, put her shoulder against her hand and wrist, and the weight of her body behind the shoulder.

Jonathan was still shouting, the men still straining. She could smell their sweat and now and then a fart. The odors did not disgust her any more than the odors of her own body. She felt the hot skin of Cook's arm slip against hers as his grip shifted. Opening her eyes an instant, she caught a glimpse of muscle bunching over ridges of rib—Davy's, she guessed, by the fish-belly whiteness of the skin.

Then the ship moved.

Only an inch, but everyone felt it. No one spoke. No one ceased to strain. Only to breathe! Again they felt it! This time the pawl clinked in the drumhead. It was coming now, the miracle. Coming…the pawls clinked again…again.

"Don't slack off! Keep her moving! Faster, so she won't settle back. You're almost there. One more heave, men. Another…another…and one more!"

She had stopped breathing so long ago that the blood had stopped moving through veins and arteries. Her muscles were starving, cramping. Only the inert weight of her body was touching the bar, but the bar moved. Her feet stumbled, hurrying to catch up. The ship was dragging men and capstan bar in her wake.

Jonathan began reeling off new commands. Men dropped the capstan bars and hurried to new posts. Amanda stood aside. Her lungs filled and she coughed. Blood stung as it returned to armpits, elbows, wrists, fingers.

Davy caught her eye as he passed; whatever had been broken was whole again. No-Name threw her a look of love. Cook's teeth flashed in his dark face as he made another turn, working the capstan bar as if it were the handle of an oar. Willy was on the bar opposite, his head thrown back as if he were laughing—or shouting.

All her life to come, whenever—if ever again—she was committed to an effort that drained all her strength (the bearing of a child, perhaps?) she would remember this moment, now already past—the human hawser, unraveling, the bundle of separate selves wound like strands of a cable: bone, muscle, blood, breath…beyond manhood and womanhood.

The wind had sprung up. She was cold. Alone in her single self and cold.

The pilot schooner *Mary Taylor* was within hail by the time they brought the *Maria M.* to the kedge. A few minutes later Captain Hustler came aboard. He and Jonathan stood on the afterdeck, talking, explaining, accounting for delays and disasters—mantalk delivered in the shorthand of a log.

A regular killer whale, that shoal. Not many got off her, once on. Act of Providence, piece of luck. The loss of three men, all drowned, bodies found by the Indians off Point Adams. Apologies: the rain and the wind, no deckhouse on the schooner. North channel or south? South, no question about it.

Later, when they were close enough to see houses on the tongue of land between the two rivers, Jonathan asked about replacements: mates and men who could hand, reef, and steer. Captain Hustler was not encouraging. Oregon was not California. But then it was not Tierra del Fuego, either. In Astoria one could do business. Produce from the Islands would bring good prices, but there would be few, if any, furs to trade.

Candor forced the captain to admit that one could do better, all things considered, upriver at Oregon City or the new town that called itself Portland, after the one in Maine. But replacements would be a problem even there, unless one was heading south to San Francisco. The gold fever was still high, and there would be many a settler willing to sign on for that passage.

Amanda stood apart from the captains. She had become invisible again.

6

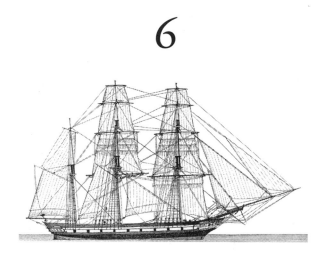

Departure

THE FIRST MONTH

October 25, 1851
Portland, Oregon Territory
Dear Mother and Father:

I am enclosing with this a family letter begun more than a
month since. Jonathan should have taken it with him to dispatch
with my letter to Aunt Aggie and Uncle Matthew, but in the
last-minute flurry of preparations for his departure there was no
time to finish it. Now there is a good deal to add.

As I foresaw, Jonathan is determined to continue on the voyage as originally planned. He was able to dispose of a good part
of our trade goods here and loaded on a quantity of sawn lumber
that will fetch a fine price in San Francisco. When he has done
his business there and found replacements for the men lost on our
passage from Ouwahoo, he will sail for the coast of China, stopping only to provision in the Sandwich Islands.

As I am not agreeable to so prolonged a prospect, I have persuaded him to leave me here (in the care of the wife of the Epis-
copal minister) until there is an opportunity to take passage in a
vessel bound for home.

Amanda stopped. If she was not yet prepared to give an account
of her separation from Jonathan by letter, it would be worse to
let the bare fact of it leak through the sieve of a clumsy deception.

Father would know that no vessels departed from this remote coast, bound round the Horn or even for the Isthmus of Panama, without stopping first at San Francisco. He would ask why she had not sailed that far on the *Maria M.*

The paragraph would have to be recast to make it appear—without actually lying—that Jonathan intended to head straight west from the mouth of the Columbia. Meanwhile she could safely expand on her hope of shortening the journey and easing its hardships by using the land bridge of Panama.

> *There is a great traffic between this place and San Francisco and an even greater one between San Francisco and Panama. I am reliably informed that a railroad is being constructed across the narrowest part of that isthmus to convey passengers from the ports of one ocean to the other. I have some hope it will be completed by the time I can reach its Pacific terminus.*
>
> *For the present, I am comfortably situated and feel closer to home than I have in over a year. That is, of course, the case, but I feel it more keenly because of the atmosphere in this house. Mrs. Holloway was raised in Rhode Island, which makes her as much a New Englander as I, and there are many touches in her home and way of keeping it that remind me of my own.*
>
> *What surprises me even more than the sharpness of my longing for home is the joy I take in the company of women. It is long since I have had intimate discourse with one of my own sex, and I did not know how badly I wanted it. I say "women" because there is a third female in our household—the Indian wife of a white settler, named Tassy. Although she learned English in a mission school in the Territory, she is not much of a conversationalist. But she is clean in her habits (it is commonly believed by the whites hereabouts that Indians are not) and adds much to our comfort by her knowledge of native foods that are free for the gathering.*
>
> *No two women could appear more unlike than these, my two companions. Tassy is small, supple, and of a color darker than her buckskin dress; Mrs. Holloway is large-boned, awkward in movement, and so pale that one feels she has not yet recovered*

from the rigors of her trek across the western desert. Yet they work together like horses long hitched to the same carriage and give every evidence of mutual affection.

Tassy's husband, John Whitt, and the Reverend Holloway took passage with Jonathan, being convinced, like every other able-bodied male, that a fortune is to be made in short order in the mines of California. The Reverend Holloway intends to use the gold he digs to finance the building of a church edifice. Services are conducted now in such places as a warehouse, a sawmill, and the residence of one of his more comfortably housed parishioners. John Whitt means to buy cattle and drive them here by the overland route. Neither man is a skilled foremasthand, but Jonathan had not much to choose from, and Mr. Smith has recovered sufficiently to continue in his lighter duties, one of which will be to assist these green hands

She had blundered into another betrayal. Everything she had written up to this point would have to be recopied. She started a new sheet and a safer subject.

Portland is a town in its infancy. It was baptized only within the year and came within the toss of a coin of being named Boston. It has other, older rivals in the vicinity, including Oregon City, the main settlement of the Territory, situated farther up the river (the Willamette, not the Columbia) at the foot of a considerable falls.

What gives Portland promise of preeminence is the deep water here. Oceangoing vessels can moor or tie up at its new wharf at any season—as they cannot farther upstream. Also there is a new road (still being planked) that leads over the crest of hills behind the town into the wide Tualatin Valley. There are many new settlers there, for the land is rich and produces as soon as it is put to the plough.

Portland aspires to be the nexus of trade between the river (and the ocean beyond) and the plains. It is growing at a pace one can actually hear. Every morning, as soon as there is light, broadaxes, saws, hammers, and the shouts of drovers make a chorus that drowns out birdsong. Not that I would lie abed and listen to that music in any case. For we too are up with the light.

Though the cabin is small, it shelters six human beings with mouths to be fed. Although fourteen by sixteen feet is not large by ordinary standards, it does not seem cramped to one who has spent a long time aboard ship. Mrs. Holloway has a three-year-old daughter and an infant son. Tassy (whose Indian name no white person seems able to pronounce) has a papoose whose age I can only guess, since she does not permit him to walk, though I believe he would be able to.

Our diet is for the most part fish—salmon—in various guises and potatoes or boiled wheat. Now and then there is white flour for a pie when Tassy has gathered berries enough to fill it. Sugar is very dear, and butter almost unobtainable. But thanks to Tassy we have an abundance of wild fruits and some palatable roots, sweet and of pleasant, if unusual, flavor. Mrs. Holloway says that in the spring Tassy will be able to provide us with fresh greens of many kinds.

There is every reason to believe I shall remain here till spring. There is little traffic on the river during the winter months, which are almost upon us. What vessels do beat up the coast from California face a return passage so perilous that I am reluctant to make the attempt. The flooding of the tributary rivers often fills the main channel of the Columbia with treacherous sandbanks. And even if a ship is lucky enough to traverse the bar unscathed, at sea it is the season of gales.

The climate is not so severe as that of Massachusetts (although the latitude is considerably north of Portland, Maine). We are to expect little snow, except in the high elevations of the mountains to the east. The rains are to be heavy. Already they are turning the unpaved streets of the town to mire. But I am content in my present circumstances and shall not be in a hurry to depart before the spring freshet, unless some irresistible opportunity offers, in which unlikely case I may embrace you both

soon after this letter arrives. Otherwise, it will surely be soon
after the summer solstice.

Your loving daughter,
Amanda

She reread the whole of her letter, noting the revisions that must be made. It was possible to explain the absence of her housemates' husbands without involving Jonathan and the *Maria M.* Simply, they had gone gold hunting, like half the men in the Territory, never mind by what conveyance. And she could easily alter the first pages to leave the impression that Jonathan intended to dispose of his cargo of lumber in Ouwahoo.

What was not so easy to remedy was her inadequate excuse for remaining in Portland till spring. Father would know that it was all but impossible to journey overland to the east or south. And he would also know—or be so informed by any seagoing acquaintance of whom he made inquiry—that many vessels put into the Columbia and left its ports during the months of September and October. Why had she not taken passage on one of them?

She could think of no explanation but the truth: she did not have the passage money and would not accept it from Jonathan. It was foolhardy bravado. She could see that now. But at the time she was too angry to be prudent.

"I quite understand your wishing to go home," Jonathan said soon after they moored at the bend of the river in front of the new settlement. (He *had* read her letter to her parents.) "If you remember, I warned you that a voyage like this was not for a woman."

Perhaps not, though this woman had weathered the voyage better than he. But Amanda said only, "It's not the hardships I mind."

Jonathan gave her a chance to continue, to expand on her dissatisfactions, but it was hard to put into words he would understand feelings he could not possibly share.

"I am...not the same person I was," she began uncertainly. "I don't believe I could...be content...unoccupied..."

"Perhaps you'd like to have the keeping of the log?" Jonathan sounded cheerful and eager. "On most vessels it's one of the mate's tasks, but I let Smith off because I don't much like his way of putting things. And I keep my own log in any case."

"And would if I were log keeper?"

He studied her as if she were a blurred chart. "Just what is it you want, Amanda?" he asked at last.

She tried again, even harder, to find words for it. "To...be useful." But that was not it. Not at all! She sounded like a humble suppliant. *"I am Ruth, thine handmaiden...."* And Jonathan was as magnanimous as Boaz.

He put his arm around her shoulders and gave them a gently playful squeeze. There would be ample opportunity for usefulness, he assured her. Though he did hope there would be no further occasion for her services as nurse. She might practice with the sextant when it was not in use. He could set her problems to solve. "I told you you'd have a knack for navigation."

She heard a note of condescension in his voice, and it blew life into a fire that had been smoldering since he proposed to put her ashore with Smith. And her anger blew life into his.

She reminded him that she had solved the problems set by the voyage itself and brought the ship safely through its perils. He reminded her that she had put the ship aground because she assumed authority she was not competent to exercise. Each accused the other of overweening pride and as many collateral sins as they could call to mind.

It ended with Amanda demanding to be put ashore at once. She had seen a small hotel on the street that fronted the river. She would take a room there until she could make arrangements for passage home.

Jonathan left the cabin without another word. He did not return till late in the evening.

"I'm sorry to have to tell you there is no room available at the City Hotel," he said, looking past her, refusing to meet her eyes.

Amanda was not entirely sorry to hear this news, but she could not think how to say so, and he gave her little time.

"I'm making inquiries about other possibilities," he said in a voice so cold it made her want to draw her shawl closer. "In the meantime you may rest assured I shall not disturb you here."

For the days it took to unload the cargo he was selling and to load the sawn lumber he was buying, he did not come near her. Whether he slept aboard or ashore, where he took his meals, Amanda did not know. Nor was there anyone to ask. She was a prisoner in solitary confinement. Even when she went on deck for air, everyone seemed to avoid her. Except No-Name. He always caught her eye and smiled—but he could not speak.

She had time to sort out her anger, to see that there was some justice in Jonathan's contention that she put the ship aground because she lacked experience and the knowledge it gave. And injustice in his overlooking all else, focusing only on her failure. If they could have begun again, she would have argued better. Perhaps he too would have given ground....

But while this anger cooled, another had begun to burn in her. She was discovering that she had run aground in another sense. Again it was because she lacked knowledge—knowledge of the world and how pitifully few resources she had with which to sustain herself in it. A common sailor who jumped ship could find his way anywhere. But who would give a berth to a woman who knew something of celestial navigation, a good deal about embroidery, less about nursing, and even less about cookery?

At home or in any civilized state she might set herself up as a shopkeeper or find work as a teacher. But here, at the edge of the wilderness, she was a beached fish.

Then one afternoon Jonathan came to the cabin to convey an invitation for her to "keep Mrs. Holloway company while the reverend is away."

His voice was not as chilling as it had been last time she heard it, but the distance between them seemed greater than ever. As if the bond had been severed so long ago that all feeling had faded. As if all that remained was items of business.

"You may stay with the Holloways as long as you like. But as soon as you can get passage to San Francisco, you should take it. There are emigrant steamers from Panama making port there every week, and most return half-empty." He explained about the new railroad across the isthmus and the regularity with which ships sailed between its Atlantic terminus and New England ports. And he laid on the green baize table a packet of money that "should cover all necessary costs."

Then for the first time, he looked at her. Straight at her. But only for a moment, and the light was behind him. Amanda could not read his face.

She accepted the offer of sanctuary because she had no choice. Jonathan had said the ship would drop downriver with the change of the tide, which left hardly enough time for her to stuff a bag with her warm clothes, Horace's journal and his copy of Emerson's *Poems,* her own journal and copy of the New Testament, comb, brush, and writing implements.

The packet of money she left untouched on the green baize table.

The first night ashore she could not rid herself of the sensation of the ship rolling under her. Mrs. Holloway saw her nodding and insisted that she retire, pulling a white muslin curtain across the corner of the cabin where a bough bed had been prepared for her. Amanda was to make herself comfortable and have a good rest. There would be time in the morning to begin to know each other and to explore the settlement.

She could smell the fir branches of the bed through the quilt that covered them and hear the murmurs of the child and the infant and the other woman. She knew where she was. And yet the sea heaved and cradled her. She closed her eyes and let it have its way....

She was in her stateroom, dressing to go ashore as soon as the anchor was let go. The vessel was still under way, and there was time, plenty of time. But just as she pulled the stays of her corset tight and tied the laces, she was called. Something had happened that required her presence on deck.

She stood in full sunshine, wearing only her low-necked chemise, ruffle drawers, and the corsets that pushed her breasts high and full. The sunlight touched the bare skin like a lover's fingers...like a lover's breath....

No one noticed her in the confusion. She herself was only gradually aware of the unseemliness of her exposure, but she pretended not to be, hoping this would prevent others from remarking it. Everyone's attention was on something else, something that did not concern her. It seemed she was not needed after all.

She would have gone below, but someone was watching her.

All the rest were hurrying here and there, pulling and hauling, making a great uproar. Were they launching the longboat? Was this a landfall? She could have answered simply by turning her head to look, but she was transfixed by desire—her own and that of the man.

She could not see his face. He was standing behind her, but she could feel his eyes. Now his hands came from behind to close over her breasts, cupping them, pulling her back against him so that she could feel his body, feel his penis swelling and pushing against her buttocks. The corsets were peeling away like leaves from a heart of palm....

Where had she seen those curled white stalks of unborn palm, pulled, one after the other, from the central bud? Somewhere along a white coral beach....

Some heavy object was dropped on the puncheon, and she awoke. While she lay with eyes closed, waiting for some other sound to follow, she breathed the smells of fir, woodsmoke, and leather, and pictured the room, its other occupants, the confines of her new life.

The noise was not repeated, and she tried to burrow her way back into the dream.

She had lost it, but she remembered where she had eaten the heart of palm. It was on the island of Maui, one of those perfect days ashore with Jonathan.... *"There are places I've wanted to show you since first I clapped eyes on them...."*

They had hired horses and ridden on the quiet leeward beach and come upon a palm that had been undermined by the surf. Two islanders with great curved knives were hacking out the treasured heart. One of them offered her a slice. It was tender and sweet, delicately delicious.

The next day they rode to the interior, over plains of red dust, through the forests of strange trees and giant ferns, through layers of cloud, across wastelands of volcano slag, up, up, to the rim of the great crater. As the sun was setting behind them, they looked down into the caldron where dead rivers of lava coiled round cones and pinnacles of ash; then wrapped themselves in blankets against the chill of the heights and slept, fitfully, in each other's arms....

THE SECOND MONTH

AMANDA BRIGHT'S JOURNAL

November 22, 1851
Portland

I have quite given up writing a journal, but not because there is too little to write about. There is too much and too little time. The days at this season are pitifully short. The evenings are very long, and there is enough light from the fire, but there is always some task at which my companions are busy—spinning knitting, mending, and when all else is done, the piecing of a quilt. It has never seemed right to open my journal and retire into my private thoughts.

Tonight is sadly different.

We are sitting vigil at the bedside of one of the Holloway children—little Janet, who is running a high fever. Mrs. Holloway sent Tassy for one of the older neighbors who is reputed to have skills in midwifery and medicine. She brought a jar of bear grease, a bottle of turpentine, and a bag full of simples. If I had my Guide *or the medicine chest to which it was* Companion, *I would have offered my own advice. Instead I have brewed tea, heated water for a bath (in case of a convulsion), and helped to rub the little sufferer with a repulsive mixture of grease and turpentine. Now, several hours later, we are still waiting for the fever to break.*

Outside it has been blowing a gale since morning. While there was light enough to see the great trees that surround us, I bundled myself in shawls and went outside to watch how they meet the wind. The cedars seem almost impervious to its force. Their thick foliage absorbs it like the feathers of a ruffled hen. The spruces and hemlocks dance to it, but in different fashions. The spruces exult. They sway and thrash in passionate abandon, while the hemlocks, whose branches droop as persistently as the spruces' reach skyward, writhe in a pantomime of grief. In the air above, the gulls hang motionless, as they do at sea.

If I close my eyes, I can see the heaving great swells, but I no longer feel them. Nor do I feel the rise and fall of pressure as I once did. I am losing my weather sense along with my sea legs. When

I have just been asked by Mrs. Holloway when I am expecting! The question so startled me that I have only a vague idea what I replied. I am writing to compose myself, to consider what I should say.

I realize now that she has never asked how I came to leave the ship. She believes I am pregnant. That I prefer to pass my waiting time ashore. That Jonathan means to return in time for the birth of our child. Whether he told them something of the kind or whether she and her husband hit upon this as the most plausible of explanations, I don't know, nor dare I inquire.

I must set matters straight. But I am apprehensive that my new and dear friend will neither understand nor approve.

·✦·

L ittle Janet stirred and whimpered. The three women were at the trundle bed in an instant, but the child did not wake. Tassy touched her forehead gently and signed that there was no change. They settled back again to wait.

Amanda knew she must not let silence lie for her. She cleared her throat and began. "I am not with child."

Mrs. Holloway caught a breath like a sob. Her eyes filled with tears, and she reached across the space between them to lay a comforting hand on Amanda's. Was she quite sure? One could not always go by the ordinary signs. How long had she and the captain been childless? Had she miscarried before?

Amanda could not frame answers quickly enough to interrupt the nervous flow of her friend's consolation.

She was not to be discouraged or downhearted. She was not old enough to give up hope, though it was not easy to bear one's first child after twenty. Many a woman who thought herself barren had conceived and carried a child to term. Some, more than one. Perhaps it would turn out that Amanda was to be blessed after all, only a little later than she and the captain had supposed. One could never be sure.

Was that possible? A child born of a union already dissolved? What if nature should play such a monstrous practical joke? Like a fairy tale in which a malevolent fairy grants a foolish wish....

Mrs. Holloway was still nibbling away at the margins of the supposed mishap. She was commiserating with Captain Bright, who would, she assumed, take the disappointment as hard as Amanda. It was almost as bad for a man—not having a son to carry on his name.

"There, now, I've said something to make you blush. Forgive me. The fact is, I've come to think of us as sisters, with no need for modesty between us."

If she was blushing, it was not for modesty. She was irritated, and it took her a moment to pin down the irritant. Mrs. Holloway's assumption that only a male child would satisfy Jonathan—or any man—was not novel. But it had never struck her so forcibly before that women thought of themselves as second best. No wonder men... But she was letting silence lie for her again.

"My husband has no expectation of being a father," Amanda said. "We have parted."

Tassy's head turned in her direction for the first time. Amanda had not thought she was listening. The two women stared at her, wordless.

"I can't believe it!" Mrs. Holloway whispered at last. "You don't mean to say Captain Bright has left...?"

"I requested to be left."

"But he'll be returning for you in the spring?"

Amanda shook her head.

What Mrs. Holloway was feeling showed in her plain, open face—a riptide of conventions, convictions, and real affection, in which she struggled for a footing.

It was Tassy who spoke next.

"I think the men not come back," she said. Without apparent emotion, halting only when she had to struggle for English words, she said what she believed: that men who left on a ship with sails seldom returned; whether or not they meant to return did not matter; women left by such men were deserted; they must fend for themselves till they could find other male protectors.

"How can you say such things?" Mrs. Holloway had struck soundings at last. She began a sermon on the sanctity of Christian marriage, reminding herself, as well as her audience, that nothing could annul vows taken in the sight of God. Not even death. To entertain a moment's doubt was unthinkable, "especially in one converted and baptized," as Tassy had been.

Tassy dropped her dark eyes in apology for the discourtesy of dissent. If a woman was not too far from her own people, she said, it was best to take her child and return to them. But for her that was not possible. She had been brought here from a place far to the south. Too far to walk with a heavy child.

But Mrs. Holloway was not to be deflected from her peroration by side issues or special instances. "We must put our trust in the goodness of Our Father...not give way to dark thoughts...keep up each other's spirits..." As for violating her marriage vows, that would be risking her immortal soul to sustain her mortal body—or her child's—and Tassy was never again to consider such a thing. "There is—there will always be—a home for you in my home. You are my sister, and your child, my children's brother."

She kissed Tassy's forehead, took Amanda into her arms and held her, whispering that she "would not ask reasons. There can be only one, and I don't blame you for not speaking of it." Then, in her normal, forthright, Yankee schoolmarm voice, "And I will say this: I can't but admire your courage. Though it will be hard…very hard."

The child's fever broke before midnight. They changed her damp clothing, wrapped her in warm dry flannel, gave her some herb tea to drink, and rocked her to sleep.

Amanda lay a long time awake, thinking of what had been said and left unsaid. She thought of the exchange between Tassy and Mrs. Holloway, of the Indian woman's passive acceptance of the odds against men returning from a voyage on "a ship with sails" and Mrs. Holloway's vigorous rejection of them. How little respect she had for the perils of a voyage by sea, this woman who had survived a land journey almost as perilous. Was it better to hope, even unreasonably? Or despair, and then take up one's life burdens and go forward?

In one sense Tassy's choice was less, not more, passive. To wait was not to act. But action to Tassy was the search for another male protector. Even Mrs. Holloway doubted that a woman could take her life into her own hands. "It will be hard…very hard." Flagg had said the same thing.

But women did! Flagg's wife and other seamen's wives, sometimes for years, sometimes for the rest of their lives. Widows with children. Women who never married. Women like—Louisa!

She had never written the letter to Louisa.

She had meant to send it by the ship that carried her letter to her parents, but she had not had time to solve the riddle of name and address. Not so. She had time enough but not the will. She had pushed it back into a dark corner of her mind because she could not summon the strength to inflict pain till her own had abated, to wound this unknown sister till her own wounds had healed.

Tomorrow she would write it. Or at the very least, she would read through Horace's journal in search of a clue—any link that would lead her to the woman he had loved.

The next day was Sunday.

In her husband's absence, Mrs. Holloway usually read from the

Scriptures to those members of her husband's congregation who could fit into the small cabin. But under the circumstances, it seemed better to use another home.

Amanda volunteered to stay with the children, but Tassy bound her papoose to his cradleboard, and Mrs. Holloway carried her little boy in her arms.

Janet was sleeping quietly, and Amanda dug into her bag of belongings for Horace's journal. From it she took the folded sheet on which Louisa had copied Mistress Bradstreet's poem.

As loving Hind that (Hartless) wants her Deer,
Scuds through the woods and ferns with harkning ear,
Perplext, in every bush & nook doth pry
Still wait with doubts, & hopes, and falling eye,
His voice to hear or person to discry.

She felt some remorse for prolonging the pain the poem described but also—more strongly—something like impatience. Like the irritation she had struggled to suppress when Mrs. Holloway was consoling her for the loss of a presumptive son. Surely Louisa did not think of herself as a timid doe. A woman who earned her own living by her art, who had the courage to engage herself heart and soul to a man without the means to support her, whose parents rejected her, threw obstacles in the path of their union, forced separation upon them….

She opened the journal, hoping to find *that* Louisa in its pages.

Horace's style of journal keeping was nothing like her own. He did not use it to examine thoughts and perceptions, to record inner as well as objective reality. Begun as an *aide-mémoire* of interesting or novel events, it had been reduced in short order to a series of jotted notes—mostly illegible—dates of landfalls and departures and ports at which he had been able to dispatch a letter to L. B.—a clue, a last initial! But nothing else.

The entries after Honolulu were different, as if they might be notes for a letter he would write when he had time. The last of all—undated—must have been written on the day of the tragedy:

·✧·

I used to want the men to like me. I felt myself one of them. When orders came from above, through me to them, my first thought was of what it would mean to whoever must spend his strength to carry it out, feeling it in my own bones and muscles. Now the orders come from me. I give no thought to the cost nor the man who must pay it. So long as the order is carried out smartly—

Will you accept this cold-hearted officer of the quarterdeck in place of the husband you cherished?

·✧·

Amanda remembered their unfinished conversation about the dark side of the joys of mastery. This entry must have been written just before that. While they were talking, he was changing his mind, deciding to reject the *hubris* of the omnipotent captain and become once more the husband Louisa cherished, the man whose heart was "tender gold."

THE THIRD MONTH

Amanda spent much of each day dreaming. Her hands were busy and her contribution to the household considerable, but her mind was in other places. In Salem, for one.

She imagined her letter to her parents arriving. If only she had not written so decisively of her intent to stay on in Portland till the spring. When spring came, she might well be no nearer a solution to her problem, and then it would take months for an appeal to reach home and help to come from there.

But perhaps her letter would not deceive them. Perhaps Mother would read between the lines, persuade Father to make a canvass of ships belonging to the firm or to friends and acquaintances in hopes of finding one that could rescue her without too great a detour from its course.

It was also possible that her letter might never reach Salem. Mails were not only slow and irregular but subject to the hazards of land journeys through hostile country or to the hazards of the sea. Perhaps no one knew of her predicament. Ought she to write again?

She decided to wait at least another month. Till there had been time for letters to go and come. Then, if she had not heard, she would write.

Meanwhile she dreamed of other, less humiliating solutions. A ship out of another New England port might drop anchor at Portland on other business, its master, hearing of her predicament, might pronounce himself happy to oblige a fellow countrywoman. Such a man would almost surely know or know of her family and might refuse all payment....

When she was not living in the future, she lived in the past. Most often it was the past before the voyage, with the Jonathan of that past—the land Jonathan, the man she had loved, longed for when he was away, given herself to gladly when he returned...the real man...given to silence but not dour...shy of words but not shallow in feeling...the man behind the mask of mastery.

It was the mask that had cut the bond between them. She saw that now. Jonathan could not accept—could not even recognize—the woman she had become, because the change in her was born of what he took to be his failure. The new Amanda was, or would have been, a constant reminder to himself and to others, that he was not the man he aspired to be—Captain Infallible. The wound to his pride was deeper than his love.

Sometimes she went over in her mind her own sins of pride. There was, for instance, her quarrel with Willy. He had struck at her pride by refusing to accept her as master. And even when he had repented, she had been unable to forgive, unwilling even to listen to his defense. Was it because she was uncertain of her "mastery"?

It occurred to her for the first time that Jonathan's rigidity might also be a sign of uncertainty. Perhaps a captain covered the chinks in his armor for fear his authority might be undermined in ways that would endanger the safety of all. She was beginning to understand many things that had seemed inexplicable, unforgivable.

But understanding—even if it had come before their quarrel—would not have resolved their dilemma. She could not change into the woman on the walrus tusk. Could not stuff the genie back into the bottle. Could not or would not—even to preserve her love.

When she was not reliving and reworking the past, she was writing letters to Louisa. Louisa B.—somewhere in the safe, snug world of home.

Because the letters could not be sent, she felt free to write whatever came into her mind, and it became one of her secret joys. She wrote to this unknown sister without fear of offending or being misunderstood. Confessed sins she would have been ashamed to confess to any other. Exposed her own insecurities and indecisions and pettinesses. Argued both sides of propositions that perplexed her. And she gave Louisa much sound sisterly advice. Especially about love.

Amanda had read and reread Mistress Anne Bradstreet's poem and liked it less and less. If the lady was truly the timid, dependent doe (and Amanda was beginning to suspect that the image was hyperbole, designed to flatter the absent husband), she was not a model to be emulated. Louisa must know that there were other, better ways to love.

She had found in Mr. Emerson's *Poems* one she thought more inspiring. Perhaps Louisa already knew it. Perhaps Horace had read it to her. Perhaps that was why he carried the volume with him. Perhaps both he and Louisa had committed it to memory, as she was doing now.

GIVE ALL TO LOVE
Give all to love;
Obey thy heart;
Friends, kindred, days,
Estate, good-fame,
Plans, credit and the Muse,—
Nothing refuse.
...
It was never for the mean;
It requireth courage stout.
Souls above doubt,
valor unbending,
It will reward,—
They shall return
More than they were,
And ever ascending.

Leave all for love;
Yet, hear me, yet,
One word more thy heart behoved,
One pulse more of firm endeavor,—
Keep thee to-day,
To-morrow, forever,
Free as an Arab
Of thy beloved.

...

Though thou loved her as thyself
As a self of purer clay,
Though her parting dims the day,
Stealing grace from all alive;
Heartily know,
When half-gods go,
The gods arrive.

Horace had obeyed most of those imperatives. He had given to love friends, kindred, estate, good-fame, even the man he might have been. If Jonathan had been able to give half so much of himself, might not he and Amanda have found some middle ground?

But Horace was dead, and Louisa must find a way to live. Not as a lonely deer but free as an Arab of the beloved. That was the promise of the final stanza, its consolation and its challenge. She, Amanda, had accepted it for herself.

To leave all for love yet keep thee, today, tomorrow, forever, free— unless one could take that transcendent paradox into one's very soul, one could never heartily know the joy of a fulfilled self that would console and heal all sorrow and loss. It was not an easy exercise. She would have given much to share the struggle with her unknown sister.

Midmonth there was a day more like late spring than early winter. There had been a respite from rain, and the sun shone briefly, but brightly, every day. Janet and the papoose sat on a log that served as a doorstep, warming themselves. Mrs. Holloway was examining the little orchard she had planted in the summer, snipping off premature buds that might be blasted in the next frost.

Amanda was knitting a pair of wool stockings. She had dried out her boots and greased them. Her feet felt warm for the first time in a month, and she was hoping to finish the stockings in time to insulate them against the next onslaught of chilblains. Tassy came running up the trail from the river with unusual animation in her face.

"A ship with sails comes up the river," she said.

"Is it my husband's?"

Tassy said no. And it brought no letters. The men at the wharf were saying that the ship was of the English. But it was stopping here. It was rare for a ship flying the Union Jack to stop short of the residence of the Hudson Bay's factor in Oregon City. Tassy seemed to expect Amanda to take particular interest in this phenomenon. "A ship with sails take you to your people," she said.

Amanda shook her head. A ship with sails would take her the first leg of her journey if she could pay for her passage, but she couldn't. Not having listened to what Jonathan said on that subject, she did not even know what it would cost. Well, at least the new arrival offered her a chance to inquire.

She put her knitting into the pocket of her apron, pulled her shawl from the peg, and set out for the wharf.

The vessel was a brig, out of Bristol. There was no officer visible on the quarterdeck. The bosun was supervising the unloading of what looked like bolts of yard goods. Mr. Leary, the dry goods merchant, was standing under the portico of the City Hotel, in conversation with a gentleman who might be either the master of the vessel or its mate.

Amanda was reluctant to interrupt them with a question she wanted to sound casual, so she settled herself on a stump that served in place of a bench and occupied herself with the heel of her stocking.

She had hardly got it turned when Mr. Leary was at her elbow, asking her pardon for the liberty and introducing the gentleman as Captain Cartwright.

"He seed you knitting, Mrs. Bright, and allowed as how he hoped to get hisself some stockings while he's here. We do sometimes have a few pairs to sell—take them from ladies to even their accounts— but at present we're out."

"And I made bold to hope you might see your way to supplying my need, ma'am."

There was a twang in the man's voice that reminded Amanda of Davy and prejudiced her in his favor. But she had to explain that she was only just learning to knit and not quick enough to finish a pair of stockings in anything less than a week.

Captain Cartwright looked dashed. He was not going to linger that long in Portland. "I'm anxious to be across that damned bar before the next set of storms comes down."

Amanda asked where he was bound. To San Francisco, he said, then down the coast of Mexico to Panama, Peru, and thence around the Horn. "Homebound for Bristol out of Boston."

Keeping her eyes on her needles, Amanda asked if the captain happened to know the fare for a passage, say, to Panama. Or all the way around the Horn and up to Boston?

Captain Cartwright named a figure that might as well have been astronomical, since she was penniless. Still, it was not as bad as she had feared. She thanked him and said again that she was sorry not to be able to oblige him.

"If you are thinking of a voyage to Boston," the captain said, "I wonder, would you be interested in working out your passage?"

Working! She saw herself standing on deck with the sextant; sitting at the desk, computing and charting; commanding;…But of course that was not what he had in mind.

The captain was explaining that his wardrobe was in a shocking state after three years at sea—linens needed washing, jackets and unmentionables needed mending. He could use some warm mittens as well as socks. And it so happened there was an empty stateroom on the brig. He did not ordinarily take passengers, but Amanda was welcome. She could share the officers' mess. Perhaps she might turn her hand to improving the fare.

He waited for her answer like a suitor who has made a proposal of marriage. She felt the tensing pull of temptation. But only for a moment. It snapped when she saw the solution she had been waiting for, the answer to prayers she had not consciously prayed.

She declined politely. The captain doffed his hat and hoped he had not given offense. She said he had not and forced herself to walk away at a dignified pace, all the time wanting to fly up the muddy street to the cabin. To pour out her plan to her companions. To engage them in it.

There were four men to every woman in Portland—not counting transients who came by ship or on horseback, from the sea or the interior valleys. Fewer than half of them were married or had a woman to "do" for them. Washing, mending, knitting, sewing, baking—there were any number of services women could perform.

For money! Not for credit at the store. Nor in exchange for fish or game or potatoes or wheat. For money—bank notes, silver, or gold. Men had money even in this place. They spent it on other needs. Why not on their personal comfort?

It was not easy to persuade Tassy or Mrs. Holloway that taking money in return for woman's work was respectable. Tassy had no objection to barter, but exchange through the medium of precious metal seemed to make her uneasy, as if it involved the breaking of some taboo. Mrs. Holloway said that her way was to give of whatever she had to whomsoever was in need of it and to accept gratefully whatsoever was given to her, without calculating reciprocal values.

"But I can see how it might be different in your circumstances," she added.

Amanda was stung to defensiveness. Men had no scruples about taking money for their labor. For example, the Reverend Holloway: "He went to the mines to earn money. And without leaving you enough for your needs. You can't depend on friends' charity for shoes or blankets or candlewick, to say nothing of pans and a shovel and hatchet to replace the ones he took with him."

Mrs. Holloway did not let herself be provoked into argument. All she would say—with wounded dignity—was that Amanda could count on her help at any time it was needed. Then she had a sudden inspiration.

"Maybe I could put by for a harmonium!" It had like to broke her husband's heart when they had to throw away that little pump organ they had carried across the plains. It was the last of all the possessions they had abandoned on one particularly bitter grade when oxen and wagon threatened to give out. "I can't think what would make him prouder than to come back and find the Lord has shown us the way to make it up!"

And with such a goal, Mrs. Holloway could recruit other women. There were only five families in the Holloways' congregation. It was not as large as the Methodists' or the Catholics' or even the Congregationalists', but five resourceful women were not to be sneezed at. And six growing girls besides, all of them able to knit.

"The thing would be to get wool enough."

Tassy knew where she could barter for raw wool.

"It's a deal of work to wash and card it," Mrs. Holloway said, "and we'll need to make a quantity of soap."

But with enough hands to share the labor, nothing was impossible. And with plenty of soap, it might even be possible to undertake real heavy washings.

So the enterprise was launched.

THE FOURTH MONTH

O n the first day of the new year they celebrated.
   Christmas had not been festive. A few days before the
twenty-fifth, Mrs. Holloway consulted Amanda on the propriety of
accepting an invitation from the Methodists, who had a church
building, to include the Holloways' congregation in their services.

Amanda convinced her that none of the differences in dogma
were as weighty as what Christians had in common on the anniver-
sary of the birth of Him through whom they all hoped for salvation.
The other members of the congregation agreed, and there was much
anticipation. Hymns of the season were hummed while the women
worked at their spinning or at their baking or even at the washtubs.

About midday on the twenty-fourth, Mrs. Holloway began to
bleed. She was diffident about explaining her sudden weakness, but
within an hour Amanda understood and went for the midwife. It
was a miscarriage, not the first Mrs. Holloway had suffered. (For the
first time Amanda noticed how little flesh the woman carried on her
heavy frame.) There was no ergot in the settlement, and nothing in
the midwife's bundle of remedies seemed to slow the flow of blood.
But when Tassy understood the nature of the trouble, she paid a visit
to the Indian encampment at the north end of the town and returned with remedies: one dried root and several species of berries.

A strong, bitter infusion was prepared, and little by little the hemorrhage was stanched.

By Christmas morning the crisis was past, but there could be no thought of leaving the cabin. Outside a heavy ground fog closed the visible world to a circle a few yards in diameter, within which even the frailest feathers of weed and grass showed frosty white against the gray. Overhead one could make out the vague forms of spruces rising out of nothingness and disappearing into nothingness, a ring of darkness like the walls of a dungeon. But inside the cabin the fire was bright, and there was plenty to eat. The women of the congregation had seen to that. Amanda read from the New Testament and sang as many carols as she could remember. Mrs. Holloway lay quiet and listened, weeping a little now and then, not from pain nor even from sorrow at her loss, but only because it was "so good…having the love of friends."

New Year's Day was different.

Tassy and Amanda had cut cedar branches to make garlands and gone into the forest for holly berries. Tassy had snared a rabbit. And Mrs. Holloway was well enough to have a try at making a New England Indian pudding, using wheat grits in place of cornmeal. It had not turned out quite to suit her, but they ate it with appetite.

After the meal there was a surprise for Amanda. "By rights we should save it for Twelfth Night," Mrs. Holloway said, "but Tassy and I are no better than children at waiting."

From under her mattress she brought a flat package. Amanda unwrapped it to find yards and yards of green merino. Enough for a dress and a shawl.

"For your voyage."

The two women had taken money from their earnings to buy the goods from Mr. Leary's store. "We knew it might be some time before you'll need it, but if we'd waited, it might have been gone. There was another shade of green—more to the blue—that I fancied because it had more the look of the sea about it. But that had already been spoken for."

273

Too moved to speak her thanks, Amanda fingered the fine wool and remembered the ship that had brought it here, the captain's proposal, how it had changed their lives.

After the dishes were washed and dried, Mrs. Holloway asked Tassy to tell them one of the legends of her people. "She knows enough of them to make a book."

Tassy obliged with the story of the war between the snow-covered mountains on the far side of the great river.

Very long ago, a beautiful, white-robed woman mountain came to live in the valley between the two men mountains. Both of them fell in love with her and began to quarrel over which should possess her. They became so angry that they took off their white coats, painted their bodies with fire, and began to hurl great rocks at each other. The whole earth trembled as the mountains spat fire and belched great clouds of smoke that hid the sun.

At last they tired and stopped to rest. The air cleared, and they could see what they had done. The land had been burned clean of all its fruits. The game had been driven away. Even the fish were gone. This was because the fighting mountains had torn a great hole in the earth, and the waters of the lake had rushed out, taking all the fish with them, leaving a stone bridge over the tunnel they carved.

All the people who had not been killed by the fire and the falling rocks were hiding in caves. They were starving and sick, and they called to Kemush, the Creator, for help.

He came to earth, and the mountains were made ashamed. As punishment, Kemush ordered them to wear their ugly black war coats for fifty seasons. After that he would decide which of them would possess the beautiful woman mountain. And to remind them that a woman's beauty is not lasting, he put an ugly, toothless old woman as guard on the stone bridge that led from one mountain to the other. If they broke their promise to be at peace, he warned, the stone bridge would fall and new afflictions would come upon the land.

For many years the mountains were at peace. They put on their coats of white buckskin again. But one day they looked upon the woman mountain and forgot their promise. They quarreled. The stone bridge fell. Many people were drowned by the wave of its falling. And neither of the man mountains was given the beautiful woman mountain to possess.

"How did she feel?" Amanda asked, when it was apparent that the tale had ended. "Did she want to marry either of them?"

Tassy did not know. The story did not say.

Mrs. Holloway was reminded of questions she had long wanted to ask about marriage customs among the Indians and how they differed from Christian practice. Tassy's answers provoked more questions. What emerged, bit by bit, was a way of life in which women had no more right of choice than slaves. Marriage was a sentence to hard labor, in return for which they received only the barest sustenance, and, when times were hard, not even that.

Mrs. Holloway's tongue clucked. She hoped Tassy was thankful to have been saved from such a future by her marriage to Mr. Whitt. But Tassy did not seem thankful. Amanda had the impression that she not only accepted but preferred a system that was patently—savagely!—unjust. Was there something about it, not yet explained, that made the bargain more bearable?

She tried some questions of her own: How was work divided within the tribe? What was expected of women, besides the bearing of children?

Tassy reeled off a list of tasks, beginning with the gathering of wild foods and medicinal herbs; the preserving and preparing of these as well as of the fish and game provided by the hunters; and other labors—all of them menial, most of them requiring great strength and endurance, some downright dangerous.

"Women do what men do not like because women cannot do what men can," Tassy finished with what Amanda took to be irony.

"And what is it men do that's too difficult for women?"

"Fight enemies. Take slaves. Build canoes. Build lodges."

Amanda was growing contentious. She was not convinced that women could do none of these things, given a motive and an opportunity. But what mattered more was that men's work seemed to be respected and rewarded, while women's work was not. "Why is hunting more honorable than gathering, for instance?"

Tassy did not find the concepts "reward" and "honor" meaningful in this context. Her view of life—the life of the group—was molded by the imperative of survival. All must contribute as they were able, or the people would die.

"Women are able to bring forth the next generation," Amanda said. "What's more important than that?"

Mrs. Holloway intervened to defuse the impending controversy. In her opinion, the heart of the matter was that woman's nature—Indian or white or what you would—was different from man's. Nurture came natural to a woman and was its own reward.

"That's what a woman is. Her nature is to give, without thought of recompense. By giving she is replenished, filled and fulfilled. It is different with a man."

Amanda could hear her mother's voice. Or was it her grandmother's? The old lies, handed on from mother to daughter, down the generations. And they *were* lies—no matter who spoke them or how often. Men and women were not different in this: either could use the other in the search for wholeness and peace, but neither was fulfilled by such usage.

Tassy and Mrs. Holloway were nodding to each other, finding common ground across the vast gulf between their worlds. Ground from which Amanda was excluded. What had she done—or not done—to deserve this? Was it because they had borne children and she had not? But she had been childless an hour ago and admitted to the sisterhood. There was the green merino wool to prove it.

Men and women were different. And she was different from both—like Eve after she had eaten the forbidden fruit. If she could not learn to hold her tongue, she too would be driven from the Garden. Without Adam. Alone in a strange land.

She thought again of Louisa. Louisa would not believe the old lies, the old laws. She and the other privileged women who inhabited the world Horrie described—they had all tasted the forbidden fruit. One day, when she had finished her voyaging, she would ask admission to that world, to a Garden from which she could not be expelled.

THE FIFTH MONTH

By the middle of February Amanda had put by the sum Captain Cartwright named for a passage to Panama. It was not enough to see her across the isthmus and north by sea to Boston, but she was confident she could manage that before the end of summer, and her confidence started her dreaming again....

Perhaps if she took passage as far as San Francisco, she would have a greater choice of options. Perhaps the fare between that place and Panama—on one of those half-empty emigrant ships—would be less than the captain had thought. There might even be a ship that carried the master's wife aboard, willing to accept a lesser payment or even none at all. If such a suppliant had come to her when she was the only woman aboard, how gladly she would have welcomed a companion.

While she dreamed, she worked. Worked hard and for long hours. Most of what fell to her share was washing—great loads of heavy cottons and linens that took boiling and bleaching and could only be dried on bright days when the wind was brisk. Her hands were chapped and cracked despite nightly applications of mutton fat. Her shoulders ached from the angle at which she leaned over the washtub. But her forearms had grown stronger and tired less easily now, and she was learning some tricks that lightened the labor.

The green wool dress was cut out and basted together. Mrs. Holloway had provided the shears and helped with the cutting. Tassy turned out to be a fine needlewoman. She and Amanda worked at the seaming whenever the weather decreed a respite from the washboard.

They sat together this morning, listening to the light rain—so fragile after the downpours of winter—and working their way toward each other along the bottom hem. There was the sound of a wagon passing outside, heading up the plank road that led to the valley.

Tassy stopped sewing to listen, and smiled—something she did so seldom that it made what followed memorable. She had intended to follow the plank road into the valley, she said, as soon as it was spring. The plains were a good place to look for a male protector. "Valley white men plant wheat. Do not go on ships."

It was Amanda's understanding that plenty of white settlers from the valley had joined the rush south when news of the gold strike came. But she did not want to disturb Tassy's rare communicative mood by arguing the point. "Have you decided not to go?" she asked.

Tassy nodded. "I stay with her. But not if he comes."

Amanda was not sure whether "he" was the Reverend Holloway or John Whitt. She was filled with curiosity, but cautious. "Is Mr. Whitt a good—" She revised the sentence before it was finished, "father to your baby?"

Tassy nodded.

"Did you marry him willingly? Or was there someone else you would rather have had as a husband?"

"I was bought by him. For horses."

"Your father sold you?" Amanda was horrified.

"Not my father. The chief of the village where the stone bridge of the gods fell into the river." Tassy and her brother had been captured returning to their home after a season at the mission school. Enslaved—but only for a short time. The boy was sold to another Indian tribe; Tassy, to Whitt. She had planned to escape at the first opportunity and return to her people. But then there was a child.

"How long ago was that?"

Five years. The first child did not live, but for quite a while Tassy was not strong enough to walk very far. Then there was another child, this one.

They sewed in silence until their needles met. The hem was finished. When Mrs. Holloway came back, there would be one more fitting. Then, if there were no adjustments to be made, the bodice and skirt would be joined to the belt.

"You will be happy to return to your people?" Tassy asked.

"Of course. Overjoyed." But the words did not ring quite true. She would be overjoyed to see her loved ones—parents, brothers, all the wide circle of relations and comrades of her school days. But after the rejoicing, or even before it, the future widened like a starless night.

What would her life be in Salem? She would not starve or be sold into slavery. She would not need a male protector who planted wheat and did not go to sea. She would not be deprived—except of a reason for living. There would be tasks for her to perform, needs to fill: the care of her parents as they grew older...of other people's children. Or she might find work that would earn her a moiety of independence—some occupation more to her liking than laundering. But even if she were able to find her way to the world Horace had described, Louisa's world—and it seemed possible only in daydreams—she would find no work that would challenge and stretch her, nothing that would fill her heart and mind.

She dreamed that night of a woman dressed in a green merino dress. Seated in a chair whose back was turned to the dreamer. A chair with a high carved back and horsehair upholstery...Such a chair belonged in a parlor, not out of doors...on the roof of a house with a widow's walk.... The wind was blowing, but not one of the woman's hairs was moved by it. Amanda sensed that if anyone were to touch her, she would topple forward and fall.

A few days later, the mail schooner brought a letter for her. It was from her mother, who was full of loving concern for her health and comfort but "glad all the same that you made so prudent a decision. We look forward to hearing that you have embarked on your homeward journey, but let it not be till all prospects are favorable." Nothing to indicate that they knew her real situation, nothing to indicate that they questioned her account of things. A conventional maternal letter from a conventional woman to the daughter she had bade good-bye less than two years ago. Still, it warmed her.

As Amanda slipped it back into its envelope, she saw a small, separate page. On it was a postscript, in her mother's hand, that appeared hastily, almost carelessly, written: "Your Aunt Agatha asks a favor. That you write of your cousin's death to a friend—a Miss Brown, of Cambridge. Your aunt does not know the lady but understands her to be the daughter of the Unitarian minister of that place. She asks also that you keep this in confidence."

Amanda sat up after the rest had gone to sleep to write a letter to be carried on the mail schooner's trip downriver. It was odd after all the other letters—some written out, some only dreamed—to find herself hard put to find words for Louisa. Words that would reach a real woman whom she did not know, whose outlines she had filled in with the lineaments of a sister she had created out of her need.

In the end, she wrote only the simplest account of "our mutual loss." She wanted to write more, to confide enough of her own situation so that Louisa might understand how closely it resembled hers. Each of them had lost the love around which she had arranged her life's plan. Each must make a new plan. They could offer each other much comfort, much support. But all she could say at this time was that she hoped Louisa would write to her in care of her parents in Salem, that one day—perhaps before the year was over—they would surely meet.

As she was melting the wax to seal the envelope, she decided to copy out Mr. Emerson's poem and include it.

THE SIXTH MONTH

It was the day of the equinox, exactly half a year since she had given the order that headed the *Maria M.* into the bar.

Spring was far advanced. Yellow trumpets of skunk cabbage blared from the low places along the river. There were bright tips of new growth on the conifers, a green haze of foliage on the hardwoods, fat buds on the apple trees. Ships were coming upriver in increasing numbers. Besides the monthly mail schooner from San Francisco, there had been this week a lumber schooner and a bark out of Halifax, loading dried salmon and cedar spars for Ouwahoo. Next week there might be a ship bound south, perhaps more than one.

Amanda was hanging out sheets and doing sums in her head: how many more basketfuls of washing would earn her the difference between what she had put by and what she would need? She did not hear Mrs. Holloway's first warning, and the second came too late for her to flee.

"It is! I'm certain of it. If you'd rather not see him, you could step behind the clothes there and slip away."

Amanda turned and saw Jonathan walking up from the waterfront. He was thinner than he had been before the illness, and there was a little gray in his beard. But he walked with strong strides, with his old erect bearing. How elegantly handsome he looked in his blue go-ashore suit. Amanda was suddenly conscious of her own appearance—her rough, unironed clothes, her dirty apron, muddy boots, and unkempt hair. If Mrs. Holloway had not been watching, she might have yielded to the impulse to dash for the cabin and make herself presentable.

"You don't want me to leave you alone with him?" Mrs. Holloway asked in a whisper.

"No, stay. Please." That was silly of her. But there was no time to take it back or explain.

Jonathan greeted both ladies with a polite bow and inquired after their health. His voice had a new timbre, lower…was it also softer? And he seemed more at ease than usual in the company of females. More at ease than either of the females present.

He had brought a letter for Amanda.

While she tore at the stiff envelope, his eyes were on her hands. Was he reading her life from the roughness of their backs? She was trembling a little—from embarrassment, nothing else—as she managed at last to pull out the letter. And a thin packet of bills.

For a moment she thought it was the money she had refused, but Jonathan forestalled her objection.

"Read the letter," he said.

It was from the owners of the *Maria M.*, expressing their gratitude for "the diligent care by which you have contributed to saving the lives of the officers and injured crewmen," and for "your energy and intelligence, which contributed to the saving of the vessel and its valuable cargo." The enclosed salvage award was recognition that "without your firmness in command and your knowledge, the ship must have been lost."

"How did they come to know?"

"I dispatched my report and rough log from San Francisco."

It took Amanda a moment or two to absorb the full meaning: He had written to the owners of her firmness in command and knowledge. He had admitted to them—men who expected him to be infallible—what he had been too proud to admit to her: that her strength had compensated for his weakness. At least for a time. A critical time.

It was an apology, a handsome, if wordless one and the only kind he would be able to bring himself to make.

Mrs. Holloway had asked if he brought news of the reverend and of Mr. Whitt. Jonathan was explaining why he had not. He had seen both men, at different times, early in the year. Both were well then. They would surely have sent word by him if they had known he would be touching at Portland, but even he had not known it at that time.

Mrs. Holloway looked to Amanda as if for prompting, and getting none, asked where the *Maria M.* was bound.

To Nootka. Then west. To Nagasaki and Shanghai.

And now, Jonathan said, he must be getting back to the ship. "Unless I can be of any further service?"

Amanda had been expecting something quite different. She had just worked it out in her head: he had waited till the letter from the owners that would make amends for him, then come to persuade her to forget their quarrel and rejoin him. She had been expecting him to make some excuse to speak with her alone and had been steeling herself to refuse.

Mrs. Holloway looked from one to the other, helplessly confused as to what role she was expected to play. She offered a cup of tea. It would take only a few moments to bring the kettle to the boil. But Jonathan was firm. There were still some supplies to be loaded, and he would be casting off at the slackening of the tide.

"By the by," he turned once more to Amanda, "I almost forgot to ask if you left any belongings aboard that you will want?"

"Indeed I did." More than once during the winter she had lamented the haste of her departure.

"Shall I have Willy fetch them? You'll probably want a word with him in any case."

"I prefer to go for them myself, thank you."

Mrs. Holloway frowned a warning, but Amanda smiled back in perfect confidence. She could walk with Jonathan to the ship, embrace her cousin, gather her belongings, and run no risk of being driven off her chosen course. Jonathan might, or might not, try to persuade her. She knew her answer. No.

The walk to the waterfront was silent. Jonathan's new ease of manner had deserted him as soon as they were alone. He was the same stiff, silent man from whom she had parted six months before. But Amanda felt herself drawn back further in time. Drawn to a younger but still silent Jonathan....

They were walking along the road to the beach...with the wind in their faces.... In a moment he would put his arm around her to protect her...and a fire from within would drown out the roaring of the wind....

They turned the corner at the foot of the slope and the ship came into view—so much smaller than she remembered. Someone waved to her from the ratlines.

"That's Willy." Jonathan found his tongue at last. "You won't know him, the way he's grown." And in more than one sense of the word. The lad would be taking Horace's place for the rest of the voyage. "He's young for such advancement, but I haven't been able to find a better man."

As they came closer, Mr. Smith doffed his cap to her from the forecastlehead, where he was supervising the stowing of the anchor chain. Davy stood with his back to her at the opening of the midships hatch. Willy and Flagg were using a yard, doubling as a boom, to lower a great, rough-hewn cedar log down to a hand who was guiding it into the hold. King John and Cook were coming up the street from the opposite direction, laden with provisions.

"Where's Crank?" Amanda asked.

"He signed off in San Francisco. Got his nose out of joint when I shifted Davidson to bosun."

"And No-Name?"

"Jumped ship. Along with the Kanaka. We've mostly new hands."

As she came aboard, Willy called down that he would be finished with his work within the hour. Amanda answered that she would be finished with hers in less time, but she would wait to speak with him before she left the ship.

If the ship seemed to have shrunk since she saw it last, the cabin seemed to have grown. She remembered it as a cell in which she had been condemned to solitary confinement, in the bolted-down chair beside the green baize table under the hanging lamp. But she had forgotten the desk, the gateway to her kingdom, wide as the sky. And the books that had taught her to rule it. There in the rack was her Bowditch.

No, not hers—Jonathan's. The papers on the desk were his. The sextant—his sextant—had been put away. To keep it safe from profane hands?

"Take all the time you need. Willy will be at your disposal to carry your things if they are burdensome," Jonathan said and left.

He was not going to try to persuade her to come back. He had come all this way to pay a debt, to wipe clean the slate. That was all. He was no longer angry or jealous. He would never have promoted Davy if he had not conquered that. He was simply indifferent, except to his obligation. He had fallen out of love.

If she had not, it was of no consequence. She would be spared the temptation, which, in the end, she would have resisted. It was to pack she had come, and she went to the stateroom to begin.

There was the double bunk—her bed and Jonathan's for many months of lovemaking and a brief, sudden violation of love. That memory seemed unreal, like gossip heard at third- or fourth-hand. Perhaps if they had talked of it afterward, when he was recovered...But having made her bed in this fashion, or having had it made for her, she would never lie in it again.

She pulled open the drawer under the bunk that had been hers. In the front, covered with a flannel sheet, was a collection of small treasures. She did not even remember having put them there. Her embroidery basket. Unlikely she would ever use that again. The lace antimacassar she bought in the Canaries. The wreath Jonathan made her from shells they gathered together. No-Name's kittiwake. What would Mrs. Holloway think of her, returning with only these trifles to excuse her coming?

Farther back in the drawer, she found a length of sprigged muslin, intended for a dress she would wear in the tropics, forgotten long before the troubles began. A fur-lined hood—that she could have used in the winter, but not now. A parasol and a badly dented straw hat—as useless as the muslin in this climate. And at the very back, her rolled-up corsets. Those she would need when she returned to New England. If they still fit. They looked small....

She stood to try them on over her dress, pulling at the laces till the panels met. There was no room left to breathe. The woman in the green merino dress was not the wirewaisted child of the scrimshaw. But the corsets would serve if she adjusted the laces.

She was loosening them when Jonathan came down the companion ladder into the cabin. He looked through the open door, saw her in this embarrassing *deshabille,* begged her pardon, and started away.

"Jonathan!"

He turned. They faced each other across the space of the cabin. He seemed to expect her to speak. But she had nothing to say—except that she was afire with longing for him.

The silence echoed with old quarrels in which they had wounded each other with ugly words and uglier silences, of which she was as guilty in her way as he in his. Jonathan had made amends—at least for those wrongs he was conscious of having committed. She could ask forgiveness for hers, but forgiveness was not what she wanted.

She took a step toward him and tripped over the trailing corset laces. Jonathan caught her as she fell. She put up her arms, tried to draw his mouth down to meet hers. He resisted, but his body betrayed him. It trembled—almost as violently as when the fever was on him. She was trembling, too. But she held on, and slowly, reluctantly, his head bowed. Their lips touched. She ran the tip of her tongue along his till they loosened. The fire caught and blazed.

She was lifted in his arms. She heard the door of the stateroom close. They lay naked in each other's arms.

Once Jonathan seemed to pull away as if he were shocked, but she would not let him shame her. *"Don't play the fine gentleman with me!"* In another moment, their bodies were folding around each other like lava, seeking a posture in which they would melt and be one. They found it. At the same moment. Together.

Later, when they lay quiet, Amanda asked, "Who was Sal?"

"Sal?" Jonathan raised himself on his elbow to look at her. "I don't know what you mean."

She told him as much as she thought he could bear to hear.

He groaned. "If you say, it must be so. I can't believe…and all the time I thought…"

She had to prod him to finish.

"I thought you'd got to where you couldn't stand the sight of me. It would have been natural enough, seeing me like that—sick as a dog and good for nothing, for so long."

Relief made him voluble, almost eloquent. He begged forgiveness for the crime committed in delirium, but he denied knowledge of any woman whose name he might have spoken, denied the implicit charge of whoring—except perhaps on his very first voyage. He would take his oath that he had kept the faith plighted in their marriage vows. If he had sinned before that, she must try to understand …men being far from angels…

She saw he was assuming that the chapter of their estrangement was closed, that it had been a tragicomedy of errors, misdirected passion, jealousy, pique—differences that could be dissolved by a word or two and a successful sexual encounter.

She would have to disabuse him. She would have to speak the words. And cherubim with flaming swords would bar her forever from the Garden. If she did not speak…if she could learn to hold her tongue…

She would be imprisoned in the green baize world of the cabin. There were worse fates. This time there would be passion within her prison walls and perhaps, eventually, a child.

When half-gods go, the gods arrive.

But perhaps a half-god was better than none, even a confined life better than the death-in-life of the woman in the chair on the roof with the widow's walk...perhaps.

While they were dressing, Jonathan asked, smiling as if it were a pleasantry, "Will you sail with me, Amanda?"

Eve spoke before Amanda could. "As keeper of the log?" Jonathan caught her by the shoulders. "What is it you want? What that's within reason? I want you with me more...more...." He was struggling so for words that his face twisted from the effort. "There's nothing I have that I wouldn't give. But you cannot be master of the ship!"

"I have been!"

Jonathan said nothing, but he let go of her shoulders. Since he did not dispute her claim, she was shamed into amending it herself. The truth was, she had been master only within narrow limits of time and of circumstance. She had learned to find the height and right ascension of a point of light in darkness and by it—sometimes—the way of the ship. She had learned to command men, not in Jonathan's way but in one that had different strengths and different weaknesses. And she had learned how much more there was to be learned. It would take her years to become truly the master of a vessel, and she did not want to spend years at such a task. Mastery was not her province, but having lived in it—even so briefly—she had tasted something she could not willingly live without.

"Tell me, Amanda," Jonathan said again. "I'm trying to understand."

How was it possible to want something so profoundly that life without it seemed pointless—and yet not be able to describe or define it?

"Maybe it's a different world that I want," she said at last. One in which men and women and the love they had for each other were not pressed into molds that crippled and warped them. A world in which the laws freed even while they bound.

"A ship is a world of sorts," Jonathan said.

She had not thought of it in that way, but it was true. On a ship

288

out of sight of land one could make one's own laws—if one were in command. One could mold a life in which...

Her imagination failed her on the threshold. But that did not negate the vision or the hope.

"Would you sign on as navigator?" he asked. Amanda tried to read his face before she answered, hesitantly, "There are no charts."

"There is a course."

Still she hesitated, unsure in what context the offer was to be understood. "There is only one sextant...."

"There'll be only one navigator, unless you jump ship again."

Amanda could hold out no longer. "Well," she said, trying not to smile, "if I am promised advancement..."

Jonathan laughed. She had not heard him laugh that way before. Not ever. As if something that had been locked was freed.

The words of Mr. Emerson's poem came to her, and she spoke them aloud:

> *It requireth courage stout.*
> *Souls above doubt*
> *Valor unbending,*
> *It will reward,—*
> *They shall return*
> *More than they were,*
> *And ever ascending.*

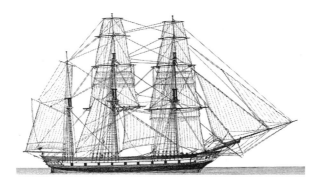